Pra[...]

THE CONTRA[...]

Hunsicker's latest book [...]
military contractors—th[...]
ing the deserts of Iraq [...]
the borders of the Unite[...]
of black humor, Hunsi[...]
What-If with an altoget[...] [...]
giving the reader a remarkable post-9/11, War-on-Drugs novel.

—David Morrell, best-selling author of *First Blood*
and *The Brotherhood of the Rose*, co-founder of the
International Thriller Writers

The Contractors is the fully loaded model with all the options.
With streetwise and wisecracking Jon Cantrell and Piper at
the wheel, they take the reader for one hell of a ride through
the drug- and crime-ravaged parts of Texas that don't appear
on picture postcards or tourist brochures. Hunsicker's eye for
detail, sense of place, and his snappy dialogue shine through.

—Reed Farrel Coleman, three-time Shamus Award–
winning author of *Hurt Machine*

The Contractors is film noir without the film, cyberpunk without the cyber. It's a world to lose yourself in, a fascinating tale
that lives in shades of grey. The prose is muscular, the images
vivid, and the pace relentless. Simply put, Hunsicker kills it.

—Marcus Sakey, author of *Good People* and host of
the Travel Channel's *Hidden City*

THE
GRID

ALSO BY HARRY HUNSICKER

The Jon Cantrell Thrillers
The Contractors
Shadow Boys

The Lee Henry Oswald Mysteries
Still River
The Next Time You Die
Crosshairs

A JON CANTRELL THRILLER

THE
GRID

HARRY
HUNSICKER

THOMAS & MERCER

Published by Thomas & Mercer, Seattle

www.apub.com

Amazon, the Amazon logo, and Thomas & Mercer are trademarks of Amazon.com, Inc., or its affiliates.

ISBN-13: 9781477827659
ISBN-10: 147782765X

Cover design by Marc J. Cohen

Printed in the United States of America

To Alison

- CHAPTER ONE -

Sarah is a bandit.

This is the gift she brings to the world: terror. The moment the gun is aimed, and the muzzle points at a face pale with the prospect of death.

The fear is sweet and succulent, like a fresh peach. A razor's edge between life and death visible in the victim's eyes.

The gun is a four-inch Colt Python. Old, untraceable. Once the property of her grandfather, who acquired it only the devil knows where.

Sarah hides the weapon in a purse designed for the concealed carry of a firearm.

The handbag, certainly not a fashion statement, offers easy access, allowing the gun to be brought to bear in seconds. Sarah is proud of the fact that in twenty outings, she's never had to fire the revolver. The mere presence of the Python, looming in front of the mark, is enough to accomplish her goals.

She's in a five-year-old Buick LaCrosse with dealer tags, idling in the far corner of a motel parking lot off Interstate 35 near Waco, Texas. An auburn wig, made for cancer patients, fits snuggly on her head, hiding her brown hair. Oversized mirrored sunglasses cover her gray eyes.

This is farm country. Sorghum and wheat, the occasional tract dotted white with cotton. The chrome-colored sky is vast, the horizon reaching as far as the eye can see.

Only a handful of cars are present on this Tuesday morning. The LaCrosse is neither the newest nor the oldest.

The motel is a chain, limited services. Not the kind of place that has a restaurant or spa. Not much traffic, few employees.

She's done her homework. No detail too small. Nothing left to chance.

The maid's rounds have been completed. Cameras are located in the lobby, the front hallway, and the main parking area by the highway. Only one manager is on duty at the moment. Most of the rooms are unoccupied.

Sarah checks the disposable phone. No messages or e-mails.

Today's location is pretty far afield from her usual territory, but as her grandfather used to say, "There's no sense hunting where there ain't no critters to kill."

She checks a second phone. No messages there either. She sticks this device in her back pocket and taps the steering wheel with her thumbs.

Almost showtime.

Adrenaline makes her jumpy.

She takes several deep breaths to calm her heartbeat, but there's nothing she can do to stop the arousal from tickling its way up her thighs, building in her belly. That goes with the territory—the gun and the danger, a heady sense of being in control.

The setup is simple. She robs men who cheat on their wives. The "horndogs," she calls them. She doesn't have sex with the horndogs, just steals their wallets. She's fucking enough guys already. No sense making her life more complicated by boinking some loser she met online.

The men are acquired via a dating service designed for extramarital affairs. Her username is "SarahSmiles," her profile pic a selfie from the neck down.

A few minutes later, right on time, today's horndog—username "RockyRoad35"—parks his Ford pickup by the rear door of the motel, just as instructed.

He exits the vehicle and scans the parking area, trying to look nonchalant, she imagines.

In Sarah's profile picture, she's wearing a black thong and matching bra, her thirty-eight-year-old body still taut and firm in all the right places. Using the disposable cell, she arranges the meetings, either by text, voice, or an e-mail account employed only for this one purpose.

From across the lot, she can see that RockyRoad35 is true to his profile and picture—a rarity in the world of online dating, an *Alice in Wonderland* kind of place where people are height–weight proportionate only if they're nine feet tall.

He is in his midthirties, a couple inches over six feet, a solid two hundred pounds, with lean, muscular flesh that fills out his Wranglers and pearl-button shirt nicely. Forearms ropy with muscles, thighs straining the material of his jeans. A good-looking man, a rancher maybe.

Sarah rubs her legs together, fantasizing for a moment about peeling off the man's clothes while they gaze in each other's eyes. She pushes those thoughts from her mind, concentrating on the task at hand.

From Rocky's vantage point, there's not much to see but a handful of cars and the Walmart behind the motel. Maybe he notices the LaCrosse with the tinted windows, maybe not.

After a few seconds, he ducks inside the motel.

For a moment, Sarah wonders who might be left back at the man's home. A couple of children maybe. A wife frayed at the edges after a decade or so of marriage, watching her man try to eke a living from the hard-packed soil of Central Texas.

She ponders this but doesn't really care. The idea is abstract, not relevant to the current situation. Everybody has left people behind. Even SarahSmiles.

Her last e-mail contained instructions for the rendez-vous, a little cloak-and-dagger routine that cuts out the window-shoppers.

The keycard to a ground-floor room will be taped to the side of the Coke machine just inside the back door, room number written on the back. Go on in, her e-mail said, make yourself comfortable.

The horndogs always do as they're told, especially after she's sent the other pictures, the ones where she's removed her bra. They are like little boys—easily manipulated, so agreeable to whatever Sarah suggests.

She counts to thirty. She exits the vehicle, chirps the locks shut.

Not even noon, and the heat and the humidity hit her like a wave, making her scalp sweat under the wig.

She strides to the rear entrance of the motel, steps into an empty, well-lit hallway. The air is chilly, smelling of lemon furniture polish.

She pads softly to number 139, three doors from the exit. She sticks another keycard in the electronic lock with her left hand. Her right hand grasps the Python hidden in the purse on her shoulder.

The horndogs come in a wide variety of flavors, emotionally speaking, and Sarah can usually get a read within a few seconds.

Some—most, actually—are scared and nervous. Others are cocky, a bravado used to disguise their nervousness. A couple have been sad, eyes welling with tears at the idea of what they believe is about to happen. More than a few have been drunk.

On the locking mechanism, a tiny light winks green.

She steps inside.

The door closes and locks behind her.

The shades are closed, the room dark except for a single light on the desk.

Rocky is sitting at the desk, one end of a straw jammed in his nose, the other vacuuming up a rail of white powder laid out on the Gideons Bible.

A pistol rests on the surface within easy reach.

He looks up, and Sarah knows she's made a huge mistake.

Rocky is not like the others. He's not drunk or nervous or sad.

His eyes are devoid of emotion, flat and empty like a mackerel on ice.

"You must be SarahSmiles." His voice is ragged, like he's been shouting.

She doesn't reply.

He points to the cocaine. "You want a little pick-me-up?"

The mackerel eyes don't blink. They focus on her face, and Sarah imagines he can read her every thought.

The room is silent, just the hum of the AC.

The man has a peculiar odor—a musty mixture of sweat, tobacco smoke, and something else she can't quite place, a faint metallic tang that fills the air.

"What's with the gun?" She tries to sound tough, but her voice cracks a little. "That's not the kind of weapon I'm looking for, stud."

He glances at the pistol but doesn't answer.

"And the coke." She shakes her head. "My profile was specific. Drug- and disease-free."

"Why don't you take off your sunglasses . . . *Sarah*." He rubs his nose.

She doesn't move. Instead she squeezes the grip of the Python hidden in her purse.

He stands. "At least sit down on the bed, make yourself comfortable."

She looks at the bed like it's covered in hot lava.

The man smiles, an expression that leaves her cold on the inside.

Her stomach churns. Her knees shake.

The idea of challenging this person fills her with dread. There's no wife and children at home. He's left horrible things in his path, and she wants no part of them or him.

"You ever done this kind of thing before?" He steps closer. "You look nervous."

She eases away. Her back hits the door.

"What's in your purse?" He cocks his head to one side.

Sweat coats her palms. Her mouth is dry.

"Have you been a bad girl, Sarah?" He pulls a pair of handcuffs from his back pocket. "Do you need to be taught a lesson?"

An image of her grandfather forms in her mind, the old man standing on the back porch of his home in Bowie County, up by the Red River. Summertime, early evening. She's maybe eight or nine. By the fading light she can just make out the scar on his cheek, the one from the German bayonet.

He's been dead ten years, but Sarah feels his strength flow through her limbs, the resolve returning. The gift is ready. She pulls the Python out, aims at the man.

"Hands on top of your head, Rocky." She cocks the hammer.

Over the hum of the air conditioner, through the blackout drapes covering the windows, comes a faint cracking noise, several in a row. Not gunshots or a car backfiring, different.

The sounds stop both of them.

A puzzled look appears on Rocky's face, one that no doubt mirrors her own. Neither person moves.

An instant later, the desk light flickers off, plunging the room into darkness.

An instant after that, the Python is knocked from her grip as a hand rips open the front of her blouse. The stench of the man overpowers her as much as the attack. Feral, like an animal.

She wants to scream, but fingers grasp her throat, squeezing tighter and tighter.

- CHAPTER TWO -

The badge felt heavy on my chest, tugging at the starched khaki shirt that made my neck itch.

A six-pointed star. Hammered tin, electroplated with a gold coating that was only a few microns thick. A wisp of metal that weighed four or five ounces shouldn't feel burdensome. But this one did.

In the center, in a circle of red enamel, were the words State of Texas—Sheriff—Peterson County.

That's me: Sheriff Jonathan Cantrell. Back in the family business, so to speak, quite a surprise to everyone.

Jerry, the county commissioner who served as my boss, sat across from me in the other side of the booth. We were in a diner about the size of a Greyhound bus, a blue-plate-special kind of place that smelled like coffee and bacon.

The diner was located in Peterson County, a few miles from a private, for-profit prison situated on the banks of the Brazos River, just south of Waco and not far from Interstate 35, the highway that served as Main Street for the entire state, running from Laredo in the south all the way up to Oklahoma.

Jerry peered at me over the top of his coffee cup. "You're gonna have to kill him. You know that, don't you?"

The diner was full of cattlemen, oil-field workers, and prison guards, in reverse order the three biggest forms of employment in the county.

"I'm not a hit man," I said.

"You ever killed anybody?" Jerry asked.

I sprinkled some Tabasco on my eggs but didn't answer.

Jerry was in his seventies, thirty years my senior, and a veteran of the Vietnam War—no stranger to the ways of violence. He lived a block away from the courthouse in a rambling brick home, an impressive structure that had been in his family since Teddy Roosevelt had been president.

"Sorry it's come to this," he said. "You being new on the job and all."

"I'm going to arrest him, Jerry. Not kill him."

We were talking about my deputy, a man who'd run his life into the weeds several months ago after he'd discovered the seductive but deadly pleasure of cocaine.

His wife was in the hospital in Waco, recovering from two broken ribs and a cracked orbital socket. CPS had taken his kids. Money was missing from one of the official accounts to which he had access.

"He's not gonna go without a fight," Jerry said. "You need to be careful."

"I've handled worse than a coked-up redneck." I paused. "But I'll do what's necessary."

Jerry nodded, an expression of approval on his face, and I wondered if my ability to "do what's necessary" was the main reason I'd been offered the job of sheriff.

My curriculum vitae was, how shall I put it, *checkered*.

After a couple of tours in Kuwait and Iraq during Gulf War I, I'd been a Dallas police officer. After that I worked as a federal law-enforcement contractor, a freelance DEA agent paid on a commission basis—the so-called eat what you kill method of compensation.

My last position was as a fix-it man for a DC law firm that specialized in handling federal contracts. Due to circumstances beyond my control, my boss at the firm had needed someone to fall on a sword, and with my record I'd been the perfect fallee.

As a way of compensating me for the metaphorical sword wounds, he'd used some Homeland Security grant money to arrange for this job, an emergency fill-in for the elected sheriff, who had died suddenly from a coronary. Normally, the deputy would have moved into the sheriff's slot, but Jerry and the other commissioners had seen trouble brewing on the horizon.

"Did you study Plato when you were in school?" Jerry fanned himself with the menu.

"Can't say that I did. What's your point?"

"That deputy, he only sees with his eyes. You and me, we see things from a higher plane."

Several of the roughnecks, heavyset men in dirty work shirts, stinking of sweat and diesel, clomped out of the diner, allowing a blast of heat inside as the door swung open.

I hoped my higher plane wasn't as hot and smelly.

The waitress brought the bill.

"He's bad seed." Jerry picked up the check. "His end is not going to be peaceful or quiet. He doesn't see that, of course, but you and me, we understand the situation."

I glanced at my phone resting by the Tabasco.

The Texas Department of Public Safety had issued a BOLO— be on the lookout—for the deputy's pickup, a late-model Ford.

They'd find the vehicle, sooner rather than later. When they did, they would send me a text, and I'd go arrest the man.

Odds were good he was still in the county. People like that rarely stray far from home.

Jerry unfolded a cracked leather wallet, then counted out several bills and laid them on the check. He looked out the window, whistling softly.

The view was unremarkable. A convenience store that sold beer and fishing supplies was next door, sharing the gravel parking lot with the diner. Both were on a two-lane asphalt road. The other side of the road was overgrown with post oaks, Mexican sycamores, and stinging nettles. Everything baking in the sun.

"Something else on your mind, Jerry?"

Two months in Peterson County, and I knew the whistling meant another topic was weighing the man down.

"Have you heard from her?" He handed the money to the waitress.

I'd arrived in Peterson County with a woman and an infant. Now I was alone.

I rubbed my eyes, an ache suddenly developing in the back of my head.

Disappearing was her way. You either accepted that or not. She'd been my partner back when we'd both worked for the same DEA contractor. We were chipped from the same piece of flint, able to operate as a single unit. But with a closeness like we had, there came a certain amount of animosity, at least on her end. I missed them both terribly, however.

My phone chirped before I could answer him.

A text message: *Ford pickup, TX license 027-HQR located at the TravelTimes Inn Express, FM 1876, McLennan County.*

"They found him," I said. "I need to go."

"You're a nice fellow." Jerry slid out of the booth. "I know a couple of women who—"

The lights flickered. Conversation petered out. People looked around. A few seconds later, the ambient noise of the AC clattered to a stop as the lights went dark. The air in the restaurant seemed to get instantly warmer—or perhaps that was my imagination.

Jerry looked at the manager standing by the cash register. "Y'all forget to pay the electric bill?"

The manager pointed outside. "Lights are off at the place next door, too."

Jerry and I looked where the man indicated.

The sign over the convenience store was dark. The neon beer advertisements in the windows were out as well.

"They got backup generators at the prison, don't they?" Jerry looked at me.

"Hope so." I stood. "Wish me luck. I'm gonna go arrest a fellow law officer."

- CHAPTER THREE -

Sarah shakes her head, swallows several times. She desperately wants the ringing in her ears to stop.

The motel room is still dark. What vision she gained after the lights went out has been destroyed by the muzzle flash from the Python, which has also done a number on her hearing.

She can still use her nose, though. And what she smells—the copper tang of blood, an ammonia stench of urine—tells her she better get moving.

The Python is in one hand. Her jeans are around her thighs. Her bra is torn, shirt buttonless.

Panties. Dear God, where are her panties? She remembers them being ripped from her body like they were made of so much paper.

She pats the carpet with her free hand, searching by touch.

Squish.

A puddle of liquid against her palm. Warm and thick, like syrup.

The smell of blood grows stronger.

She tries to quell the nausea but can't. She leans to one side, vomits, stomach heaving, bile dangling from her lips.

Tears fill her eyes, run down her cheeks.

The weeping makes her angrier than anything that has occurred in the crappy motel room. SarahSmiles does not cry. Ever.

A few seconds go by. The ringing in her ears lessens slightly.

Then, the desk light comes back on, and the AC begins to rumble.

Sarah blinks, looks around the room.

Rocky is on his back a few feet away, dead, a bloody hole in the middle of his shirt where his sternum is. His bladder has opened. There's a damp spot on the floor, separate and distinct from the blood.

One of his ears has an imprint of Sarah's teeth, where she bit down before shoving him off and retrieving the Python. He'd been pressing against her throat with one hand while the other tried to get her jeans off so he could—

Dear God. This animal almost raped her.

Another wave of nausea ripples through her stomach. Her teeth chatter, skin clammy.

How long has the electricity been off? Five minutes? Ten?

She finds her panties. They are unwearable, of course, resting by her purse. Both items are under the desk, the top of which contains Rocky's drugs and pistol.

Blood coats her hand from the puddle by the dead man's body. Blood that is tainted by cocaine and who knows what else. She stares at her palm, imagining the diseases burrowing under her skin.

She struggles to her feet, starts to walk to the bathroom. The jeans trip her. She falls to her knees, head banging against the wall.

Groggy. Double vision. Wig askew. Tears dripping on the carpet. Hysteria slithering its way up her spine.

Thump-thump-thump-thump-thump.

Outside the door. Soft, then loud. Then soft again. A person running down the hall.

How long before somebody comes to investigate the sound of a gunshot? She tells herself it will take a while to pinpoint this particular room, especially with the confusion of the power outage.

She gets up again, pulls her jeans on her hips, staggers into the bathroom. There, she yanks off the wig, turns on the hot water in the sink, and scrubs her hands.

The porcelain grows red from the blood, droplets staining the counter as well—a forensic clusterfuck, especially when combined with the mess in the bedroom.

Sarah looks at herself in the mirror. She's wearing a blouse with no buttons and a ripped bra dangling off one shoulder. Her ribs on the right side throb; a bruise is forming there. Somehow, her face is speckled with Rocky's blood. Her hair is, too, even though it had been covered by the wig.

She closes her eyes, and this time instead of hearing her grandfather's words of strength, her father appears, drunk, standing on the balcony of the house in Bowie County. He's looking out over the field where the cotton used to grow. He is waiting for Sarah's grandfather to return, an unpleasant meeting.

Sarah feels small and helpless at the memory.

It's the 1980s, and her father has lost more money than most people will ever see in a lifetime, the old man's money, gone in a swirl of headlines as the oil bust and savings-and-loan crisis in Texas deepened.

Two things her grandfather hated more than anything: losing money and headlines.

Sarah opens her eyes. Steam fills the bathroom.

Make that three. The old man hated her father, his only son. Thought him weak and ineffectual, a simpering drunk. Which he was, up until the day he died in an alley behind that gay bar in Dallas.

Sarah realizes the stench filling her nostrils now is from her own body—sweat and fear and more sweat. She shuts off the hot water in the sink and turns on both taps in the bath. Then she removes what's left of her clothes and takes a hurried shower, scrubbing herself raw with soap, shampooing her hair.

Four minutes later, she's putting on her jeans and blouse, underwear balled up in her purse. The blouse won't fasten, so she finds a lightweight plastic jacket in her handbag, an oversized, shapeless raincoat type of thing you can buy at a dollar store, something that folds to a compact size and is kept for emergencies.

Sarah always has one handy in case she needs to change her appearance after an encounter with a horndog. She puts the coat on, zips it up to just below her throat.

The garment reaches to her thighs and completely hides her shape. She could be anorexic or morbidly obese.

Satisfied with her appearance, she wipes down the sink and counter with toilet paper and flushes the sodden ball. Then she gingerly steps into the bedroom, avoiding Rocky's blood and her vomit.

Outside, the sound of car doors slamming, people talking.

The wig has been torn somehow. She jams it in the purse and removes a Dallas Cowboys ball cap. With the cap on her wet hair, oversized sunglasses, and the jacket, she's unidentifiable, unless a close friend is doing the looking, which is highly unlikely since SarahSmiles doesn't have many of those.

There's nothing she can do about the mess she's leaving behind, though.

The thought gives her pause, but only for a moment.

More movement from the hallway.

She takes a deep breath, stares at the door, wonders what's on the other side.

Are the police waiting for her?

A lungful of air catches in her throat, makes her gasp. Fear paralyzes her limbs.

Her grandfather's words reverberate in her head: *Don't be like your daddy, Sarah. Don't be a fucking pussy.*

- CHAPTER FOUR -

I parked my squad car by the front entrance of the TravelTimes Inn, underneath the porte cochere. The deputy's pickup was in the back, along with a half-dozen other vehicles. A slow day at the inn.

My phone dinged with a text message at the same time as the car's two-way radio squawked. Both communications were about the power outage, which apparently had involved several counties, a pretty big swath of Central Texas in the dead of summer.

Fortunately that was someone else's problem.

I got out, left the car and AC running, and went inside.

A clerk stood behind the front desk, watching me as I crossed the lobby.

He was short and scrawny. His skin was the color of cinnamon, and he wore a name tag that read, IRVING PATEL, ASSISTANT MANAGER.

I stand a little over six feet, about ten inches taller than he was. A Stetson rested on my head, mirrored Ray-Bans perched on my nose, a pistol on my hip.

Irving Patel smiled. "What may I do for you, officer?" He spoke with a thick Indian accent.

I took off my glasses, tried to look less intimidating. "I need to see your register."

Irving's mildly puzzled expression disappeared from his face, replaced by a frown.

"That is not possible, officer."

"I'm the sheriff, Irving. Not an officer."

He nodded but didn't speak.

"Your guest list. I need to know who's staying in what room."

"I am sorry"—he squinted at my name tag—"Sheriff Cantrell. This I cannot do."

I sighed.

Stupid TV. Everybody'd seen a zillion episodes of *Law & Order* and thought they knew how to be tough with the po-po. Based on our limited interaction, Irving Patel seemed like an all-right guy, as assistant managers go, and I hated to bring the hammer down. But I had an armed, coked-up deputy somewhere on the premises. That trumped being nice.

I pointed in the direction of the interstate. "You know the truck stop up the road?"

No reply.

"The one with the girls hustling tricks in the parking lot?"

Irving frowned but didn't speak.

"Maybe you know the guy named Wally who hangs out in the coffee shop there."

Silence. After a moment, he licked his lips.

"I'm sure you know Wally," I said. "He sells Mexican crank to the truckers when he's not pimping out the girls."

Irving rearranged some pens in a coffee cup. His eyes wouldn't meet mine. "We do not allow Mr. Wally on the premises anymore."

"That's swell, Irving. We all have to do our part to keep crime in check." I paused. "Say . . . did you ever tell anybody at the home office about Wally?"

Irving chewed on his lip, stared off into the distance.

"What I hear, the franchisee rules are pretty strict," I said. "Be a shame for the home office to yank your logo."

Roadside motels live and die by their brand, the goodwill associated with a particular chain as well as their vast reservation system. If a motel owner lost his logo, then the rack rate went down. If the rack rate went down, then people like Wally would be back, and pretty soon what started out as a nice, clean family hotel would end up a flophouse with HBO.

We were both silent for a few moments. Then Irving said, "Do you know why I cannot show you the register, Sheriff Cantrell?"

I shook my head. "Tell me, Irving."

"The electricity was cut off," he said. "And the server hasn't rebooted yet."

I rubbed my eyes. "You coulda mentioned that on the front side."

"You didn't ask."

My walkie-talkie dinged, another call about the power outage.

"Let's try this from a different angle." I turned down the volume. "I need to know who's checked in here in the last day or so. Can you do that without the server?"

"Perhaps this I can help you with." Irving smiled again. "Who are you looking for?"

"A man about my size," I said. "Caucasian, a few years younger than me. Drives that Ford pickup out back."

"No man has checked in." Irving shook his head.

Silence. I waited. Irving smiled expectantly.

I tried not to sound exasperated. "Has a *woman* checked in sometime during the last twenty-four hours?"

"Oh yes." Irving nodded. "A woman arrived last night while I was on duty."

"What room?"

He consulted a slip of paper. "Number one three nine."

"What'd she look like?"

"She was white. I could not tell her age. Somewhere between forty and, I do not know, sixty perhaps."

A heavyset guy in Dockers and a golf shirt, a traveling salesman probably, emerged from the elevator. He waddled over and asked about breakfast.

Irving said, "I am sorry, sir. Coffee only this morning because of the power outage."

The man looked like he was about to argue but shook his head instead, muttering under his breath. He wandered over to the coffee bar.

I spoke to Irving. "Was she closer to forty or sixty? Give it your best shot."

The ageless woman was probably nothing, a traveler stopping for the night, but since she was the only person who'd checked in during the past twenty-four hours, I decided to find out what I could about her.

"Her name. Would that help?" Irving consulted his paper again. "Mildred Johnson."

"Mildred . . . So closer to sixty," I said. "Or older, maybe?"

"Perhaps." Irving smiled nervously. "Forgive me, Sheriff. But all of you people look the same to me. I do remember that she had red hair, lots of it, and much makeup."

Swell. He just described Sylvester Stallone's mother, Jackie.

"Where's room 139?" I asked.

"Ground floor. At the other side of the property."

"Is the rear exit unlocked? I'm gonna drive around back."

I could have just as easily walked through the corridors, but I wanted to block the deputy's pickup in case he tried to flee the scene.

Irving nodded as the salesman appeared at the front desk again, coffee in hand. He looked at me and said, "Are you here about the gunshot?"

Before I could answer, the power went out again.

- CHAPTER FIVE -

As Sarah touches the handle of the motel room door, the lights flicker off again.

The AC rattles to a stop, and there's no noise anywhere. Nothing but the ringing in her ears from the Python—lessening bit by bit—and the thump of her heart.

The silence is stronger than the darkness.

A minute or more passes, fear paralyzing her. Finally, she opens the door and steps into the gloom of the hallway.

From the direction of the lobby, raised voices. From the rear exit, nothing.

She walks away from the lobby, purse on one shoulder. She moves with purpose but not fast. Confidence, that's the key. She has somewhere to go, but she is not afraid.

As the exit draws near, she reaches for her sunglasses, finds them resting against the Python in her purse. She pushes the door open with one hand, slides on the shades with the other.

The sun is fierce, the heat more oppressive than before, especially under the shapeless plastic raincoat. She is grateful not to be wearing the wig, though, and even more grateful to have not seen anyone.

A sense of euphoria washes over her. She's going to make it.

Then the police car squeals to a stop behind RockyRoad's pickup, which is still parked about twenty feet from the rear exit of the motel.

Twenty feet from her.

The euphoria disappears. She hesitates for a moment—like any normal person would, she tells herself—and continues walking, heading down the steps that lead to the parking lot. The direction will take her right past the front of the squad car.

There's no other choice. To deviate now would attract attention. She concentrates on putting one foot in front of the other.

She has nothing to fear. She's just a traveler, anxious to be on her way. She didn't even take the time to dry her hair. Just tucked it under a ball cap.

The door to the squad car opens, and a man in a cowboy hat and mirrored sunglasses gets out. A sheriff. He's wearing jeans and a starched khaki shirt with a gold badge on the breast.

He's somewhere in his forties. He's fit, with broad shoulders, muscular arms. Good-looking, too—a thin nose, strong chin.

Despite what she'd left behind in room 139, what she'd . . . *done* in that room, Sarah slows just a little.

From the dark places in her mind, the thoughts come without warning. Images splatter across the screen in her brain like paint flung by a child.

Naked bodies, skin coated in sweat, mattress springs squeaking.

She imagines an encounter with this man.

Sex, an anonymous coupling like the kind advertised on the sites where she arranges her meetings. Afterward, she robs him, a deviation in her usual pattern, which up to now has not allowed for any physical contact with the horndogs.

Those thighs between hers, their lips pressed together as her hands pull on that ass. The Python rests on the nightstand, next to a half-empty bottle of wine.

The images start coming faster, like they always do with a person she's attracted to—an out-of-kilter blur, a movie reel that's jumped its sprockets. Flesh against flesh. Tangled bedsheets.

In her imagination, the danger and the sex and the gun all ball up into one throbbing sensation that settles in the pit of her stomach until she feels faint and aroused at the same time.

"Ma'am? You all right?" The sheriff cocks his head.

Sarah realizes he's talking to her, that's she's been daydreaming the whole encounter. The reality is that she's standing in front of the squad car, sweating, wobbly on her feet.

She takes a deep breath. "I'm fine. The heat, it gets to you when you first walk outside."

He chuckles, a sound full of warmth and caring. The sound a man might make while standing around a barbecue in his backyard, playing with his kids.

"I grew up around here," he says. "Every year, I think it's gonna be different. But it never is."

She smiles, a small moment between two people who have no other connection except a few seconds of banter about the weather. Then she imagines the sheriff's warm voice growing cold, whispering in her ear about how hard he is going to fuck her.

Her thighs tremble with pleasure, skin sensitive to the texture of her clothes.

She pushes the thoughts back to the dark corners of her mind. She's a traveler again, anxious to get home to her family.

She heads to her car. "Take it easy, Sheriff."

He pinches the brim of the hat with his thumb and forefinger, a gesture reminiscent of her grandfather. "You too, ma'am. Be safe now."

She strides across the parking lot. The LaCrosse is where she left it, parked by the Dumpster near the property line between the motel and the Walmart.

The interior of the vehicle is as hot as a steam bath.

She cranks the ignition, turns the AC to high, and looks across the parking lot.

The sheriff is standing by the back entrance, staring at her car. At her.

- CHAPTER SIX -

I was pretty sure Irving Patel had never seen a dead body up close and personal. I based this hypothesis on the fact that as soon as he peered around my shoulder into room 139, he vomited.

I've seen a lot of death in my time, the results of natural causes and otherwise. *Lots* of otherwise. What always strikes me is the utter stillness of the deceased.

An anatomically correct doll left lying where some over-sized child had dropped it, tired of playing for the day. An empty vessel—the spark that made us more than just a slab of meat never to return.

My deputy's corpse was sprawled at the foot of the king-sized bed, a bullet hole in his chest. His jeans were unzipped, pulled down around his hips like he was trying to get them off but got stopped.

The room smelled like vomit, blood, urine, and that hot, soapy aroma that comes after someone takes a shower.

I shoved Irving toward the door. "You're contaminating the crime scene."

He stumbled to the hallway, wiping his mouth. "What should I do?"

"Wait for me in your office. Don't do anything until I get there."

"But—"

"Go." I pointed toward the lobby.

He stared at me for a moment, a worried expression on his face, then trotted away.

After he disappeared from view, I called Jerry, relaying the information to him as quickly as possible.

Our deputy had been murdered. There was evidence of drug use. The main suspect was a woman with red hair—age and a more detailed physical description to be determined after I'd secured the crime scene. Jerry started to say something, but I hung up.

My next call was to the Department of Public Safety in Austin, the statewide police agency and parent organization to the venerable Texas Rangers, the special forces of law enforcement.

Peterson County had a population of about twenty-five thousand, not counting the inmates in the penitentiary by the Brazos River.

Like many rural areas, the population was getting smaller every year and couldn't support the law-enforcement infrastructure that a larger county could. So there were no *CSI*-style crime labs or homicide squads waiting to spring into action. There was only me, my remaining deputies—ten total—and several woefully understaffed police departments in the larger towns of the county.

In cases like this, the protocol was to contact the Texas Rangers, tasked by the DPS to handle crime scenes and murder investigations in areas where the local authorities were unable to proceed, for whatever reason.

I spoke to a man who handed me off to a woman who was the officer on duty at the Texas Rangers' desk. I gave her my name and title and callback number, as well as the situation. She repeated everything, told me to sit tight. Help was ten minutes out—several DPS officers, the closest resources available.

While I waited, I took photos of the crime scene with my phone, dozens of them.

The deputy's body. The sleeping area, the bathroom, the short hallway leading to the door. I got several shots of the white powdery residue on the Bible, as well as the Glock, which appeared to be the deputy's service weapon.

Even though an official photographer would come along later and do exactly the same thing, an extra set wouldn't hurt.

Nine minutes later, a group of DPS troopers—big burly men in khaki uniforms and polished black boots—marched through the rear door of the motel.

I had one secure room 139 with crime-scene tape and asked the others to start doing door-to-doors. The hotel was mostly vacant, but we had to make sure every avenue was covered.

After that, I went to find Irving.

• • •

The manager's office was behind the front desk, a windowless room about twelve feet by twelve, crammed with a particle-board desk and credenza, several cheap chairs, and a copier.

The air smelled like print toner, stale coffee, and Irving's aftershave: Old Spice.

"This is a problem." Irving held his head in his hands, staring at the surface of the desk. "A very, very big problem."

"Yes it is, Irving. For now, I need everything you've got on the person who rented room one three nine."

He nodded, took several deep breaths, and went to work.

To his credit, he had a lot of information on the unknown woman who'd used the name Mildred Johnson. He had a home address in Austin, her method of securing the room—a prepaid Visa card that could be bought in any grocery store—and a description of her car, a Buick LaCrosse, license plate number 512-AML, the number undoubtedly a fake since the car I'd seen had dealer tags.

I called the DPS again, got the same woman on the Ranger desk, gave her the license plate info. I also told her about the LaCrosse and the person in the sunglasses and Dallas Cowboys ball cap who'd been leaving as I was parking in the rear.

About a minute passed before the woman came back on the line. "That license plate doesn't exist."

There was a shocker.

"Can you check an address for me?" I recited the information that the woman had given to Irving Patel. A house on Lamar Boulevard, a street that ran through much of central Austin.

She stayed on the line this time, keyboard clacking in the background. "That's not a residence; looks like a vacant lot." More keyboard noises. "You have a TDL?"

I glanced at Irving. "What about her driver's license?"

Irving looked away. He stared at a picture on the far wall, a dark-skinned woman in a sari standing behind several children, Irving next to her.

I said to the Ranger, "Let's do a BOLO on a late-model Buick LaCrosse, color gray, dealer tags. Female driver between thirty and forty years of age. Caucasian, five foot six. Wearing a Dallas Cowboys ball cap and oversized sunglasses."

The Texas Ranger read it all back to me, while Irving rubbed his head with one hand, looking like he was going to be sick again.

I ended the call.

Irving stared at the picture of his family. "She did not have a driver's license."

"What about an ID card?"

A moment of silence.

Then he said, "She told me her purse had been stolen."

"Her wallet or her purse?" I remembered the woman in the ball cap. She'd been carrying a large handbag.

"Her wallet, not her purse. That is what she said."

"And you let her check in without a valid ID?"

Irving crossed his arms. "It was late at night. I took pity on her. She seemed nice and harmless."

Not getting a photo ID was a big no-no according to franchise rules, state law, and common sense.

"I'm not blaming you, Irving. I just need to know the facts."

He nodded, a glum look on his face.

Sirens sounded outside. More troopers were arriving, hopefully a medical examiner from Waco, too.

"The guy that died," I said. "He worked for me. For what it's worth, he was going to come to a bad end one way or the other. Either here or in some other motel or bar."

My cell rang, a number I didn't recognize, area code Dallas. I sent the call to voice mail.

"I shall be fired, of course," Irving said. "My employer is my uncle. I have caused a rift in the family, dishonored the name Patel. This is very, very bad."

"Nobody's getting fired." I shook my head. "Have your uncle call me. I'll tell him Mildred gave you a fake ID."

Irving looked up, a faint expression of hope on his face. "Thank you, Sheriff. Thank you very much."

"In the meantime, get me a list of every woman who's checked in here in the past week." I told him briefly about the person in the Cowboys cap.

He nodded, started tapping on a keyboard.

Then his desk phone rang. He stared at it for a moment before answering. His expression went from fearful to confused. He pressed the receiver to his chest and looked at me.

"It's for you."

My cell buzzed; Jerry's number appeared on the screen. I sent him to voice mail, too.

Irving said, "Do you know a man named Price Anderson?"

A thousand lifetimes ago, an alley in Kuwait City filled with dust and heat and the stench of rotting flesh. Price Anderson had saved my life.

Irving pointed to the phone. "He needs to talk to you."

An insurgent with an AK-47, barely old enough to shave. The muzzle of the rifle pointed at my face.

The end of everything I'd ever been or ever would be, peering into my eyes.

Price Anderson fired at the insurgent, and I was still alive.

The memories were strong. The smell of the alley filled my nose.

Irving said, "Sheriff Cantrell? Are you all right?"

- CHAPTER SEVEN -

I stepped into the coffee shop located a few hundred yards north of the motel. It was a dismal place attached to one end of a truck stop. On the other end was a strip club.

The investigators with the Texas Rangers had arrived at the motel a few minutes before, and I was mostly getting in their way, so I decided to accept Price Anderson's request to meet. He'd indicated it was urgent.

Unlike the diner where I'd had breakfast with Jerry an hour or so ago, this establishment was windowless and dirty, dimly lit by wagon-wheel chandeliers draped with cobwebs. The worn linoleum floor felt sticky, and the Naugahyde booths were patched with duct tape.

At the hostess station was a waitress in her sixties with a Farrah Fawcett hairdo dyed the color of tar. She stood about five foot nine but looked like she weighed only a hundred pounds. A cigarette dangled from her lips.

"Can I help you?" Her voice was raspy, like she'd been gargling fiberglass.

The place was about half full. Truck drivers and day laborers. Drifters. By the salad bar were several bikers who looked like they hadn't slept or bathed since Bush had been president. Everyone was smoking.

"What's the special today?" I asked. "Chicken-fried meth?"

"The old sheriff useta come in here all the time," she said. "Only he weren't no asshole."

"He's dead. Now you have to deal with me."

She shrugged.

"I'm meeting somebody," I said. "Last time I saw him, he had all his teeth. That ring a bell?"

With her cigarette, she pointed to the back. "Try our non-smoking area."

The tiny room was on the other side of the kitchen. The walls were decorated with pictures of World War II bombers and Lyndon Johnson.

Price Anderson was the only person in that section. He was also the only person in the entire restaurant wearing a decent set of clothes—a dove-gray suit and a lavender dress shirt with French cuffs.

I slid into the opposite side of the booth. We shook hands.

"How long's it been?" he said. "Fifteen years?"

Despite the fact that he'd saved my life, Price and I were not friends.

Call it a clash of personalities. Price was a narcissist, always preening in front of a mirror, his combat fatigues altered to accentuate his broad shoulders and tapered waist. Price was the kind of person who applied hair gel before going on patrol.

"More like twenty," I said. "We were on leave in Manila. You stiffed that hooker. Asked me to watch out for her pimp."

"Oh yeah." He chuckled. "Boy, was she pissed."

"What I told you on the phone, Price: I can give you about ten minutes. Things are a little busy right now."

"The homicide, right?"

I didn't reply.

Price was showing off, telling me he was plugged in enough to know about a murder where the victim was still warm. I'd already surmised that, since he knew to reach me at the scene of the crime.

"Last I heard," he said, "you were a DEA contractor."

This little tidbit was not a secret. Not by a long shot.

"That's been a while," I said.

"You settled down, right? Somebody told me you were married and had a kid."

Silence.

I lived alone now, and not by my choice. I saw no reason to discuss my domestic situation with a supposed old friend who'd dropped in out of nowhere.

"Me, I was in-country until a couple of years ago. Working for a division of Halliburton. We were revamping the electrical grid in Baghdad."

I remembered the two power failures in the past ninety minutes. A large section of Central Texas without electricity.

"Who you working for now?" I asked.

"Ever hear of a company called Sudamento?"

I nodded.

The company was a huge operation, one of the largest employers in the region.

"Sudamento owns a third of the electrical plants in the state," Price said.

"And here you are. Right after the power goes out."

"I'm head of security." He slid a card across the table.

The waitress brought me a cup of coffee, even though I hadn't asked for one. She refilled Price's cup.

His business card was made from ultrathick cardstock the color of buttermilk. The lettering was navy blue. Expensive, as befitting the corporate address, which was a skyscraper in downtown Dallas.

"What do you know about the electrical grid?" He stirred sugar into his coffee.

"Not much. And I'd like to keep it that way."

He took a sip and stared at the waitress, who was across the room, filling saltshakers.

"I bet she's free tonight," I said. "Why don't you ask her out?"

In addition to being a vain, self-centered egotist, Price Anderson was also a man-slut. He'd screw the crack of dawn, given half a chance.

"The power outage today was not an accident," he said.

I didn't reply. Electrical demand surged during the summer. Temporary brownouts, euphemistically called "rolling blackouts," were not uncommon. That's what I'd figured today's occurrence had been.

"Why are you telling me all this?" I looked at my watch.

A task that I dreaded still awaited me: notifying the deputy's widow.

"We're being attacked, Cantrell. Sudamento's ability to generate electricity is threatened."

"Who's doing the attacking?" I asked.

No answer.

"Are you talking about an act of terrorism?" I lowered my voice. "You think it's domestic or foreign?"

There were two ways to disrupt the grid—this much I knew. A software hack, something that could be initiated by people on the other side of the globe. Or a physical attack on the hardware—transmission lines, generators, turbines.

"If we knew any of that, do you think I'd be here?"

"What do the feds say?"

He didn't respond. After a moment, he shrugged.

"You have brought them into this, right?"

"Of course." He rolled his eyes. "Homeland Security, the FBI, and a bunch of other alphabet agencies are crawling over each other. It's like a dick-measuring contest." He paused. "But none of them have any viable leads at the moment."

His statement implied the feds were on-site, which meant a hardware attack, not a network breach.

I took a sip of my coffee and then pushed the cup away. I wondered why Price had contacted me but decided not to take the time to ask. Minutes were dribbling away. Time for me to leave.

"Do you know what happens if the power grid goes down?" he said. "I'm talking more than just a few counties in Texas for an hour or two."

"People go all *Mad Max*?" I asked. "And the doomsday preppers get to say I told you so?"

"Always the wisecracks." He shook his head.

I sighed and then ran down the checklist for him—the stuff any military personnel or law-enforcement officer knows—just to prove I wasn't a total smart-ass.

Most grocery stores only have three days' worth of inventory. Perishable goods would spoil within a day or so. Gas pumps wouldn't work, so food trucks couldn't deliver non-perishable items. Banks wouldn't be able to keep track of their money. Hospital generators would run out of fuel.

"And the economy grinds to a halt." I finished my little speech.

He nodded. "Which means tax revenues drop, so Uncle Sam starts to run out of money."

I looked at my phone. Nine text messages, all of them concerning the murder. I needed to get back to work. Coming here had been a mistake.

"The attack feels like a probing action," he said. "Testing our security, the integrity of the grid. Our thinking is this is just a warm-up, getting ready for something big."

We sat in silence for a moment. The waitress left the room.

"Sudamento would like some fresh eyes on this situation," Price said. "We're willing to pay you a substantial consulting fee."

"When you were looking on Craigslist for 'fresh eyes,' did my name pop up?"

He didn't reply.

"Is this the part where you remind me how I owe you?" I said. "The brothers-in-arms routine?"

I felt a momentary twinge for bringing up our history in such a manner. The feeling passed.

"Best of luck to you." I slid from the booth, stood. "In case you haven't noticed, I already have gainful employment. I'm a sheriff now, not a fed or a contractor."

Price stood as well, moving close enough that I could smell his cologne, a subtle fragrance that made me think of sage and limes. Expensive, unlike Irving Patel's drugstore brand.

"Skip the Andy Griffith routine," he said.

We stared at each other, not blinking.

"Your former employer strong-armed you into this job," he said. "You'd never even set foot in Peterson County until three months ago."

I tried to control my anger. The sheriff's job represented a chance at stability and a new start. I didn't want people like Price Anderson screwing that up. I also didn't want to admit, even to myself, how bored I was. The job really only occupied half my time. The rest of the day I spent wondering about Piper—the mother of my child—who had disappeared soon after our arrival in the county, along with my infant daughter.

"Let the feds do their job," I said. "This is their turf."

He chuckled. "Who do you think sent me?"

- CHAPTER EIGHT -

Sarah knows the LaCrosse is compromised.

The good-looking sheriff with the mirrored sunglasses is not stupid. She sensed that during their short encounter a few minutes ago. By now he's found RockyRoad's body, dead from a gunshot wound, with his cocaine and pistol and his pants pulled down.

Mildred Johnson, the identity she used to check into the motel, doesn't exist. The only real information she's left in her wake, other than a bucket full of forensics evidence that will take time to process, is the Buick LaCrosse.

Therefore, the vehicle has to go.

She speeds north on the access road, past the skeevy truck stop with its diner and strip club. She merges onto the highway, going the speed limit.

With the growth in Texas's population in recent years, the interstate has become more—oh, how to put it—upscale. Gone for the most part are the biker bars, one-room liquor stores, and mom-and-pop porn shops.

Now it's chain restaurants, outlet malls, and service stations advertising clean bathrooms. This, coupled with the advent of cheap video-monitoring systems, makes it damn hard to get rid of a hot car and find a new one.

Ten or twelve miles blow by before Sarah sees what she needs, a VFW hall with blacked-out windows, set back from the highway.

The building is cinder block, surrounded by a gravel parking area with only a handful of cars. Older models, easy to steal. No fancy electronic key fobs or LoJack systems for the VFW crowd.

She exits the interstate, doubles back, does a drive-by.

The building doesn't have cameras.

At the rear of the structure, hidden from the road, sits a lime-green, late-1970s Monte Carlo.

Next to the VFW hall is an abandoned Whataburger.

Sarah parks at the shuttered fast-food restaurant. From the rear floor, she grabs a coat hanger and a rag. She wipes down the inside of the LaCrosse with the rag, gets out, does the same to the handle.

Her brother, Elias, two years older, had taught her how to steal an automobile. After getting out of the army, he'd learned the skill from a Mexican in Shreveport who used to boost cars for a chop shop in Sabine Parish.

With an old General Motors car like the Monte Carlo, all you need is a flat-head screwdriver. Sarah finds one in the trunk of the LaCrosse.

It's a little after lunch. The sky is a cloudless haze, the color of pewter. Heat radiates off the cracked asphalt beneath her feet.

Purse on her shoulder, hanger and screwdriver in hand, she trots to the VFW hall, sweat trickling down the small of her back. She's still wearing the shapeless raincoat and Dallas Cowboys ball cap.

No one is outside. She imagines the inside of the bar, dim and cool, full of day drinkers—old men talking about the price of corn and the way things used to be.

The driver's side of the Monte Carlo is unlocked. Small mercies.

She throws the coat hanger across the lot. Opens the door, tosses the purse inside. She's just about to slide behind the wheel when the rear exit of the VFW hall swings outward and a guy in overalls staggers into the heat, blinking, clutching a Schlitz tallboy.

Mr. Overalls is in his seventies and wobbly, drunk like a redneck at a tractor pull. He's got the distended stomach and burst capillaries of someone whose natural state is soused.

He squints at Sarah, eyes watery.

Please go back to the bar, Sarah says to herself. *I do not want to hurt you.*

"Hey." He points at her. "W-what are doing with Charlie's car?"

His words slur. Charlie sounds like Sharley.

"Charlie said I could borrow it." Sarah smiles.

"Charlie don't loan his car out," the old man says. "Are you his daughter?"

Sarah's pocket vibrates, her real cell phone.

"Wait a minute." Mr. Overalls scratches his head. "Charlie's daughter is dead, right?"

Sarah doesn't move. No sense boosting a car if it's going to be reported stolen in the next thirty seconds. She could get back in the LaCrosse and look for another suitable vehicle, but she doesn't want to take the time.

That leaves plan B. Take out Mr. Overalls.

The thought makes her stomach churn. The drunk is innocent. He shouldn't have to die for her sins.

The old guy takes a long pull of beer. He squints at her like maybe he's not sure what he's seeing.

She imagines what her grandfather's reaction to this current predicament would be. He'd have no hesitation. The old drunk would be on his way to the great VFW hall in the sky.

The cell keeps vibrating. She continues to ignore it. She touches the folding knife in the waistband of her jeans instead, her hand slick with perspiration.

"I never did like Charlie much." The old drunk tosses the beer can away.

Sarah doesn't say anything. Seconds tick by. Sweat beads on her forehead.

He peers into the distance, like something important is out there in the heat and the dust.

The vibrating phone stops.

Sarah slides the knife from her waistband.

The old drunk doesn't appear to notice. He burps and walks away, headed down the side of the building.

She watches him for a moment. Then she hops behind the wheel, jams the screwdriver in the ignition, and starts the motor.

The old man seems to have forgotten Charlie and his Monte Carlo. At the corner of the building, he unzips his overalls, urinates into the gravel.

Sarah puts the car in reverse, backs out of the parking space. She glances once more at the old man, realizing he's too drunk to remember her. Then she drives off.

Thirty seconds later, she's on the interstate. The Monte Carlo is in pretty good shape, considering its age. The seat is worn and the carpet has holes, but the motor runs strong, as does the AC.

She pulls her cell phone out, checks the messages.

A recorded voice. Fear clutches at her heart like a talon. She jams the accelerator to the floor, ignoring the speed limit, and heads to Dallas.

- CHAPTER NINE -

I walked down the hall of the hospital in Waco. The air was cool and clean, smelling like a hospital should, a heavy mixture of rubbing alcohol and disinfectant that implied everything was going to be okay.

The deputy's wife, Kelsey, was in a room on the third floor, recovering from the injuries she'd received during an argument with her now-dead husband. Her window overlooked the only shopping mall in town, giving her a nice view of the parking lot for Bed Bath & Beyond.

Before she took off for parts unknown, Piper had shopped there, buying stuff for the nursery.

I put the past back where it belonged and turned my attention to Kelsey.

"They're not gonna give you his benefits," I said. "Wish there was something I could do, but there's not."

She wiped a tear from her good eye with a Kleenex.

Her other eye, the one with the cracked orbital socket, was swollen shut. That side of her face was the color of eggplant, like she'd gone a couple of rounds with Mike Tyson.

"The county commissioners," I said. "They'd already filed the paperwork to fire him."

She shook her head slowly, a lost expression on her face, the emotional weight of everything obviously pressing down on her. She'd known as soon as I'd walked in that her husband was dead. People usually do. Not getting the benefits, that was a low blow, but government agencies live and die by their policies and procedures.

I skipped the more lurid details surrounding her husband's death. The cocaine, the indication that another woman was involved. I told her I was sorry, and that we'd find whoever was responsible.

"I got three kids and no job." She crumpled the tissue. "What am I supposed to do?"

Kelsey was twenty-nine, born and raised in Peterson County. For her honeymoon a decade before, she and her husband had gone to Fort Worth, the farthest north she'd ever been in her life.

"We'll figure something out," I said. "Not sure what, but I won't let you end up on the street."

She blew her nose into a fresh tissue.

"When do the docs think you can leave?" I asked.

"Couple days."

"Me or one of the other deputies will pick you up," I said. "Make sure you've got everything you need."

"That include my benefits?"

I didn't reply.

"Who's gonna help me with those kids?"

She wasn't talking to me. The question appeared to be addressed to the universe in general, a place that wasn't very kind to single mothers with only a high school diploma.

I walked to the window.

The Bed Bath & Beyond was doing a thriving business.

Young people walking hand in hand, newlyweds and freshly engaged couples, imagining married life as a happy blur of Hallmark memories. With a wedding and the rest of your days before you, nobody ever thinks about cracked orbital sockets or cocaine addiction.

"Kelsey, I'm sorry to get into this right now, but I have to ask you some questions."

"Whatever," she said. "You're a cop. That's what cops do."

I turned away from the window. "You know anybody who'd want to kill him?"

She took a sip of water from a cup with a straw. "Other than the husbands of the sluts he was screwing?"

I didn't say anything. Her good eye filled with tears.

"Or whatever dope dealer he stiffed?" she said.

"I'm gonna need a list. Sorry to put you through this."

A nurse came in, carrying a cup of pills. She stared at me, said, "Everything all right in here?"

Kelsey nodded.

"I have to go." I headed toward the door.

The nurse handed Kelsey the pills and then adjusted her IV.

At the door, I stopped. "I'll come back when you're feeling better."

"Wait," Kelsey said. "You checked his computer yet?"

I didn't say anything.

"He was meeting women online. One of those places on the Internet for people looking to cheat."

A website for people looking to step out on their spouse.

That's the type of place where you might arrange a rendez-vous at a motel on the interstate.

- CHAPTER TEN -

My office was on the ground floor of the county courthouse. The building was two stories, limestone and granite, constructed in the 1920s when cotton revenues swelled the local tax coffers and black people had to drink from a separate fountain.

The structure was in the middle of the town square and completely at odds with the current economic climate, which could barely support the construction of a Quonset hut. The building itself wasn't in very good shape either. The plumbing leaked, as did the roof. The marble flooring was worn into grooves in the middle of the hallways. The air smelled like old paper and mildew.

As was my habit, I circled the square before parking, looking for anything out of the ordinary. Usually that meant a drunk sleeping in the shade of the bus station or an elderly runaway from the nursing home two blocks over.

Today was different.

Three black Suburbans, antennas sprouting from their tops, idled underneath the canopy of the gas station by the funeral home. Through the SUVs' front windows I could see men in suits, wearing sunglasses.

By the entrance to the courthouse were two vehicles that clearly didn't belong.

A Lincoln Navigator, hunter green, marked on the side with a decal that read, SUDAMENTO: CLEAN POWER FOR A CLEAN TEXAS. Next to the Lincoln was another black Suburban, similar to the ones at the gas station.

I parked in the spot reserved for the sheriff and got out.

Midafternoon. The sign on the bank across the street indicated it was 101 degrees. No breeze. The leaves on the trees hung listlessly, curled at the edges.

Jerry marched out the front door of the courthouse, his lips pressed together, eyes narrow. He intercepted me at the curb.

"What's going on here, Sheriff Cantrell?" He pointed to the Suburbans. "Who are these people?"

Sheriff Cantrell? He always called me Jon. He must be really upset.

"My guess is they're feds of some sort."

"When we hired you, we were told this wouldn't be a problem."

"This what?" I asked.

"We wanted somebody to keep order in the county," he said. "Not have a bunch a damn G-men running around here."

The past was a bitch, always sitting on your shoulder, waiting to pop her head up when you least expect it.

My time as a federal law-enforcement contractor had generated a certain amount of headlines and notoriety, an unsavoriness that Jerry wanted kept out of his county. Who could blame him?

Nevertheless, I was hot and tired and not in the mood to rehash ancient history.

"Kelsey's benefits," I said. "The commissioners need to reinstate them."

He mopped his brow with a handkerchief, a blank look on his face.

"She's in a tough spot," I said. "The county shouldn't make her situation worse just because it can."

"Jon . . . I'm, uh, sorry. Didn't mean to snap at you. It's this damn heat."

"No worries." I forced a smile.

"Do you have any leads on who killed our man?" He put his handkerchief away. "This is an affront to the county. We can't rest until the murderer—"

"Our man?" I said. "You were trying to fire him twenty-four hours ago."

He didn't reply, suddenly looking every bit of his seventy-odd years.

"He was catting around," I said. "Looks like his murder was somehow related to that."

Jerry nodded.

"The Texas Rangers are handling the investigation. We're gonna find who's responsible."

He looked across the square to the Suburbans idling at the gas station.

I followed his gaze. "They're here about the power outage, if I had to guess."

"The what?" He seemed confused.

"The brownout this morning, remember?"

"Oh yeah."

"You feeling okay?"

He nodded. Then shook his head. "The deputy's grandfather. He and I were friends way back when."

Neither of us spoke for a moment.

"Kelsey and her benefits," I said. "Don't forget."

He pinched the bridge of his nose, eyes closed for a few seconds. Then he wandered down the sidewalk to his car, a freshly washed Cadillac sedan.

I took one last look at the Suburbans, then went inside the courthouse.

- CHAPTER ELEVEN -

Sarah's making good time. The speedometer is pegged at ninety, and there's not a cop in sight.

Then the tire blows.

A loud thud followed by a slapping noise.

The Monte Carlo tilts to one side. Smoke and road dust gush from the back right of the vehicle. The steering wheel rattles. She hangs on with all her strength, knuckles white.

Instinctively, she takes her foot off the gas but does not apply the brake, instead letting the vehicle slow on its own. She aims toward the shoulder on the right side.

Just north of Hillsboro, this stretch of the interstate is empty of houses and commercial buildings. Nothing but heavily wooded land and roadside billboards.

The car comes to a stop, and the AC starts blowing hot air for some reason. She leaves the engine running because starting it again with a screwdriver can be tricky.

Traffic whizzes by, a never-ending stream. Cars and pickups, the occasional motorcycle. Eighteen-wheelers that buffet the old Chevy like it's a tin can.

Dallas is maybe an hour away.

There might as well be an ocean between her present location and the safety of the city. She's in a stolen car with a blown tire and no key to the trunk, where there might be a spare. Also, the state police are probably looking for her by now.

Her whole body shakes. Sweat pops up on her forehead, trickling into her eyes.

The voice of her grandfather echoes in her head: *You really shit the bed this time, didn't you?*

"Shut up." She yanks off her sunglasses.

Whatchoo gonna do now, girl?

On the opposite side of the highway, separated by forty yards of grassy median, a Texas Highway Patrol unit speeds south.

Sarah hyperventilates.

The correct word hasn't been invented yet for how fucked she is.

Inside the Monte Carlo, everything feels like it's getting smaller, the air hotter.

She rips off the ball cap and her hair spills out, dry but tangled. She unzips the raincoat, flings it open, not caring that she's naked underneath.

Her chest is slick with perspiration.

She leans her head back against the rest, eyes closed, trying to control her breathing, slow her heart rate.

Rap-rap-rap. Knocking on the glass by her head.

Sarah jerks her eyes open, looks out the windshield.

A man in a plaid shirt, the sleeves ripped off, stands there, staring at Sarah's breasts, his eyes wide.

She hurriedly closes the jacket. Grabs the handbag with the Python from the passenger's seat, slides it onto her lap. The weight of the revolver is comforting.

"What do you want?" Sarah says.

"You all right?" The man's voice is muffled by the glass.

Sarah stares at the stranger, at the tattoos around his neck. He's in his forties and pudgy, pear-shaped. His hair is dyed black, shaved on the sides, spiky on top.

"I thought you were gonna roll over back there." His voice sounds husky but vaguely feminine.

Sarah squints at the stranger's throat. After a moment, she realizes the man doesn't have an Adam's apple.

He is a she.

"I'm fine," Sarah says. "Just a little shaky."

"I got a flat, too," she says. "We must have hit the same patch of bad road."

Sarah realizes that if she's going to get to Dallas, she needs to be nice to this person. Her other options are limited at the moment.

She glances in the rearview mirror and sees a gray van, a Ford, maybe twenty yards back. One of the front tires is shredded. The woman with the spiky black hair had no choice but to stop where she did, right behind Sarah and the stolen Monte Carlo.

Sarah opens the door and gets out. She slings the handbag over her shoulder. Wind from passing vehicles ripples their clothes, whips Sarah's hair around her head.

"My name's Cleo," the woman says.

"I'm Sarah. You don't by any chance have a jack and a spare tire for an old Monte Carlo, do you?"

"What about the trunk?"

"I lost the keys," Sarah says. "All I have is the spare to the ignition."

The woman stares at the Monte Carlo and then at Sarah. "That's a problem, isn't it?"

Sarah nods.

"Aren't you hot in that jacket?" Cleo says. "I'm sorry, couldn't help but notice earlier when, well, you know."

"It is pretty warm today." Sarah unzips the coat about half-way. "I didn't pack very well for this trip."

Cleo stares at her cleavage.

"Maybe you could give me a ride?" Sarah smiles. The feeling of control allows her a sliver of hope that she might make it home.

Cleo gulps. Takes a step back.

"I just need to get to Dallas." Sarah wipes a trickle of sweat from her left breast. "I won't be any problem at all."

Cleo closes her eyes, mumbles to herself, an expression of extreme distress on her face.

Sarah tries to figure out what's wrong but draws a blank. Maybe her new friend only goes for other butch types. Maybe she's not into girlie girls.

"Are you okay?" Sarah asks.

Cleo opens her eyes. She hugs herself, stares off into the distance.

Sarah wonders if the keys are in the van. That would be the easiest solution. Leave the dyke on the side of the road and high-tail it in a new vehicle.

"You are a temptation," Cleo says.

"Uh, look, I just need a ride to Dallas." Sarah zips up her coat. "I won't be doing any more tempting."

Cleo opens her eyes. "You are an offspring of Satan himself. I must be strong."

Sarah hears a loud whooshing noise, a roar that is above and beyond the traffic on the interstate. She is thirteen again, and her cousin is in town. He's two years older, her mother's nephew. He's good-looking, like a Ralph Lauren ad, and Sarah is just starting to have that tickle between her legs when she's around an attractive boy.

They're in the pool house when they get caught, half naked, groping on each other.

Sarah touches her cheek. She can still feel the sting of her mother's hand, smell the wine on her breath. Hear the hate-filled words: *You are the devil's own child.* Her mother's face inches from her own. *You are as bad as your grandfather.*

"What did you say?" Sarah's back in the present. She looks down at Cleo.

"You think I want this burden?" Cleo opens her eyes.

"Did you call me the devil?"

Cleo wipes a tear from her cheek. No one speaks for a moment.

"The keys to the van." Sarah slides her hand into the purse. "Where are they?"

The woman reaches toward her back pocket.

"Don't surprise me, Cleo." Sarah grasps the Python. "I'm not what I seem."

Cleo smiles, eyes still teary. "Me neither."

A convoy of eighteen-wheelers blows past, making conversation impossible.

Cleo pulls an item from her pocket, something small and shiny that looks sort of like a gun.

Sarah tenses. Her finger tightens on the trigger of the Python hidden in the purse. The barrel is pointed at the woman's chest.

"It's a lock pick." Cleo points to the trunk of the Monte Carlo. "I'll change your tire."

Sarah nods. Maybe that's for the best. One more stolen vehicle will only hurt her chances of reaching Dallas.

"Just don't tempt me again," Cleo says. "That opens doors that ought to stay closed."

Sarah lets her breath out. "Whatever you say."

Cleo kneels by the rear of the Chevy, jams the tool into the lock. She works for a minute or so and then says, "So what's in Dallas you're in such a hurry to get to, Sarah?"

Sarah doesn't answer. She thinks about the message on her cell from earlier. Trouble ahead of her, trouble behind.

The trunk pops open.

"My child is hurt." Sarah can't help herself; the words blurt out.

The pain she feels is real, an ache in her chest, and she is surprised at her reaction to the child's injury. The maternal instinct is not a large part of her makeup.

"That sucks. Me, I never had kids." Cleo pulls the spare out. "They say you never quit worrying about them."

Sarah nods in agreement but doesn't speak.

"You ever wonder if you can change what you are?" Cleo grabs the jack and tire iron. "I mean really change yourself. Deep down."

Sarah thinks about that all the time. But she'll be damned if she has a conversation like that on the side of the highway with Cleo the Bull Dyke.

"I want to change, Sarah. I really do. But I don't think I can."

Cleo rolls the spare to the side of the Chevy and goes to work. A few minutes later, the car is operable again. She pitches the flat into the ditch on the other side of the shoulder.

"The Monte Carlo," Cleo says. "How hot is it?"

Sarah doesn't answer.

"I'm gonna need to trade cars," Cleo says. "You cool with that?"

Even though she'd been thinking about making just such a switch, Sarah is not cool with that, not at all. Why would Cleo want to trade her late-model van for a Chevy that came off the assembly line the same year that *Saturday Night Fever* was in theaters?

Sarah strides to the van, Cleo trailing after her, the tire iron still in hand.

The vehicle is running. It has sliding doors that face away from the highway.

When Sarah gets to the side of the van, Cleo says, "Remember what I said about opening doors?"

Sarah grasps the handle. Her other hand still has ahold of the Python in her purse.

Cleo smiles expectantly, like she really wants Sarah to see inside the van. Like that's been her goal all along.

Sarah yanks open the door.

Inside are two women and a whole lot of blood.

The women appear to be in their early twenties. They are naked and hog-tied, blindfolded, mouths gagged. One is dead, her throat cut. The other is whimpering, thrashing about.

Sarah jumps back, aghast. She jerks the Python out of her purse but not fast enough.

Cleo swings the tire iron for the hand holding the gun, connecting with Sarah's bicep. The whole limb goes numb. The Python clatters to the ground.

Cleo jumps on top of Sarah, pins her to the dirty asphalt. The van is between them and the traffic. They are out of sight.

"You stupid little slut." She wraps a hand around Sarah's throat. "Flashing your tits like that. *Tempting* me. I oughta put you in the back with those other two. Have us a real party."

Sarah, vision blurry, tries to speak but can't. She claws at the hands around her neck.

"You're a fighter, aren't you?" Cleo squeezes harder. "I bet you and me could have a lot of fun if I wasn't so pressed for time."

The tire iron is to Sarah's left, where Cleo dropped it.

Feeling is coming back to Sarah's right arm. The limb hurts but doesn't feel broken. Sarah reaches her right hand toward Cleo's face, fingers going for the woman's eyes.

Cleo turns her head, closes her eyes.

With her left hand, Sarah grabs the tire iron. She swings at Cleo's head. From the ground, flat on her back, she can't muster much force, so she does little more than rap the woman's skull.

That's enough to make Cleo let go of her throat.

Sarah grabs one of the woman's breasts and squeezes as hard as she can.

Cleo screams, rolls off.

Sarah hops up. She swings the tire iron with all she's got and hits Cleo in the temple.

The woman with the spiky hair collapses on the ground, unconscious. Maybe dead. Sarah can't be sure and doesn't really care.

She stands, shaky. She scoops up the Python, sticks it in her purse. Traffic continues to rush by, but Cleo and the open door of the van are not visible from the highway.

Sarah heads to the Monte Carlo. She gets about ten feet and stops. She walks back to the van and pulls the knife from her waistband. She climbs inside, carefully avoiding the blood.

The bound woman who is still alive hears her. She whimpers, tries to move.

"I'm not going to hurt you," Sarah says.

The woman stops moving.

"I'm gonna cut your hands free. But you have to promise me something."

The woman holds completely still.

"You have to promise you'll count to one hundred before you take off your blindfold."

The woman nods.

"Once you do that, untie your feet and start running south. Away from the back of the van."

The woman nods again.

Sarah eases closer. She slices the ropes around the woman's hands. "Good luck."

The woman whimpers what sounds like "Thank you."

Sarah hops out of the van and runs to the Monte Carlo.

Dallas is still an hour away.

- CHAPTER TWELVE -

Price Anderson and two other people were in the waiting area of my office.

One, a burly guy about six and a half feet tall with a buzz cut, was obviously with Price. His suit was not as expensive as Price's, but it was better than what you'd get at the Men's Wearhouse closeout sale. He was in his late twenties and should have been wearing a sign that said Ex–Special Forces.

Across the room was a woman, a government employee if I had to guess.

She wore a navy skirt and matching blazer. She was in her late thirties, pretty in an L.L.Bean kind of way. Straight, shoulder-length brown hair, parted on one side. Minimal makeup, no jewelry except for one of those wristbands that sync with your phone to keep track of how many steps you walk in a day.

She was leaning on the receptionist desk and talking on her cell when I walked in. She hung up and said, "You must be Cantrell."

I nodded. "That's me. *Sheriff* Cantrell."

Her accent was East Coast, Boston or somewhere nearby. Elongated vowels, a clipped inflection.

"So . . . *Sheriff.*" She fanned herself with one hand. "Is it always as hot as Satan's butthole around here?"

Price sighed and stared at the floor, an embarrassed expression on his face.

"Who the hell are you?" I said. "Ted Kennedy's love child?"

The woman glared at Price Anderson. "You didn't fill him in, did you?"

"Fill me in on what?" I asked.

Price looked at his associate, the ex–Special Forces guy. "Wait for me in the car."

Special Forces stood. His jacket shifted, revealing a semiautomatic pistol on his hip.

"You got a carry permit for that?" I said.

"Don't be a dick, Jon. We don't have time." Price snapped his fingers at the man. "Go."

Special Forces left the room, hardly making a sound as he opened and shut the door.

Price pointed to the woman. "This is Whitney Holbrook. She's the chief investigator for FERC."

I didn't speak.

Whitney shook her head. "What's the matter, Sheriff? Is it so hard for you to believe that a woman could be a chief investigator?"

Price rolled his eyes but didn't reply.

I let the silence drag on for a moment. Then I said, "I was wondering what FERC stood for. Not how a ballbuster like you got to be chief investigator."

Price chuckled until Whitney cast a withering look his way. He said, "FERC is an acronym for the Federal Energy Regulatory Commission."

"Let me guess," I said. "They're the outfit that investigates power outages of a suspicious nature."

"Score one for the local guy." Whitney Holbrook wagged her finger at me. "We also interface with Homeland Security when there's evidence of an attack on the grid."

"Interface," I said. "Why can't you people just speak English?"

Price said, "Don't stir the pot, okay, Jon?"

Whitney held up her cell. "Homeland. That's who I was on the phone with. The undersecretary . . . Office of National Protection."

She spoke the last few words very deliberately, as if they possessed some intrinsic importance. There was a gleam in her eyes peculiar to government types, the infatuation with titles and positions and the proximity to power.

"Look, the county will do whatever it can to help with the outages." I glanced at my watch. "But right now I've got an active murder investigation to take care of."

"You've got to be kidding me." Whitney shook her head.

"What?" I looked at her and then Price. "I'm not following."

"He's still a county sheriff, Whit. He's got a job to do. Responsibilities. You understand the concept."

"You know what really pisses me off?" I said. "When people talk about me like I'm not even there."

"Don't be so sensitive, Sheriff." Whitney pointed to the door. "We're gonna take a little ride and explain to you about your new job."

- CHAPTER THIRTEEN -

Sarah parks the stolen Monte Carlo beside a 7-Eleven. The convenience store is across the street from Baptist Memorial in an old section of Dallas near Fair Park, the central part of the city.

Both she and her brother, Elias, had been born at this hospital. Sarah tries to envision the day of her birth, what it was like to be truly innocent, if only for a moment.

She rubs the bruised spot on her bicep from where Cleo had hit her with the tire iron. She hopes that old bull dyke is dead.

A flash of worry enters her mind, concern for the naked girl she'd cut loose. She wishes she could have done more. But life demands you make hard choices. At least this way the girl had a chance at surviving.

Sarah wipes down the inside of the car, then tosses the rag on the pavement and dashes across the street to the main entrance of the hospital.

The handbag with the Python hangs on one shoulder. She's still wearing the oversized raincoat and Dallas Cowboys ball cap.

Her four-year-old daughter, Dylan—her only child—is at the hospital.

The nanny had called right as Sarah was stealing the Monte Carlo, leaving a frantic, garbled message—people talking in the background, intercoms blaring. Sarah had tried to return the call, but her efforts went straight to voice mail.

The hospital's foyer is marble and polished wood, a large open area decorated with oil paintings of past administrators.

The receptionist watches her stride across the room. An armed security guard stands to one side of the large check-in counter.

Sarah stops, breathless.

The receptionist says, "May I help you?" Her tone sounds accusatory, anything but helpful.

Sarah realizes how she looks and that she's not at the emergency entrance. This part of the hospital is for the well dressed and the well insured.

She tells herself to be calm, to resist the urge to scream at this person who is looking askance at her. She takes a deep breath and says, "I need to see my daughter. She was checked in this afternoon."

The receptionist raises one eyebrow.

Sarah says Dylan's full name.

The eyebrow lowers halfway. The receptionist taps on a keyboard, squints at a screen, and then looks at Sarah.

"Yes, I see her information." The woman's tone is deferential. "And you would be . . ."

"I'm her mother." Sarah says her real name.

The security guard stands up straighter. The receptionist gulps, jumps from her seat. "I'm so sorry, ma'am. I didn't recognize you."

"My daughter," Sarah says. "Where is she?"

The receptionist motions to the guard. "Please, ma'am. Let us escort you to her room."

The extreme deference, which normally makes her teeth gnash, is comforting today.

The guard hustles around the desk, keys jiggling, and does a little half bow. He points to a hallway.

Sarah knew, of course, that would be the location of her daughter's room.

A weird twist of fate. Karma enjoying an inside joke.

She nods gratefully and follows the guard toward a large entryway on the far side of the foyer, a different wing of the hospital.

Looming over the entryway is a bronze sign commemorating the philanthropist responsible for the wing's construction.

Sarah feels a twinge at the base of her spine as she walks under her grandfather's name.

The purse hangs heavy on her shoulder, pulled down by the Python, the old man's gun.

- CHAPTER FOURTEEN -

The power plant sat on the far eastern edge of Peterson County. The facility was surrounded by a lake on one side and a whole bunch of nothing everywhere else. Pastures dotted with mesquite trees, dried-up stock tanks, rusted windmills.

I drove alone in my squad car, the middle vehicle in a convoy of five. Two black government Suburbans behind me, another matching SUV directly in front, Price and his man driving the Navigator as the lead.

Since it was my county, I normally would have been in the lead, but with the feds, it's usually best to let them think they're in charge.

The plant looked like something from a science-fiction movie, a massive complex centered around two towers, each ten or twelve stories tall. Pipes and conduit encapsulated the towers like an exoskeleton, a silvery spray of high-voltage transmission lines spewing out of the bottom of each.

We didn't stop at the plant.

Instead Price led us to a crossroads about a quarter mile away, the intersection of two farm-to-market highways.

Three of the four corners were open land, sandy soil baking in the afternoon sun, and were crisscrossed by dry creeks and tangles of what had once been barbwire fencing.

On the fourth corner was a small square tract about the size of a basketball court, covered in white gravel. In the middle sat a metal building on a concrete slab. The building was a little bigger than an average-sized walk-in closet, and the logo for the local telephone provider was emblazoned on the doors.

Price parked on the shoulder, and the rest of the convoy stopped in sequence behind him. He got out and removed his jacket, then tossed it in the backseat. He motioned to me to follow him.

I opened the door to the squad car, stepped outside.

August in Central Texas. Not a cloud in the sky.

The heat smothered like a warm, moist blanket, clouding your mind, pressing down on your limbs.

I began to sweat immediately.

Behind my vehicle, the passenger door of one of the Suburbans opened and Whitney Holbrook exited. She took off her blazer, too, and together we crunched across the gravel to where Price was standing by the shed. Whitney wobbled on her heels as she walked over the uneven surface.

About halfway to the metal building, she stopped for a moment to remove a pebble from her shoe.

"Need a hand?" I asked.

She glared at me, face red, sweat trickling down her brow. She didn't speak.

I shrugged and continued.

She followed right behind me.

After about five yards she lost her footing and stumbled forward.

I caught her elbow, kept her from face-planting in the gravel.

"Thanks." She wiped perspiration from her forehead with the back of one hand.

"This time of year, it's a little warmer here than on the Cape, isn't it?"

"You know Boston?" she said.

"Been there a time or two."

"I'm a Southie. The Cape's for rich kids." She paused. "You a rich kid, Cantrell?"

Before I could reply, Price shouted at us: "Let's go, ladies. It's hot as two camels fucking in a sauna out here."

Whitney and I continued trudging across the gravel to the metal shed. We arrived a few seconds later, and Price flung open the doors of the building.

The interior was filled with circuit banks, row after row of tiny connectors with thin, multicolored wires feeding into each side. On one wall of the shed, various boxes had been mounted, each with network cabling and larger-gauge wires running in and out.

One of the circuit boards, on the far right, was blackened, like it had been burned. Insulation had melted, wiring curled.

"What's this got to do with the outage at the power plant?" I asked.

Price said, "You know anything about how phone lines work?"

I didn't reply.

"Get to the point, will ya." Whitney picked another pebble from her shoe.

"I told you not to wear heels." Price stared at her legs.

Whitney's eyes formed slits. She opened and closed her mouth several times but didn't speak. I wondered if Price had told her not to wear heels this morning when they were getting dressed together.

"Maybe you two could stop with the foreplay," I said, "and tell me why we drove out here to look at a junction box?"

Whitney and Price glared at each other. After a moment, Price turned to me and said, "You see any houses nearby? Anywhere that would need this much bandwidth?"

I shook my head.

Whitney pointed to the metal building. "The technical term for this is an 'SAI.'"

"A whatsit?" I looked at both of them.

"A serving area interface," Price said. "It's an access point to the telecommunications network. A junction box is the thing on your house."

I nodded, understanding all of a sudden. "This is the main line into the power plant."

Price smiled. "See, Whit. I told you he was a smart cookie."

I knelt beside the burned section. "What happened here?"

"An incendiary device, very small, remote controlled." Whitney leaned over my shoulder. "Took out the phone lines to the plant. Not much louder than a car door slamming."

"The FBI has a forensics teams on the way," Price said. "We'll know more later today about the specific explosive used and all that."

I looked up. "They cut the lines to the plant so your people couldn't call 911?"

Blowing the plant's communications had nothing to do with shutting off the flow of power. I assumed Price and Whitney would get to that in due course.

He shook his head. "They cut communication so the substation couldn't interface with the rest of Sudamento's facilities."

I turned to Whitney.

"Think of the electrical grid as one big organism," she said. "Lots of tentacles going everywhere."

"Okay." I closed my eyes, envisioning Whitney Holbrook with snakes coming out of her head.

"When one tentacle gets sick," she said, "it tells the others, so that they can take up the slack."

"So they can generate more power." I opened my eyes.

Price nodded. "If the other tentacles don't know about the sick one, then they can't gear up to throw more juice."

"Which leads to a brownout," Whitney said.

"And this is the choke point for all the data?" I stood, brushed dust from my knees. "The only way information can get in or out?"

Across the road a large panel van stopped and several men in white overalls got out. The FBI crime-scene people had arrived.

"Redundancy is the name of the game," Whitney said. "There're two more boxes just like this one on the other side of the plant."

"Both of them have been sabotaged," Price said. "Same MO."

"Somebody who knows their business," I said. "They're jacking with the tentacles, aren't they?"

"Bingo." Price nodded.

I stared at the horizon. Heat waves shimmered on the two-lane highway.

Price shut the doors. "Imagine a coordinated attack like this, only on a larger scale."

"Communication lines are cut at the same time as the grid is attacked," I said. "Pick the right spots, and you could take out a state or two."

Price nodded. "Not to mention that if the damage to the generators is severe enough, you're looking at weeks if not months before power is restored."

"That leads to a bit of unpleasantness we call 'societal breakdown,'" Whitney said. "Homeland Security runs models of various scenarios. None of them are pretty."

"Who do you like for it?" I asked.

Neither replied.

"Domestic or foreign?" I said.

Silence.

"Let's check out the power plant and the substation." Price pointed in the direction we'd just come. "They actually attacked a substation, but the damage rippled back to the plant itself. You need to see for yourself what happened."

Whitney said, "It's a simple question, Price."

He ignored her, spoke to me. "We can talk about that someplace other than here on hell's back forty."

"Let's talk about it now," Whitney said. "I'm starting to like the heat."

Sweat poured down her face.

"It's not that simple," he said. "We both know that."

Whitney shook her head and trudged back toward her vehicle. About halfway to the road, she tripped again. There was no one to help her this time, so she fell to the gravel, landing on her hands and knees.

- CHAPTER FIFTEEN -

Dylan's hospital room is really a suite, a large living area plus a bedroom, two baths, and a small kitchenette.

Everything is tastefully decorated like at a nice, midlevel hotel.

Not the Ritz, but not that place outside of Waco where Sarah had arranged to meet RockyRoad.

Two people are milling about in the sitting area when Sarah storms in.

Dylan's nanny, a Hispanic woman in her fifties named Rosa. And the head of Sarah's home security team, a lanky ex-Marine in his early thirties.

The Marine, good-looking in a muscle-car kind of way, oozes masculinity and confidence. He is a distraction, and Sarah can't have any of those at the moment. So she marches over to him and says, "Get out. Now."

The Marine gives her a slow stare. He nods once and leaves.

Sarah strides into the bedroom, Rosa trailing in her wake.

Dylan is asleep, IV in her arm, dark hair sprayed across the pillow.

She appears tiny, a wisp of flesh, matchstick bones. Pale skin, tendrils of blue veins visible under the surface of her cheeks. Beneath the bedcovers, one leg appears larger than the other, swaddled in a bandage or a brace.

"W-what happened?" Sarah's breath catches in her throat.

The pain she feels looking at her offspring's injury surprises her. The mother-child bond exists between the two but in a curious, nonemotional way.

"She's asleep now," the nanny says.

"I can see that. But what happened to her?"

"They gave her a sedative. She was in pain."

"Rosa." Sarah grasps the older woman's arm. "Tell me why my daughter is in the hospital."

"The playroom upstairs." Rosa pulls free. "She fell."

The lump in Sarah's throat grows larger. She sits by the bed, takes Dylan's hand in her own. The child's flesh is cool, muscles slack.

"She was playing with that horse." The nanny's voice lowers. "You know how she is."

"That horse" is an enormous stuffed toy, a life-sized Shetland pony. The toy's place of honor is at the top of the stairs, standing guard over all who try to enter Miss Dylan's domain.

"She was trying to ride him," Rosa says. "I told her to get off."

Sarah stares at her daughter, and the memories of trying to get pregnant wash over her.

The fertility specialists, so many tests and procedures. Invasive and painful, humiliating. Endless efforts to make her body function like it should. Like a woman's.

Sarah's skin grows cold, her vision tunnels. "The doctors. What have they said?"

"I called your husband." Rosa crosses her arms.

The nanny is passive-aggressive in a way that borders on insubordinate. She does not answer directly. She prefers to shift the topic toward an area of her own choosing or respond with a question that she deems more appropriate.

Sarah turns toward the woman, her skin hot now, her breathing shallow.

Rosa takes a step back. "When I couldn't reach you. What else was I supposed to do?"

The older woman has a point, though one that will never be admitted.

Sarah's schedule is full. She doesn't devote the time to Dylan that she should.

Shopping, planning sessions for the next charity ball—long, boozy lunches with women she can barely stand. Then there are her extracurricular activities: the horndogs, a time-intensive series of events that require a lot of planning to be carried out successfully.

"He is coming back from New York," Rosa says. "He was very busy, he told me. But he is coming."

Her husband is an empire builder much like her grandfather, only his tools are legal briefs and leveraged buyouts, not sawed-off shotguns and hit men imported from the Ninth Ward in New Orleans.

He is always busy, Sarah thinks, always on the move. His position demands long hours, dinners with investment bankers, breakfasts with lawyers. But precious little time for his family.

"He is a good man." Rosa juts her chin out. "He will be here."

The nanny's message is clear. You should be a better wife.

Sarah's relationship with her husband is complicated at best, little more than a marriage of convenience at this point, a veneer of respectability so that both of them can lead their separate lives.

She'd loved him at one time, attracted to his drive and ambition, the very characteristics that forced them apart now.

Dylan stirs in her sleep.

"Her leg," Rosa says. "It's fractured in three places." A pause. "I am sorry."

Sarah pulls out her phone, scrolls through the contacts, looking for the name of the hospital's CEO, a man she knows from the country club.

"They mentioned something about surgery," Rosa says. "That's what I heard."

Sarah looks up from the phone. "Surgery? On a four-year-old?"

Rosa trembles in the corner. Before she can respond, the door to the suite swings open and three people enter.

Two are medical professionals, wearing scrubs and lab coats. A nurse and a man in his late forties, the latter with a stethoscope hanging around his neck. The third is the CEO of the hospital, a heavyset man in his fifties, wearing an Armani suit.

The man in the lab coat is a doctor, the head of pediatric orthopedics. While the nurse checks Dylan's vital signs, the doctor and the CEO usher Sarah into the living area, where the three of them sit around a coffee table like they're at somebody's house waiting for drinks to be served.

The orthopedist's words run together—anesthetic protocols for young children, damage to the growth plates, rehab options.

Sarah sits very still, trying to maintain her composure, to process it all.

The CEO assures her that everything that can be done will be done to see that little Dylan has the best care available. Sarah can practically see the dollar signs floating over his head.

Sarah nods and asks questions where appropriate, seething on the inside. Her daughter, her flesh, should not have to undergo this assault. She is too young, too innocent.

The desire to crawl into the bed with Dylan and hold her is overwhelming. After a moment, however, another desire surpasses that urge—the craving to get online and set up an anonymous meeting, something closer to home this time.

Right now, that would be like a cup of water in the desert.

The physician drones on, and Sarah wonders why neither man has so much as looked askance at her clothes, the ratty raincoat and the Dallas Cowboys ball cap.

It's because I am rich, she thinks. *Rich and powerful. And the regular rules don't apply.*

She begins to weep.

- CHAPTER SIXTEEN -

Our convoy left the damaged telco station and drove the few hundred yards back to the power plant itself, a facility called the Black Valley Generating Station.

Two guards wearing Sudamento uniforms waved us through the gate. The guards had pistols on their hips but gave the appearance of hourly security personnel the world over: pudgy and tired-looking, a mite slow in the thinking department. I imagined they were very effective at checking credentials and not much else.

We parked by a low brick building that served as the main office for the plant, several hundred yards in front of the two towers and their smokestacks.

Price and Whitney exited their vehicles, took up position at the front of my car, waiting.

I got out as well, and the enormity of the place became apparent. Everywhere you looked, there were power lines and storage tanks and about a billion miles of metal piping, everything clustered around the two towers.

Whitney pointed her index finger at me like a gun. "Cantrell, you and me are gonna take a ride. Price, you stay here."

Price shook his head. "I don't think that's a good idea. I need to explain to Jon—"

Whitney aimed the gun finger at him. "I'm not asking. I'm telling."

Price said, "Oh, c'mon, Whit. Seriously?"

"Round up those personnel files I asked for." She pointed to the office. "We'll be back in a little while."

Trying not to laugh, I shrugged at Price, waved good-bye, and followed Whitney Holbrook to one of the black Suburbans. She got behind the wheel; I hopped into the passenger side. The doors slammed shut, and it was just the two of us. Her security team stayed behind.

"How come you're so mean to Price?" I asked. "Did he give you chlamydia or something?"

She cranked the AC to high. "Your file doesn't adequately communicate how big of an ass-munch you are."

"Don't take anything he does personally," I said. "Price is the master of the hump-and-dump. If there were an Olympic slutbag team, he'd be captain."

"For the record, I am not sleeping with Price Anderson." Whitney pointed the SUV down a gravel road that cut across the site and headed toward the rear of the property.

"Not sleeping with him *now*?"

"Why do you care who I'm bumping uglies with, Cantrell?" Her fingers were white on the steering wheel. "You looking to hook up? Maybe brag to all your friends about how you nailed a Southie?"

I didn't reply.

"I thought you had a wife and a kid at home." She slapped her forehead. "Oh, that's right. Your old lady hit the road right after the baby was born. Went off the reservation, total radio silence."

"We weren't married. That should be in my records, too."

She slowed to drive through an open gate. "And you're not even sure the kid is yours, are you?"

I didn't take the bait. A tiny current of anger pulsated in my stomach, quickly squelched.

The child was mine. The color of her eyes, the shape of her mouth. No DNA test was needed.

Two months after the birth of our daughter, Piper had disappeared with the infant. The stress of the pregnancy and the hormonal cocktail flowing through her veins had exacerbated her normal state of mind—a base level of paranoia, which manifested itself in a burning desire to remain hidden from view.

I had no idea where she was. I searched for her when time permitted, using the resources available to a county sheriff. But my efforts to date were futile, as Piper was a master at staying out of sight. She knew how to reach me, though, and I felt fairly certain she'd return in due time. Fairly.

I missed my daughter, though, missed her more than words could express.

No one spoke for a few hundred yards.

Then: "Sorry," Whitney said. "The life of a cop isn't very good for relationships, is it?"

More silence. We passed a series of ball-shaped storage tanks about twenty feet in diameter, and then several massive mounds of coal, each as tall as a two-story house.

"The actual attack occurred at a substation just outside the plant," she said. "Whoever was responsible knew exactly what to hit."

"You mean like taking out the telco boxes?" I said.

"That, and more." She stopped at the rear gate.

"How big is Black Valley?" I asked. "Electricity-wise."

"Both boilers going, the plant generates fourteen hundred megawatts, enough to power about a half-million homes."

"That's a lot of juice," I said. "Considering I saw only two security guards."

"A single plant is not that important to the grid. Sudamento has nineteen more in Texas alone. Plus the other providers. All of whom are feeding into the grid."

She picked up a remote control from the console, clicked a button. The gate swung open.

"You take one plant out," she said, "even a big one, and the others pick up the slack."

"So why did half of Central Texas go dark today?"

The gate led to a dirt road that cut through a pasture that was not part of Black Valley, outside the chain-link fence. A series of high-voltage transmission lines ran on a parallel course with the dirt road, leaving the plant.

Whitney drove through the gate. In the distance, another facility appeared.

This one was smaller, maybe an acre, white gravel surrounded by a ten-foot chain-link fence.

"That's a substation," Whitney said. "Electricity from several different plants goes there and is increased to seventy-two hundred volts so it can be transmitted for a long distance."

The substation had no buildings for use by humans, just rows and rows of metal structures, beige, each about the size of refrigerators, and an equal number or more of gray canisters. The canisters looked like two smooth fifty-five-gallon drums stacked on each other. Ceramic insulators and large-gauge wires sprouted from everything.

I sniffed as a foul odor filled the interior of the SUV.

"Five plants total send their juice here," she said. "Then the power is dispersed to population centers."

The smell got worse, the acrid stench of a house fire, things that weren't meant to be burned. Combusted insulation, scorched metal, burnt plastic. Noxious, poisonous smelling.

"Those are transformers." Whitney pointed to the gray canisters. "They increase the voltage. There's another series of substations at the end of the line that steps the volts back down so the power is useable."

On one side of the substation, about a half-dozen utility trucks were parked. Men in hard hats and work boots scurried around one of the larger transformers. The trucks all had the Sudamento logo on their doors.

"If a substation goes down," she said, "especially one like this where several streams meet, then you cut the power to a lot of people."

I got out of the Suburban, walked to the edge of the fence, ignoring the heat. Whitney followed.

The gravel around the transformers closest to the edge of the property line was stained a dark brown. The stench of burnt chemicals was overpowering.

"The transformers are oil-cooled," she said. "That's what you're smelling."

"So what exactly happened?"

"They knew which ones to take out—the units that serviced the entire substation."

"Just like the telco boxes," I said. "Destroy the right transformers and everything downstream goes dark."

She nodded.

"Not to mention the juice from Black Valley has nowhere to go, and the plant doesn't know until it's too late because the phone lines are down."

"Right again," she said. "The juice backs up, and a couple of million volts go the wrong way, frying everything they hit."

"How bad's the damage at the plant itself?"

"Don't know yet. Worst case is Black Valley is offline for a month if the turbines are fried."

"What about the other plants, the ones that fed into this substation?"

"They're not so bad," she said. "They're down for a couple of days, tops."

I did some rough calculations in my head. Five hundred thousand homes with an average electrical bill of one hundred dollars per month. Say the wholesale value of the electricity was only fifty bucks. That was twenty-five million dollars in lost revenue from Black Valley alone.

Whitney seemed to read my mind. "A lot of money, isn't it?"

"So how did they do it?"

She held up a small plastic bag. A spent rifle cartridge was nestled at the bottom. With her other hand, she pointed to the horizon.

About a hundred yards outside the perimeter of the substation was a low tree-lined ridge.

"A sniper," she said. "These transformers are not exactly a hard target to hit. Like shooting a cow on the other side of the field."

"It's that easy?" I asked. "Half of Central Texas goes dark because of a couple of guys with rifles?"

She nodded. "Guys who know what they're doing, yeah."

"So who pulled the trigger?"

"We're spinning it as a couple of rednecks with deer rifles," she said. "You know, Bubbas will be Bubbas."

I didn't reply. I got the feeling that there was more to come vis-à-vis the Bubbas.

"Long term that's gonna be a hard sell," she said.

"How come?"

"This is the part where I remind you of the paperwork you signed when you were a federal agent, the fine print regarding the penalties for releasing classified information."

"Duly noted."

She stared at the ridgeline.

The trees rustled in the afternoon breeze. A cattle egret glided over the pasture, a flash of white in an otherwise empty sky.

"The redneck angle won't work for long," she said. "Because we caught one."

I stopped looking at the ridge. Turned, stared at her.

"A Chinese guy," she said.

I let out a long, slow breath.

"He had a copy of the Koran in his pocket."

A Muslim extremist in the heartland. Middle America would never feel safe again.

"Have you ID'd him yet?"

She shook her head.

"Who knows about this?"

"Counting you? About ten people."

"Where is he?" I said. "Have you interrogated him yet?"

"He's at a military hospital." Whitney headed back to the SUV. "He's about to die."

- CHAPTER SEVENTEEN -

Sarah and her husband live in a thirteen-thousand-square-foot home on Strait Lane, a tree-lined street in North Dallas populated by the top end of the one percent—billionaires and bankers, captains of industry, people with good tans who play a lot of golf while living off trust funds.

The home is a Spanish colonial, white stucco walls, long sweeping arches, a terra-cotta tile roof. Her brother, Elias, once likened the house to a high-end Mexican brothel but not as classy. Sarah's husband had been unamused.

An enormous living area dominates the first floor. The room is designed for entertaining, bracketed on either end by matching fireplaces big enough to hold a minivan. This section of the home is the main reason her husband purchased the monstrosity. "A good place to entertain prospective clients and business associates," he'd said at the time.

Sarah is in her bathroom in the master suite, a ground-floor wing on the opposite side of the house from the kitchen. She's showered again, washing off the grime from the stolen Monte Carlo and any remaining traces from her encounter with the coked-up man in the motel.

Dylan had still been asleep when she left the hospital forty-five minutes earlier. Sarah wanted to be there when the girl woke up, but she needed to change. The clothes are a link, however small, to the dead man.

Her bathroom looks like a Persian disco, ridiculous even by the gaudy standards of North Dallas, decorated with gold leaf and green marble and curtains made from burgundy silk. Her husband's idea of what would please her.

Sarah stands in front of the mirror, naked, the only moment all day she's had to be still. Her skin is damp, face flushed from the heat of the shower.

The body reflected back at her is lean and taut, the skin unblemished except for the large bruise on her arm from where the dyke hit her with the tire iron. Her appearance—*her beauty*—is soothing in ways she doesn't understand.

She tries to envision all the men who've gazed upon her nakedness. She can't. Faces and places drift away, half remembered, gone from her mind like a swirl of smoke.

In their stead, an image of the sheriff at the motel appears. Her mind's eye lingers over the line of his jaw, the flatness of his belly.

She blinks and he goes away, too, leaving her alone, as always.

In the mirror, for an instant, she sees her mother. The swell of her hips, the slender valley between her breasts.

What would her mother say now if she could see how her only daughter's life had evolved?

Sarah turns away, combs her wet hair.

Her mother, who longed for nothing more than a good game of bridge and a perfectly decorated tree at Christmas, had died when Sarah was sixteen. Valium and chardonnay hadn't mixed well with a sexually conflicted husband and an overbearing father-in-law.

The thought of the old man makes his presence loom over the steamy air. His raspy voice is in her ear: *What are you gonna do now, girl?*

Sarah says the words out loud: "Dylan. I'm going to take care of my daughter. She's my priority."

That's all that matters. Flesh of my flesh, bone of my bone.

In response, an invisible hand presses on the back of her head, forcing her to look at the crumpled rain poncho lying on the floor next to a sweat-stained Dallas Cowboys ball cap.

What about that? her grandfather says. *What are you gonna do when they come looking for whoever was wearing those clothes?*

Sarah wraps herself in a robe and rushes from the bathroom, the grotesque furnishings and the steam too much.

You messed up today. Left stuff behind they can use to find you. The old man's voice is loud in her skull. *I raised you better than that, didn't I?*

Sarah's phone is on the desk on the other side of the suite, by the fireplace.

"You didn't raise me," she says to the empty room, her voice shrill. "I raised myself."

She marches across the thick carpet, grabs the device, googles "Waco News."

In her head, the old man cackles, a cruel sound she's heard often.

She knows what's coming next. The truth. Cold steel on a winter's day, a wedge of metal that burns and cuts at the same time.

Sarah, darlin', you and me, we're cut from the same cloth, the voice says. *Ain't that a pisser, you being a girl and all?*

She leans against the desk for a moment, dizzy. Then she continues scrolling through the links on her phone.

News about the power outage dominates. Seven counties affected, a hundred thousand people still without electricity, authorities frantically trying to piece together what happened.

Normally, Sarah would have spent some time reading these stories.

That many counties just don't go dark, not in Texas, which has one of the most robust electrical grids in North America—a tidbit she's picked up from the people who manage her investment accounts.

She continues clicking until she finds a story about a murdered man discovered at a motel on the interstate. The words ricochet inside her skull.

Deputy Murdered. Police Search for Woman in Cowboys Cap.

She devours the story, every word, searching for hidden meaning in each phrase.

Shot in the chest with a large-caliber handgun. A decorated law-enforcement officer, husband, father of three. The Texas Rangers are handling the investigation under the supervision of the sheriff of Peterson County, Jonathan Cantrell. The only lead thus far is a woman aged thirty to forty, wearing oversized sunglasses and a ball cap, seen leaving the hotel.

The phone slips from her fingers.

She's killed a cop.

No place is safe. They'll scour every inch between the Rio Grande and the Red River looking for her.

She rushes into the bathroom, grabs the raincoat and cap from the floor, then dashes to the fireplace.

Rap-rap. Somebody's knocking on the door to the bedroom.

She throws the coat and cap into the fireplace, cranks on the gas.

An instant later, flames engulf the clothing, and black smoke wafts up the chimney.

More knocking.

"Ma'am." The muffled voice of the ex-Marine. Walden, head of house security.

"What is it, Walden?" She watches the last of the rain jacket melt and burn away.

"You wanted a car and a driver at five o'clock," he says. "To go back to the hospital."

Sarah looks at her watch. It's 4:55.

Her robe stops at the middle of her thighs. She tightens the sash, walks to the entryway, opens the door.

Walden is standing on the other side, wearing his usual outfit: a pair of cargo khakis, a black polo shirt, and dark athletic shoes.

"I'm glad you're here." She points to the window. "I heard something outside."

The movement shifts her robe open slightly, and Walden tries not to stare at her cleavage.

"What, uh, did you hear?" he asks.

She motions him in, shuts the door. The warmth starts in the pit of her stomach, spreads upward.

He walks to the window, looks outside. She stares at the khakis, tight around his ass, the biceps straining the material of his shirt.

"When does my husband's plane land?" Sarah says.

Walden doesn't answer.

"He'll go straight to the hospital, I would imagine." Sarah's thighs tingle.

"An hour." Walden turns around, no longer making a pretense of looking outside. "Touch down a little before six."

Sarah tugs on the robe's belt.

The garment falls open. The material feels rough as it moves across Sarah's skin, delicious against her breasts. Cool air washes over her body.

"We shouldn't do this," Walden says. "Not again."

She walks toward the man, a smile on her face, a feeling of peacefulness in her soul.

The voice of her grandfather: *Fuck him, Sarah. Fuck him good and hard.*

- CHAPTER EIGHTEEN -

Whitney and I got back into the Suburban, the AC a welcome relief.

A large panel van with government plates pulled up next to us. Several people in hazmat suits got out. They waved at Whitney and trudged over to the nearest gate leading to the transformers.

"Oh joy. The EPA is here." Whitney rubbed her eyes. "Just in case we were running short on paperwork."

"Hope those suits are air-conditioned," I said. "Otherwise, you're gonna need an ambulance crew for when they get heatstroke."

She put the transmission into drive. At the same time her cell rang. A one-sided conversation ensued, Whitney doing most of the listening. She was finished by the time the main office for the power plant appeared.

"The sniper's location." She stopped in front of the office but didn't park. "The crime-scene guys are finished. We can check it out now."

Price Anderson stood on the curb by the front door of the building, watching.

"This has been fun," I said. "Really it has. But I need to get back to work."

"The Texas Rangers are sending another team to help with your murder investigation," she said. "Your boss, Jerry—he's signed the paperwork granting you extended leave."

"Jerry wouldn't do that without talking to me."

"He's probably too busy figuring out what to do with all the money from the new USDA housing grant that just came through this afternoon."

Overhead, a pair of buzzards circled a spot on the other side of the switching station.

"There's this undersecretary at the Department of Agriculture I know," she said. "He fast-tracked the county's application."

"Well played." I nodded in admiration.

The Bible says faith can move a mountain. So can the US government, if they turn on the money spigot.

"But I'm going to pass on this one," I said. "No more contracting work for me."

A moment of silence. Whitney picked at the nail on her ring finger with her thumb.

"You still have active indictments on the books," she said. "I hate to bring those up, but I'd be more than happy to get the DOJ involved if need be."

I didn't say anything.

During my time as a DEA contractor, I'd been an unwilling participant in actions where a number of felonies had been committed.

"Leavenworth sucks the big one," she said. "From what they tell me."

Several years before, I had been involved in a situation where a lot of lives had been lost as a result of clashes between a competing contracting firm, the feds, and several drug cartels.

Shit rolls downhill, as they say, and, being at the bottom, I'd found myself neck deep. The government didn't want to prosecute me because I might name names in an open court. That didn't mean they wouldn't, or threaten to at least, if they felt the need.

We were still in front of the main office for the Black Valley Generating Station, idling on the gravel road, cool air blowing on our faces.

Price glared at us, hands on his hips. He looked hot and sweaty standing there.

"Why are you doing this to me?" I asked.

She turned, looked in my eyes.

"I'm not a fed anymore, or a contractor," I said. "You have access to a lot of qualified people for something like this."

"The FBI as well as my best agents," she said. "They're going to be handling the investigation. We'll be throwing everything we've got at this."

"See?" I smiled. "That's how it should be done. FERC and the FBI. An alphabet-soup operation all the way."

"But I want an extra set of eyes."

"Why?" I asked.

A few seconds of silence. Then:

"You know who the attorney general is, right?"

I nodded.

The AG was the cousin of the treasury secretary, both scions of an old East Coast family. Regattas at the yacht club, summer homes on the Vineyard, custom-made Brooks Brothers underwear. That sort of thing.

"The attorney general owns a very large chunk of Sudamento stock," she said. "One of his family's trusts does, technically."

I swore under my breath.

Sudamento was a publicly traded company, a perennial Wall Street favorite, like Enron but without the scandal and ruined lives.

If Whitney's team uncovered anything that might affect the stock price, there would be pressure to change the course of the investigation. Because money trumps everything, even terrorism.

"Do you think Price is involved?" I asked.

She shook her head. "But he's a college dropout making a hundred and a quarter a year. You tell me where he'll end up in a showdown between his boss and the feds."

Outside, Price Anderson continued to stare at us like he was trying to read our lips.

"Obviously, I'd prefer to use federal agents for everything."

I nodded. "Obviously."

"But after the first incident, and considering the AG's potential—oh, how shall I put it . . . *entanglement*—I decided that we needed an outside perspective."

"The first incident?"

"We'll get to that later." She waved a hand dismissively.

"How many have there been?"

"I cast a wide net, looking for the right person," she said. "Contractors, ex-military, retired federal agents. You're the most qualified for what I need."

"And what, pray tell, made you think that?"

She ticked off the list on her fingers. "Your military back-ground. You have a pretty long resume in law enforcement, both federal and local. You've had extensive counterterrorism training."

Her voice trailed off, one finger left to go.

"And . . ." I arched an eyebrow.

"Your personnel file. Quite an interesting document. If you read between the lines, it's almost like you don't know how to quit." She paused. "That's what I'm looking for. Someone who won't quit."

I didn't say anything.

"Your job is to run a parallel investigation," she said. "Off the books. You report to me only, and I go straight to my boss at Homeland."

"How come Price knows about me? Doesn't that kinda negate the off-the-books part?"

She didn't reply.

"He told me this morning that the feds sent him."

Whitney chewed her lip.

I remembered the rest of the conversation. "Hell, he said that Sudamento was going to pay my fee."

"FERC doesn't have any money in the budget right now for outside investigators," Whitney said.

"So the people I'm potentially going to be investigating are paying my bill?"

"You'll be a licensed FERC agent. Working undercover."

"*Ferc* that," I said. "I'm liable to end up roadkill. Literally."

She remained silent, staring out the window.

"But that doesn't matter, does it?" I finally understood. "Because one of the other criteria you're looking for is someone who's expendable."

My initial reaction to her manipulations was anger. Then came a level of excitement that I hadn't experienced in a long time. It felt good to get back into something other than the business of being sheriff in a sparsely populated county.

A crew of workers emerged from the office and strode toward the towers.

"I picked you," she said, "because you once broke an FBI agent's jaw. Shit that petrifies normal people seems to have no effect on you."

"Did you ever consider that maybe I'm slow in the head?"

Price marched to Whitney's side of the SUV, stood by her window. She didn't appear to notice.

"Are you gonna take the job, Cantrell? Or do I call the DOJ?"

I looked at Price. He was scowling at Whitney, his lips pressed into a thin line.

"Are you in love with him?" I asked. "Or was it a friends-with-benefits kind of thing?"

"He's got a good line of bullshit," she said. "You'd think at my age I'd be immune to that."

"We all have our hang-ups." I shrugged. "He's not a bad guy, really."

She sighed. "Yes, he is."

Price tapped on the glass.

Whitney unlocked the doors, rolled down her window. "Get in already. I'm tired of watching you sweat your nuts off."

- CHAPTER NINETEEN -

The ridge above the substation, the sniper's perch, was part of a farm owned by a man named Thompson.

Whitney parked under a live oak tree that was in front of a one-story wood-framed house. The home was old but freshly painted, white with navy-blue trim. An ancient AC unit the size of a small refrigerator hung out of the front window.

Thompson was sitting on the steps leading to the porch. He was drinking a can of Keystone Light, wearing a pair of overalls and a faded denim work shirt. His skin was creased and leathery from the sun, age hard to determine, sixtyish or older.

Whitney, Price, and I exited the black Suburban. Because I was the county sheriff, I was designated as our spokesman.

"Howdy, Mr. Thompson," I said. "How're you doing today?"

He spat in the dirt.

"You get much rain this summer?" I took off my hat, fanned myself.

No reply. Just a deadpan stare and a long pull of beer.

Whitney sighed loudly. Price shushed her.

"Heard you had a little excitement this morning," I said.

He didn't speak. Instead he stared at Whitney like she was from Neptune.

"We're gonna go up yonder." I pointed to the ridge. "Have a look around."

Thompson crushed his beer can. "Don't suppose there's nothing I can do to stop you."

A moment of silence.

"No. Afraid not." I shook my head.

This was hard country—the loamy steppes of Texas, an area romanticized as the birthplace of the rugged individual, a lone pioneer braving the elements and standing on his own two feet. People here valued their privacy and didn't much like the government nosing around. Unless there was a farm subsidy check involved.

He stood, turned his back to us, and walked inside. The screen door slammed shut.

"I thought people in the South were friendly," Whitney said.

"We're not in the South," Price said. "We're in Texas."

The three of us climbed back in the Suburban and headed toward the ridge. Whitney drove down a dirt road lined with hackberry trees, past a barn gray with age and a pen with several swayback horses.

A few moments later, we parked by a stock tank at the foot of a small hill where two vans were idling. Yellow crime-scene tape encircled the entire ridge.

A man in a sweat-stained T-shirt and black fatigue pants got out of one of the vans. He carried a clipboard, an FBI badge dangling from a chain around his neck. We hopped out of the Suburban and met him halfway between the vehicles.

"About time," the man said. "It's hot as fuck out here."

A vein in Whitney Holbrook's neck pulsed.

"I think you need to canvass the entire farm," she said. "Inch by inch. Today."

The agent swore.

I looked at Whitney. "Give it a rest. Everybody gets that you're Alpha Woman."

She glared at me.

"Walk us through it." I spoke to the agent. "One step at a time."

He shook his head slowly and then gave us the rundown, starting with the dirt track where we were all standing.

"A gray Chevrolet pickup came through here about 9:00 A.M." He pointed to a set of tracks in the dirt. "Farmer Thompson leases the back pasture to a neighbor for his cattle. He thought that's who it was."

"You checked the neighbor, right?" I asked.

The agent nodded. "He hasn't been here in a wee—"

Price interrupted. "Did you take plaster molds?"

The agent looked at me, one eyebrow arched, the unspoken question: *Who the hell is the doofus in the fancy clothes?*

"He's head of security for Sudamento," I said. "Ignore him. You're talking to me."

Whitney nodded approvingly.

"Yes, we took casts," the agent said. "Won't have anything from those until tomorrow."

The agent then explained they were in the process of contacting all the businesses within a five-mile radius to see if any had video-monitoring systems. If so, they would get the footage and look for all Chevy trucks, hoping to get a glimpse of the occupants.

I did a rough calculation in my head and figured there were zero businesses within five miles other than the power plant.

The agent motioned toward the top of the hill and looked at Whitney. "Ladies first."

She took a sharp intake of air but didn't speak. Instead she began hiking up a narrow path dotted with cow manure, her heels sinking in the dirt. Ninety seconds later, the four of us were at the top, sweating like we'd run a marathon.

"Two sets of footprints," the agent said. "Work boots like you'd buy at Walmart. Size ten and eleven. Eight spent cartridges. Remington, thirty-thirties. You can get those at Walmart, too, or any sporting goods store."

At the base of a mesquite tree, the brown grass was stained burgundy. Ants swarmed the discoloration.

"That's where Thompson found the wounded guy," the agent said. "He was the size ten."

"And Thompson calls 911." I looked at Whitney. "A call which should have ended up with my people."

No one said anything for a few moments.

Whitney spoke to Price. "Go wait in the car."

"What?" His eyes went wide.

"This is a crime scene," she said. "Law enforcement only."

Price turned to me. "Can you believe this shit?"

I shrugged.

"Un-fucking-believable." He shook his head. After a moment, he marched down the hill. When he was out of earshot, Whitney said, "Thompson's call to your dispatcher was intercepted. Happened right after Black Valley went dark. So we sent our own people in."

"Intercepted" was a polite way of saying that the NSA, who eavesdropped on about half of all electronic communications on the planet, heard Thompson's call.

I knelt by the bloody grass, tried to imagine what had occurred here a few hours earlier.

"We figure Size Eleven shot him," the agent said. "Then he took off in the Chevy."

I looked at the substation in the distance. The transformers were an easy target.

"A Chinese guy with the Koran in his pocket." I stood. "Almost like they wanted us to go straight for the Muslim-boogeyman angle."

Whitney nodded. "They succeeded."

- CHAPTER TWENTY -

Dylan is awake now, eating dinner.

Her favorites—hot dogs, mac and cheese—specially prepared by the hospital's kitchen.

Sarah cuts the hot dog into bite-sized pieces while her husband paces in the suite's living area, a cell phone pressed to his
ear. As usual, a business crisis of some sort is brewing.

Dylan has stopped asking about going home after Sarah
told her she could stay up past her bedtime and watch anything
she wanted on TV.

The meal finished, Dylan flips on the television and is soon
engrossed in an episode of *The Simpsons*, much too old for her,
but Sarah has made a promise and won't go back on her word.

Walden is in the hallway outside the suite, briefing the men
who will be there through the night. Rosa, the nanny, sits in the
corner of the bedroom, a rosary in one hand. She has spoken
very little since Sarah came back from changing clothes.

Sarah moves the dinner tray to the other side of the room
near where the nanny is rubbing her fingers over the beads.

"I will stay with the child tonight," Rosa says, not looking
up from her rosary.

"That's not necessary," Sarah says.

"Then who shall be with her?"

Sarah doesn't reply. She loves Dylan, of course. But both Sarah and the nanny understand that mothering is not part of Sarah's makeup.

The crying and the thousands of tiny traumas that form the bulk of a young child's existence—the neediness—all those pieces of a parent's life leave Sarah petrified, staring blank faced at her daughter, confused as to how to proceed, how to react.

"You were late coming back," Rosa says. "She asked about you."

Sarah doesn't speak. Lately, the nanny has been figuring out the discrepancies in her employer's schedule, chunks of time unaccounted for.

"That security man," Rosa says. "He won't look you in the eye."

"I'll stay with Dylan tonight." Sarah crosses her arms. "You can go home."

In the living area, her husband's voice raises and then lowers. Something about a lawsuit and a hostile takeover. How he'll be back in New York in a day or two.

"A child shouldn't be alone," Rosa says. "Not in a place like this."

"Perhaps both of us should stay," Sarah says.

"With the security man as well?" A faint smile on Rosa's face.

Sarah clenches her fists, struggles to control her anger. "Why do you say these things to me? Do you want to be fired?"

Rosa chuckles softly. "If I go away, then who will take care of your daughter?"

Checkmate. Sarah has longed to terminate the insolent nanny's employment. But if she did so, she would have to find a replacement—an arduous, time-consuming process. Plus, Dylan adores Rosa, and getting a new caregiver would cause untold heartache and drama for the child.

Sarah grabs her purse, a slim Hermès. "I'm going to take a walk, clear my head."

Rosa stares at her beads but doesn't speak. Dylan is still engrossed in the TV.

"I'll be back . . . in a while." Sarah marches out of the suite. She ignores her husband, who is tapping on his tablet computer, oblivious to her movements.

In the hall, Walden is at the nurses' station with two other security men. He's wearing a sport coat to cover the pistol on his hip.

He breaks away, approaches Sarah as she stands by the elevator.

"Are you going somewhere?" he asks. "Do you need a ride?"

He's just doing his job, but the questions grate on Sarah's nerves.

An hour ago, Walden had been naked on top of her, pounding away. The thought makes her stomach churn. What kind of person is she that she would find comfort in an encounter with a man like Walden?

The doors slide open.

"Stay with Dylan." Sarah steps onto the elevator.

The doors hiss shut.

A few moments later, she is outside in front of the hospital.

It's early evening and the traffic is thick on Gaston Avenue. The air smells of exhaust and cigarettes, the latter from a sitting area where the smokers have congregated a few hundred feet from the entrance to the hospital.

Sarah heads to the smokers.

There are about ten of them, half in pajamas and wheelchairs, the other half wearing hospital scrubs.

Sarah hasn't had a cigarette in two years, ever since she chaired that stupid cancer fund-raiser at Southfork Ranch. She asks a man in his twenties, an orderly, if she can bum a smoke.

The orderly, the youngest, most attractive man among those gathered, takes a long look at her. The Prada pumps, the skinny jeans, the creamy silk top open to display a healthy amount of cleavage.

He gives her a Marlboro, flicks a match.

Sarah draws in a lungful of smoke. The nicotine jets straight to her brain, giving her an instant head rush as everything turns rosy and warm. She thanks the man and stares off into the distance, letting her mind drift to an empty, serene place, courtesy of the tobacco.

It takes a few seconds to realize what she's looking at: the 7-Eleven where she ditched the stolen Monte Carlo.

Two Dallas police cars are parked at an angle behind the elderly Chevy. An officer stands by the driver's door, peering through the glass.

She wonders if the car has been reported stolen. She supposes she should feel some amount of fear, but between being back in Dallas on her own turf, and the mental glow provided by the cigarette, she doesn't much care. She is SarahSmiles, stickup artist extraordinaire, granddaughter of a man who started his fortune with nothing more than a gun and a hunger for success.

Sarah closes her eyes and wonders if the old man would be proud of her.

Movement in front of her, feet shuffling.

She opens her eyes and sees her grandfather standing there.

He is tall and thin. His eyes are like slate—gray and hard, unyielding. Handsome with a long nose, high cheekbones, and a thick head of wavy black hair.

"Hello, Sarah."

She gulps, drops the cigarette.

It is not her grandfather of course. It's her brother.

Nothing good can come from Elias showing up unannounced. He is trouble, and Sarah's got a full tank of that particular commodity at the moment.

"There's a joint across the street," he says. "Let's get a drink, catch up."

"How did you know where I'd be?"

"I know everything, Sarah." He chuckles and strokes her cheek, his tone gentle.

She recoils from his touch.

"Don't be that way," he says. "We're family, after all."

She stares at him for a moment and then nods, relenting as she always does.

He smiles, a look of supreme confidence on his face.

Together they zigzag through the traffic, heading to a tavern with neon beer signs in the window and a parking lot full of Harleys.

The place looks dangerous, the kind of bar where there might be a dice game in the back or a guy in a corner booth selling weed.

The kind of place where both Sarah and Elias feel at home.

- CHAPTER TWENTY-ONE -

As we headed back to the power plant from Thompson's farm, a call came in on Whitney Holbrook's phone. She listened for a long time, driving slowly down the two-lane highway.

She hung up, turned onto the gravel road leading toward the boilers, and said, "The Chinese guy's dead. We have a name, though. Got a hit off the fingerprints."

I was in the front passenger seat, Price in the back. He leaned forward.

"Jimmy Wong," she said. "Street name: Jimmy the Weasel."

"I'm guessing that Jimmy wasn't a Chinese national," I said.

She nodded. "You are correct. Mr. Wong was born in Galveston in 1978. His most recent address was the Texas Department of Corrections."

"A local boy," Price said. "So he was recruited in the joint? A Nation of Islam convert?"

"I wouldn't bet on that angle," I said. "The only people Louis Farrakhan hates more than whitey are Asians."

Whitney parked in front of the office. "He was serving a five-year sentence for armed robbery. Running concurrently with an assault-and-battery conviction."

No one spoke for a moment.

"Jimmy beat up a hooker with a shovel," Whitney said. "Put her eye out."

"Anything on known associates?" I asked. "That's the best starting place."

A guy named Jimmy the Weasel who gave smackdowns to working girls sounded like a street thug, not a radicalized fanatic. The people he ran with when he was on the outside would be a good indicator of what kind of hood he actually was.

"They have to pull his file by hand," Whitney said. "The power outage, all the servers haven't come back up yet."

The sun was setting. The clouds on the horizon were thin, streaked by the fading light to the color of rust.

While we'd been gone, the activity level at the plant had increased significantly.

Sudamento pickups and utility trucks were everywhere. Men in hard hats and orange vests swarmed around the two towers like safety-minded cockroaches.

The black Suburbans and my county squad car seemed out of place.

Price's phone dinged, a text message. He read the screen and said, "They had to shut down both boilers. The transformers are fried. Nowhere for the juice to go."

"What about the other Sudamento plants?" I said.

He continued reading. "They'll be back online tomorrow. Black Valley is out of commission for at least thirty days."

A man wearing a short-sleeve dress shirt and carrying a clipboard came out of the office. He stood on the front steps and surveyed the scene.

"That's the plant manager. I gotta go." Price jumped out of the SUV, slammed the door.

Whitney and I sat in silence. She turned the blower on the AC down a notch; it was getting chilly.

"I'll need a badge," I said.

She opened the console, handed me a slim leather wallet.

"That was quick." I flipped the wallet open. One side was my Texas driver's license picture laminated on an ID card, which read, FEDERAL ENERGY REGULATORY COMMISSION—DIVISION OF INVESTIGATIONS. The other side was a gold shield.

"I plan to keep investigating the murder of my deputy, too. That's nonnegotiable."

A fellow law-enforcement officer had been murdered. Even though he appeared to be crooked, the killing still had to be solved, those responsible brought to justice. Every cop on the planet could understand that.

After a moment, she nodded.

"How many other attacks have there been?" I asked.

"This is the second incident. The first where there was an outage, however."

"Were they both Sudamento facilities?"

She nodded.

"I'll need a vehicle and a list of the company's plants."

"There's a Suburban just like this one at your office now," she said. "I'll e-mail you a list later tonight as soon as I get back to my motel."

I got out of the passenger side and stood in the doorway, looking back at her.

"This doesn't feel like an Islamic terrorist operation to me," I said. "What's your take?"

"Shut the door, Cantrell. You're letting the cold air out."

• • •

An hour later, I was sitting in the same booth in the same diner where I'd had breakfast with Jerry that morning.

It was dark now. I was the only customer. The electricity was back on, thankfully, and the room felt cold enough to chill beer.

I was having the daily special—meat loaf with mushroom gravy, fresh green beans, mashed potatoes—and reading a series of e-mails from the Texas Rangers regarding the investigation into the murder of my deputy.

The Rangers had been busy but had little to show for their initial efforts.

A video camera at a service station across the highway had a two-second sliver of footage that showed the LaCrosse getting on the northbound lanes of the interstate.

The fake address the woman had given the hotel clerk was to the south, in Austin.

I kept reading. A canvass of the hotel guests had yielded nothing. The crime-scene investigators had recovered a lot of DNA evidence, though the material would take time to process.

I looked up from my phone and glanced outside as a black Suburban pulled up next to my squad car. The driver's door opened and Whitney Holbrook got out. She stared at my vehicle for a few moments before entering the diner.

The waitress seated her in the booth next to mine so that we were facing each other. Whitney ordered a salad with chicken and an ice water. Then she looked over at me and said, "This is the only place to eat in town."

I didn't reply.

"Not counting Dairy Queen," she said. "Which is where my crew decided to go tonight."

"Where's Price?"

She didn't reply, just gave me an irritated look.

The waitress brought her a glass of water and silverware.

After she left, Whitney said to me, "How do you live somewhere so small?"

"Texas?"

She rolled her eyes.

"It's quiet around here," I said. "People keep to themselves."

"Parts of Manhattan are like that, too. But you can still get Thai takeout at 4:00 A.M."

I shrugged, continued to eat and read e-mails.

The waitress brought Whitney's salad.

I pointed to the empty side of my booth. "You want to join me?"

After a moment's hesitation, she picked up her plate and slid in across from me.

"This afternoon." She stabbed a chunk of lettuce. "I never said thank you."

"For what?"

"For taking the job."

I shrugged again. "You're welcome."

We ate in silence for a few minutes.

Whitney said, "How's the investigation of your deputy's murder going?"

"Slow. Whoever killed him planned ahead. But there's a lot of physical evidence at the scene, so we may get lucky that way."

"Do you know about the stolen Monte Carlo?"

I stopped eating.

"After the attack on the power plant, we cast a wide net," she said. "Any police reports, we wanted to see."

"Keep talking."

"A VFW hall about ten miles north of your murder scene. Two old boozehounds got into a fight. Apparently one of the drunks had his car stolen and was blaming the other one."

"What's that got to do with my murder?"

"One of the drunks said that a woman took the car."

I put my fork down.

"Before you get too excited, remember it's two wet brains who haven't been sober in years. Police could hardly get a coherent word out of either of them."

The waitress refilled our water glasses.

"The bartender," Whitney said. "He had to confirm that Boozie Number One's Monte Carlo was in fact missing. A 1978 model. Lime green."

I pushed my plate aside.

She took a bite of her salad, chewed thoroughly, swallowed. "Boozie Two. He said he saw a woman in the car, and she was wearing a Dallas Cowboys hat."

I stared out the window into the darkness, wondering how many women in Central Texas at any given time were running around wearing a Cowboys ball cap.

Whitney slid a piece of paper across the table. "Here's the location of the VFW hall and the witness's address."

I looked at the paper. The place where the car had been stolen was on the highway. The drunk man's location was in a small town thirty or so miles away.

"Why are you being so helpful?"

"A cop got killed," she said. "I want to see whoever is responsible nailed just as much as you do."

I nodded but didn't speak. Some things are universal, such as the desire for justice when one of your own is harmed.

"I wouldn't count on doing an interview tonight," she said. "They field-tested him. Old guy blew a point two four."

I put the paper in my pocket and figured tomorrow around noon would be a good time to drop in. The waitress came by, asked if we wanted dessert. We both declined.

"My room won't be ready until tomorrow." Whitney dropped her napkin on her plate. "Something about a cockroach infestation."

She told me the name of the motel, a rundown place where you might go to commit suicide or hook up with a waitress from Sizzler.

"Any other lodging options in the area?" she asked. "The joint where your deputy died is full tonight."

Those were the only two places to stay in the county. I told her so, and she muttered under her breath.

"Where's Price staying?" I asked.

"He got the last room at the cockroach Hilton. But I'd rather spend the night in the men's room at the bus station than with him."

There was something about Whitney Holbrook that made me imagine a sad and lonely childhood, a young girl fearful and timid, overcompensating as an adult. Both parents working, maybe, a child at home alone in a bad neighborhood in South Boston. She brought out my desire to protect, to shine a light into the darkness and say, *The bad guys aren't out there. You're safe.*

Only that would be a lie and we would both know it.

I put some money on the table. "I've got a couch you're welcome to. My place is not far from here."

She didn't reply, her expression that of someone watching events spiral out of control.

"I'm not hitting on you."

"I know." She nodded. "You're not that way. I can tell."

A few moments of silence ensued. She made no move to leave.

"Talk to you tomorrow then." I slid out of the booth.

"You sure you don't mind a houseguest?"

I shook my head.

Whitney stood. "Wait up. I'll need to follow you."

- CHAPTER TWENTY-TWO -

The bar across from the hospital is full of tweak-heads and guys watching ESPN like they've bet their last dollar on a preseason game between the two worst teams in the NFL. Other than Sarah, there are only two women present; both look like day-shift strippers with drinking problems.

Sarah knows there will be a fight, because trouble finds her brother like water seeks a low spot.

They sit at the bar.

Elias orders bottles of Coors and shots of tequila. Then he says, "How have you been?"

She doesn't reply.

"I'm fine," he says. "Thanks for asking."

"Why are you in Dallas? I thought you weren't, you know, supposed to travel."

Sarah doesn't mention the probation officer who must give permission for Elias to leave Travis County.

"I had some things I needed to attend to." His tone is light, but the words are ominous. Elias harbors a well of anger deep inside, more so than even she does.

"You have to let stuff go," she says. "Resentments will eat you up."

"Look at you, being all Dr. Phil." He smiles. The expression is not pleasant.

They drink in silence for a few minutes.

"How's Austin?" Sarah figures this is a safe topic.

The state capital is a good fit for Elias. It's full of pothead musicians, hippies and burnouts, college students majoring in going to college. A perfect place to get lost among the other bits of human flotsam and jetsam.

Elias sighs. "I needed a change of scenery."

On the TV over the bar, the sports coverage disappears for a moment, replaced with two still pictures: RockyRoad35 in his uniform. And the motel where he died.

The text underneath the photos reads, DEPUTY MURDERED; WOMAN IN DALLAS COWBOYS CAP SOUGHT AS PERSON OF INTEREST.

Sarah stares at the screen, everything crashing back on her, the enormity of what she's done. Her teeth chatter even though it's warm in the bar. She feels Elias staring at her.

Finally, the picture of the deputy goes away, replaced by an image of a power plant, Black Valley Generating Station.

Sarah takes several deep breaths and looks at her brother.

He is staring intently at the screen. At the power plant that has shut down because of what the news anchors are saying is too early to be called a terrorist attack.

An unthinkable question forms in her mind.

"What have you done?" she whispers.

He shrugs and takes a long drink of beer.

Elias has always been full of grandiose plans to avenge a litany of perceived wrongs. Several months ago he'd mentioned how easy it would be to take down the power grid.

Sarah points to the TV, lowers her voice even more. "*You* did that?"

"Shouldn't you be getting back to the hospital?" he asks.

Sarah doesn't reply. A sense of despair envelopes her. She can't discern if it's because of her current predicament or what her brother's done. Or, are they one and the same in some weird way?

"Are you okay?" Elias asks. He almost sounds genuinely concerned.

She struggles to control her emotions, surprised that she cares this much about what happens to her brother. After a few moments, she realizes how much she wants to share her burden with him, to confess what happened in the motel room.

Rocky's death presses down on her shoulders like a sack of lead.

"I've done a bad thing." Sarah blurts out the words, a tear trickling down her cheek.

"My darling sister?" His expression is one of mock surprise. "Did you cheat at bridge?"

Tequila burns in the pit of Sarah's stomach, and her head feels wobbly. The glow from the alcohol is threatening to overwhelm her. She takes a drink of beer to cool the fire.

Elias chuckles. "Or did you murder someone in the throes of passion?"

She shudders, an image of Rocky's body flashing in her mind's eye.

It would be a mistake trying to talk to her brother. He's mean, and what little compassion he had disappeared during his time in prison.

Fuck him.

She leans close, whispers, "What's it like to kill another human being?"

An awkward stillness descends upon their impromptu family reunion.

Elias flexes his finger, a murderous expression on his face.

Sarah wonders why she always brings up topics that cause pain. Oh yeah. Because it's fun.

"Do you think I like to talk about that?" Elias says.

"It's just a question." She downs her third shot, liquid courage coursing through her veins. "Don't get your panties in a wad."

Rocky's stench fills Sarah's nostrils. The room is spinning. She is drunk, words starting to slur.

They drink in silence for a bit, each wallowing in their respective anger. The news comes back on, more images of Rocky and the motel.

"Why do you keep looking at the TV?" Elias asks.

Sarah shakes her head, reaches for her fourth shot. Tears well in her eyes, and she doesn't know why.

The news ends. Sports coverage returns to the television.

A man in a blue work shirt with a Jiffy Lube emblem on the breast is sitting on a stool next to Elias. He is watching the TV over the bar as well, drinking a mug of beer. Every so often he glances at Sarah, a look of concern on his face.

Even drunk, Sarah recognizes the man for what he is, a white knight looking for a damsel to save.

Elias's eyes are filmy and moist, clouded with alcohol.

Jiffy Lube eases closer. "You all right, ma'am?"

Sarah nods, wipes her face.

Elias turns slowly on his barstool, stares at the man. "She's fine."

"She don't look fine." Jiffy Lube puts his beer down. "She looks upset."

"It's all good," Sarah says. "We're just catching up, me and my brother."

Jiffy Lube, who is about forty pounds heavier than her sibling, nods slowly.

This should be the end of it, but with Elias, shoulds and coulds are just puffs of smoke in a mountain breeze. Meaningless, inconsequential.

"Okay then." Jiffy Lube nods like he's done some great service to humanity.

Elias doesn't respond.

Then, like a stack of plates teetering too high, the final words are uttered and the whole thing comes crashing down.

Jiffy Lube picks up his beer. "Ain't no need in making a lady cry, now is there?"

Elias slides off his stool. "What'd you say?"

Jiffy Lube doesn't respond, a slightly befuddled look on his face, like maybe he's just now realizing that the skinny guy with the thick hair and the glassy eyes is capable of more than his appearance indicates.

Elias says, "What are you trying to tell me, chubby boy?"

Jiffy Lube frowns. He puts his beer back down. "You looking to get your ass kicked?"

"When I was in the joint," Elias says, "I used to fuck fat guys like you."

Jiffy Lube gulps, clenches his fist.

Before he went to prison, Elias had been in the military, a demolitions expert with the Eighty-Second Airborne, well trained in armed and unarmed combat. He can do amazingly horrible things to another human being with just his hands and feet.

Sarah almost feels sorry for Jiffy Lube.

Elias moves like a ballerina, his actions elegant and choreographed. He turns away like he's thought better of the path he's chosen, this meaningless altercation. Then he rears back his arm and slams an elbow into Jiffy Lube's nose, one smooth motion.

There is a noise like a side of beef being hit by a brick, wet and sloppy, a slight crunch.

The other man falls to the floor with a thud.

Conversation in the bar stops. Everyone stares at Sarah and her brother.

Elias tosses money next to their empty shot glasses.

The bartender doesn't move. His eyes are wide.

Jiffy Lube is groaning on the floor. Blood coats the lower half of his face.

Elias grabs Sarah's elbow, guides her to the door. No one stops them.

Outside it is dark and the heat of the day has begun to dissipate.

"You really hurt that guy," Sarah says. "He was just trying to be nice."

"He disrespected me." Elias leads her toward a gray Chevy pickup. "I think Papa would have been proud."

Papa was their grandfather.

Sarah looks back at the bar, wonders if the police have been called yet.

"Do you want to take a ride with me?" Elias says. "Or do you want to go back to the hospital?"

Her husband and Rosa are with Dylan. Perhaps it's better that way.

Sarah heads to the passenger side.

Elias says, "Watch out for the gun on the floor. I have Papa's thirty-thirty with me."

- CHAPTER TWENTY-THREE -

Sarah's brain spins as her stomach rumbles and the back of her throat burns from the tequila.

Elias guns the motor of his pickup as they speed down Gaston Avenue away from the bar where they left the man in the Jiffy Lube shirt bleeding on the floor.

Streetlights flash by, strobing the interior of the Chevy.

The neighborhood is bleak. Rundown apartments. Stately old homes that have been converted into boardinghouses. Convenience stores that sell sweet wine and discount-brand diapers.

Elias makes a couple of turns, and a few minutes later, they are on Garland Road. They drive past pawnshops and bars and used-tire stores.

"Where are we going?" Sarah's words slur.

He doesn't answer. Instead he pulls into the parking lot of a liquor store. He gets out, goes inside, and emerges a few minutes later with a paper sack under one arm. Back in the pickup, he puts the sack on the seat, pulls out two cans of Coors.

"I'm drunk," Sarah says. "I don't want a beer."

He hands her one anyway. She opens the can of course, because there's no such thing as enough in their family, only the hollow feeling that nothing ever seems to satisfy. She longs to get online and set up another meeting with a horndog.

Elias pulls out of the parking lot and drives north for a few miles until they reach the spillway at the bottom of White Rock Lake, a large body of water in East Dallas surrounded by expensive homes.

He parks at the foot of a small hill. Together, they climb the steps to the crest, Elias carrying the sack, Sarah wobbling, using the handrail. At the top, they sit on a bench and take in the view of downtown, an array of lights that look like pale stars in a cosmos full of dark haze.

Elias retrieves a pint bottle of Cuervo tequila from the sack and takes a drink, followed by a sip from his Coors.

"I left my daughter alone in the hospital," Sarah says. "What kind of mother am I?"

"Why'd you have a kid anyway?" Elias asks. "We're not exactly parental material, you and me."

"You're not a woman." Sarah feels a flash of anger. "You wouldn't understand."

"Oh yes." He chuckles. "The ovaries, the need to nurture, blah-blah-blah."

"Why are you so mean?" Sarah yanks the bottle from his hand. Takes a long swig.

Elias laughs, a deep-throated noise like their grandfather used to make.

Sarah wipes a drop of tequila from her chin. "You sound like him."

Elias opens another beer as a phone rings.

Sarah looks at the screen of her cell. Her husband is calling, no doubt to ask where the hell his wife is since their only child is alone in a hospital room with only a platoon of nurses and a superstitious nanny to care for her.

This is a conversation Sarah would rather not have at the moment, so she sends the call to voice mail.

"Have you been back to Papa's house lately?" Elias asks.

An image of the dead deputy flashes in Sarah's mind.

"A hot day like today," Elias says. "Makes me remember eating watermelon on the back porch."

Summer heat always makes Sarah think about the August afternoon when she'd been eight and her grandfather had locked a Mexican guy in a car with the windows rolled up. The Mexican's hands had been duct-taped behind him.

The old man had set out a picnic for Sarah and Elias, and together all three of them watched the car. Two hours went by. Then the old man said, "That's what happens when you don't pay what you owe." He'd packed up his grandchildren and left, the Mexican still in the stifling car, fortunately no longer kicking and screaming.

"I was at the house not long ago," Elias says. "Going through his things."

The home in Bowie County remains as it had been when the old man died. His clothes are still in the closet, dishes stacked in the cupboard. Ten-year-old newspapers resting on the coffee table in the den.

The county talked about turning the house into a museum, the years having whitewashed the owner's reputation, a favorite son of East Texas who overcame staggering hardship to become a man of wealth and influence.

"The old Colt of his," Elias says. "Remember the Python?"

Sarah doesn't reply. Elias and his obsession with guns, almost a fetish if you ask her.

"I couldn't find that one," he says. "You know how I like to keep his things in order."

"Are you even supposed to have firearms?" Sarah says. "I thought felons couldn't own guns."

Elias slides one hand down Sarah's thigh to just above her knee. He grabs the flesh and squeezes.

Sarah gasps.

He applies more pressure, fingers digging into muscle.

Sarah squirms, tries to get away, a futile move. "Please. Stop."

"Where's the gun, Sarah?"

She doesn't reply. The pain in her leg shoots its way up her torso.

The revolver is in the wall safe in her closet along with the prepaid cell phone, her little stash of tools she uses with the horndogs.

She longs to tell him where the Python is, what she's been using it for, aching to share her adventures with someone. Her brother is the obvious choice. But sharing is dangerous, a display of weakness. So she remains silent, breath coming in heaves, sweat dripping down the small of her back.

A period of time passes, a few seconds that feel like an hour. Then, Elias moves his hand and the pain goes away.

"We're not finished," he said. "I want that gun."

Sarah stands, wobbly. "You think that makes you a tough guy, roughing up your sister?"

He stares at her like she's an animal at the zoo, one who's doing a particularly interesting trick.

"The power plant was a bad play, Elias. You screwed yourself with that little move."

He tosses an empty beer can down the hill.

"You don't understand how they'll react." She rubs the spot on her leg where his fingers had been. "If they catch you, all the lawyers in the world won't be able to protect you."

"If they catch me. Ha." Elias stands and cups his hands. He shouts toward the sky: "CATCH ME CATCH ME CATCH ME."

Sarah realizes her brother is insane. The time in prison, their upbringing, how could he be anything but damaged?

A jet flies overhead, gray contrails against the night sky.

Elias sits back down, cracks another beer. "What'd you do today that was so bad anyway?"

She doesn't answer.

He stares at the downtown skyline. "It's a big city, isn't it? All those lights."

Silence.

"I like to hurt people," Sarah says. "I wish I knew why."

Elias rubs his eyes with both hands, taking several deep breaths. Sarah wonders if he's having a mental breakdown of some sort.

"It's a nice night." He stands, walks toward the steps. "You don't mind walking home, do you?"

Her house is ten miles away, across an entire city.

"You're leaving me?" she says.

"Good night, Sarah." Elias heads down the hill, gets into his pickup.

She watches him go. When the lights of the Chevy disappear, she pulls out her phone and dials a number she knows by heart. She leaves a message—the make and approximate year of Elias's truck and the license plate.

Then she calls Walden and asks for a ride home.

- CHAPTER TWENTY-FOUR -

I lived in a house behind the post office, a rental which was a few blocks from the town square.

The home was made from red brick. The front had a wide porch with swings at either end. An old magnolia grew in the yard along with several crepe myrtle trees.

The house and the neighborhood reminded me of where I'd grown up, a small town just south of Dallas, a Norman Rockwell setting marred only by my mother's never-ending battle with drug addiction and my father's bitterness toward her. He'd been the county sheriff at the time.

A little after seven in the morning, I padded into the kitchen and started the coffeemaker.

In the living room, the couch was empty except for a tangle of sheets and a rumpled pillow. Whitney's bag sat by the coffee table. The second bedroom didn't have a bed, only a bassinet, hence the sofa as a guest room.

By the time the coffee was ready, Whitney had returned, carrying a white paper sack. She wore a pair of yoga pants, a gray T-shirt, and athletic shoes. She was sweating, face flushed.

"I went for a run," she said. "Picked up breakfast while I was out."

She was breathing heavily, too, making her Boston accent more pronounced.

I looked at my watch. "Coffee's ready."

"There was a lot of traffic at this one store." She opened the sack. "They were selling something called . . . *kolaches*?"

The middle section of Texas had been settled by central Europeans in the nineteenth century—Germans and Poles, Slovakians. *Kolaches* were a Czech pastry, kind of like a donut stuffed with a fruit filling.

"Thanks." I got out some plates. Glanced at my watch again.

"Why are you checking the time so much?" She poured a cup of coffee.

Cops always notice stuff like that. Why should Whitney be any different?

I looked at the phone mounted on the kitchen wall. If the call came, it was usually at about seven fifteen.

The house had been furnished by the owner, down to the books on the shelves, a collection of airport thrillers. The only personal touches were my clothes in the closet, the items for an infant in the back room, and a framed eight-by-ten photograph by the coffeemaker. My daughter, Elizabeth, age one month, with her mother, Piper Westlake. The snapshot had been taken a few months earlier, before Piper had decided to cut and run.

Whitney picked up the photo. She tracked my eyes as they drifted toward the phone.

"You're expecting a call. The mom?"

"Every few days about this time," I said. "She doesn't say anything. Sometimes I can hear my baby in the background."

"You trace it?"

I nodded. "Piper, that's the mother, she's exceptionally good at hiding her tracks."

"That's a pretty baby." Whitney put the photo down. "Bet she'll be a knockout like her mom."

I didn't reply. We puttered with the coffee and *kolaches.*

A few minutes later, the phone rang. Caller ID read "000-000-0000."

"I'm gonna hop in the shower." Whitney grabbed a *kolache* and left the room.

I waited for another couple of rings and then picked up the receiver. "Hello?"

Silence.

"Anybody there?"

Nothing.

"Piper, is that you?"

A faint echo on the line. Then, the sound of breathing. Or perhaps that was my imagination.

"How is Elizabeth?"

More breathing.

"Our daughter. Tell me how she's doing?" I tried not to let myself get angry. "You owe me that, Piper."

Nothing. A few seconds passed.

I took a deep breath. "Next time you call, I may not be at this number."

In another part of the house, the sound of water running.

"A couple weeks, tops. I'm, uh, taking a leave from the county."

The echo on the other end grew louder, electrons reverberating in an open space.

I lowered my voice as a tingle of excitement ran up my spine. "I'm back in the game. A federal gig."

Silence.

"Piper? You there?"

The line went dead.

• • •

Thirty minutes later, Whitney and I were showered and dressed. We were in the kitchen, drinking the last of the coffee.

I wore civilian clothes—a pair of khakis, a white button-down shirt, and heavy work boots. On my hip was a Glock .40 caliber in a tooled leather holster opposite my sheriff's badge fastened to the belt. The credentials Whitney had given me were in my back pocket.

She handed me a sheet a paper. "The information you wanted. Sudamento's plants."

I skimmed the list, nineteen different facilities, each in a rural area.

"McCarty." She pointed to one in the middle. "That's where the first attack occurred. Four days ago."

McCarty was in East Texas, nearly halfway to Louisiana.

"What happened?"

"Somebody shot out the main transformer for the plant," she said. "They used the same type of gun. A thirty-thirty."

"Is there a record of who comes and goes to the plant?"

She didn't reply. Instead she went into the living room and packed her things.

I followed. "What aren't you telling me?"

"I didn't find out about McCarty Creek until two days ago." She paused. "Price mentioned it in passing. He said since there wasn't an outage, it wasn't worth calling in the cavalry."

I didn't say anything.

Whitney zipped her bag shut. "That's when I decided to find someone like you."

"Someone off the books."

"Yes," she said. "But the credentials I gave you are legit. You're a federal agent."

I turned off the lights. We headed to the door. On the front porch, I locked the dead bolt and heard Whitney say, "Crap."

I turned.

A Lincoln Navigator was parked in front of my house. Leaning against the side of the SUV was Price Anderson.

"Well, look what we have here." He crossed his arms.

Whitney said, "What do you want, Price?"

"I was about to head to the plant." He spoke to Whitney. "I asked the manager where your room was. Thought maybe you'd want to ride along."

"They didn't have a place for Whitney last night," I said. "So she stayed here. On the couch."

"You're a piece of work, Cantrell." He shook his head.

"I'll need to get with you later," I said. "We're gonna have to go over the security procedures for Sudamento's facilities. Each one."

He shook his head again and spat in the dirt. Then he got in the Navigator and drove away.

I sighed. "That went well, I think."

Whitney headed toward her Suburban. "Call me when you get to McCarty."

- CHAPTER TWENTY-FIVE -

I parked my squad car behind the county courthouse, underneath an old sycamore tree. The government Suburban that I was to borrow was in the front, the keys on my desk, according to Whitney. I headed to my office on the ground floor, one of several surrounding an open area where an administrative assistant usually sat. This early, the admin's spot was empty.

The paperwork on my desk took about twenty minutes to plow through. I sent a half-dozen e-mails to the county admin and then dropped several files on his desk, notes attached.

The office of the deputy who'd been murdered was next to mine. A strip of yellow crime-scene tape cut diagonally across the door.

I stepped under the tape and entered the room.

The deputy had been a big fan of Texas A&M University, and his work space was full of memorabilia, everything maroon and white. Commemorative footballs, pennants, framed posters.

I sat at his desk and turned on the computer.

A yellow Post-it note was taped to the bottom of the monitor. The note contained the phrase "12thM4n!" I entered those characters when prompted for a password.

The computer came to life. So much for network security.

I opened his e-mail program first. A dozen unread messages were in his inbox, all of them regarding county business. A quick scan of old messages indicated nothing out of the ordinary.

Next, I clicked the browser icon and tapped the History button.

A moment later, all the sites the deputy had visited in the past week displayed.

None of them appeared to be what I was looking for. The most frequently accessed location was a forum devoted to discussing Texas A&M's football team. He'd also visited Amazon, Weather.com, Yahoo, three Ford dealerships in the area, and a website for law-enforcement officers in rural areas.

I closed the browser, drummed my fingers on the desk.

The deputy was using either a different computer or his phone to visit the sites that Kelsey had mentioned. Or he'd enabled "private browsing" on this machine.

The phone was part of his personal effects, which were now with the McLennan County coroner's office. I could get access to the device, but that would take time, something that was in short supply since I now had two jobs.

My to-do list for the day: Investigate an attack on the power plant in McCarty, nearly two hours away. Talk to an old drunk an hour in the other direction from McCarty, a person who might or might not have seen the woman who murdered my deputy. Avoid Price Anderson.

From the desk chair, I surveyed the office, trying to imagine what else might be hidden amid all the collegiate knickknacks. There were too many pieces of kitsch to search, too many nooks and crannies.

I turned my attention back to the computer, clicked open the folder "My Documents."

Inside, I saw what you'd expect to find there. Arrest reports, files on crime stats, interoffice memos, and the like.

Nevertheless, I clicked on each one and scanned the contents. The documents were what their names indicated—routine, nothing out of the ordinary.

I closed the computer folder and searched each drawer in his desk. Nothing there that aroused any suspicion.

The top drawer stuck a little when I tried to shut it. So I pushed harder until it slammed home, shaking the desk.

The disturbance caused a small ceramic figurine to fall over. The figurine was shaped like the Texas A&M mascot, a border collie named Reveille, and sat by the phone. It had been designed as a card holder. The dog held a basket in its mouth; cards fit into the basket.

A stack of the deputy's business cards splayed across the desk.

I returned the figurine to its regular position, picked up the cards, started to put them back in the basket.

I stopped.

The last card in the stack, the one at the rear, had two lines of handwriting on the back. Line one: "RockyRoad35." Line two: "12thM4n!"

I got back on the deputy's computer, opened a browser, and googled both phrases, individually and together.

Nothing.

Then I googled "websites for affairs" and got back a long list of Internet locations devoted to infidelity. The first seven required an e-mail address as the username. The eighth, an anything-goes kind of place with the phrase "I want to screw a stranger" in the URL, asked for a username instead. I entered the name from the back of the business card and then "12thM4n!" as the password.

That was the magic combo. A few seconds later, I was logged on as RockyRoad35, and a picture of my late deputy wearing sunglasses and a straw cowboy hat appeared, the photo taken from about twenty feet away.

The top bar was a list of possible search parameters—"M4M," "M4F," etc.—a pretty fascinating and all-encompassing strata of human behaviors, at least until you got to the drop-down menu on the other side: "Favorite Sexual Activity."

I scanned the list, more than a little taken aback. There were a lot of freaky people out there.

On the left was Rocky's profile, a mishmash of *Penthouse Forum* outtakes and *Cosmo* sex advice. Just to set the record straight, however, under "About Me" he indicated that he was looking for a "real woman who's not into playing games."

On the right side of the screen were the private messages.

The last five were between RockyRoad35 and a woman who called herself SarahSmiles. They were flirtatious, full of double entendres. Evidently, a separate conversation was also occurring via e-mail, as both Rocky and Sarah referenced information that was not in the string of messages I was reading.

Sarah asked if Rocky had gotten the pictures. Rocky replied in the affirmative, saying she was "hawt" and that he was looking forward to seeing her in person.

Sarah told him "the room's all lined up." Then: "Check your e-mail for the details, stud. Can't wait to meet in person! See you tomorrow. ☺"

That message, the last one, had been sent two nights ago at 10:27 P.M.

The room's all lined up . . . See you tomorrow.

I clicked the link for SarahSmiles's profile.

A picture of a woman appeared, her body visible from the neck down, wearing a black bra and panties. She was fit, arms toned, stomach flat. Below the photo was her profile.

Age/Gender: 35; female

Height/Weight: 5'8"; 125 lbs.

Status: Married, seeking males for short-term fun.

About Me: North Texas hottie looking to step out. Financially secure. Not looking for sugar daddy, just fun and adventure. The past doesn't define me. It's all about what's to cum. Will that be you?

About My Match: Men, white or Latino, age 30 to 50. Height-weight proportionate. No fatties! Must be financially secure. Mandatory that you be drama, drug, and disease free as I am. No mama's boys either. If you can't stand the heat, then don't message SarahSmiles. Cuz you'll get burned!

I called Irving Patel, the clerk at the hotel where my deputy had been murdered. He answered after one ring. We greeted each other.

"Two nights ago," I said. "The woman who booked the room, the one with the red hair."

"Yes?"

"What time did she check in? Exactly."

Keys clicking. Then: "10:23 P.M. Exactly."

"Thanks, Irving. I'll be in touch." I ended the call.

The woman with red hair had checked in four minutes before SarahSmiles sent the message to my deputy, telling him the room would be ready for their encounter the next day.

Four minutes seemed to be about the right amount of time it would take for the woman to leave the lobby of the hotel, get into her car, log on to the website, and leave the message.

My phone rang, Price Anderson calling. I sent him to voice mail and left for McCarty.

- CHAPTER TWENTY-SIX -

Sarah's head feels like it's in a bucket lined with steel studs and somebody's banging on the outside. The Starbucks latte she's drinking tastes bitter despite the milk and sweetener, and it makes her stomach queasy.

Fucking tequila. Never again.

Dylan stirs in her hospital bed. Sarah puts the coffee down and takes her daughter's hand.

It's nine o'clock in the morning, the day after her drunken encounter with Elias.

In a few minutes, Dylan will head off to surgery for her leg. The nanny dozes in an armchair across the room.

"Mommy, I don't feel good." Dylan's voice sounds tiny.

The pain meds are making her tummy upset.

"It's okay, baby. The doctors are gonna make everything better."

Dylan wipes a tear from her eye. "Where were you last night? I missed you."

Sarah hesitates, the old, familiar self-loathing washing over her. She doesn't want to lie. Nor does she want to say that she was drunk, just like her own mother had been the night before Sarah had her tonsils out.

Six-year-old Sarah, alone in a hospital room much like this. Her mother passed out at home. Her father shacked up at some hotel with his latest pretty boy.

Papa, her grandfather, had been with her, however. He'd spent the night in the hospital room, sleeping on a recliner, one hand grasping hers through the bars on the bed. The old man had fully comprehended the weakness of his son, Sarah's father. He'd known that no adult would be present for what was sure to be the most traumatic event up to this point in his granddaughter's life.

Rosa walks over, yawning. "Your mother, she was sick. That's why she wasn't here."

Dylan looks aghast. "Are you all right, Mommy?"

"Mommy's fine." Sarah strokes the child's head. "Just a touch of the, um, stomach flu."

Rosa's and Sarah's eyes meet. The nanny's expression is blank.

"Where's Daddy?" Dylan asks.

Sarah doesn't know. Walden had picked her up after Elias left, driven her home in silence. Sarah had passed out on the bed, fully clothed. This morning, the other side hadn't appeared to be slept in.

"He had to go to Houston," Rosa says. "Business."

"Today?" Sarah tries not to sound incredulous. "He's not going to be here for her surgery?"

No one speaks. Dylan whimpers softly, plucking at the IV in her arm.

"That's what mothers are for, yes?" Rosa heads toward the door. "I'm going to get breakfast."

Sarah doesn't respond.

"Mommy, I'm scared." Dylan fidgets in the bed.

"When will you be back?" Sarah calls out after the departing nanny.

No response. The door shuts, and Sarah is alone with her daughter.

Dylan looks up. "If I die, will I go to heaven and see Papa?"

- CHAPTER TWENTY-SEVEN -

I started the government Suburban Whitney Holbrook had provided and cranked up the AC. When the cold air started blowing, I called the Texas Rangers and relayed the information gleaned from the deputy's computer. Told them to get an IT specialist to the dead man's office as soon as possible and to check the cell phone at the McLennan County morgue. Gave them the username and password to the website.

Then I left town, driving in the general direction of Louisiana, away from the stony hills and scrub brush that most people associated with the Lone Star State, heading toward the thickets of East Texas.

Two hours later, I arrived at McCarty, a tiny town between Palestine and Lufkin, deep in the piney woods, not far from the Davy Crockett National Forest.

The town was not much more than a cleared patch among the trees—ten, maybe twelve blocks in either direction. Old wood-frame houses topped with satellite dishes. A Dollar General store and a Dairy Queen.

Not counting the power plant, I figured the town's three biggest industries were food stamps, bass fishing, and diabetes.

The McCarty Creek Generating Facility was located on the eastern edge of the metropolis, just past a mobile-home park that looked like it had been recently hit by a tornado.

The plant was smaller than Black Valley, only one tower—what's called the boiler, according to Whitney Holbrook.

Four guards were at the gatehouse. All of them were in their twenties, fit and alert. They were carrying machine guns and wearing black tactical vests marked on the back with lettering that read, SUDAMENTO SECURITY.

I stopped at the gate as the head guard stepped in front of my SUV, one hand held up even though I wasn't moving. After a moment, he walked around to the driver's side.

"May I help you?" He stood about two feet from the window, fingers on his gun.

I displayed the FERC badge. "I need to speak with the manager."

He gave me and the Suburban a long look and then disappeared into the gatehouse. A moment passed, and he came back out, handing me a visitor badge and a one-page map of the facility. The gate swung open.

I thanked him and drove down a gravel road toward the boiler tower.

The terrain was rolling, covered in native grasses that were dormant from lack of water, the color of dried sand. Most of the trees had been cleared from the site, allowing for an unobstructed view of the boiler and the surrounding equipment, as well as the small lake that served as a cooling source for the plant.

The road forked at the entrance to the boiler compound, an area separated from the rest of the facility by a chain-link fence topped with barbed wire and an open gate.

I took the road to the right, which led to the administrative office, a low metal building about three hundred yards away.

A man in his forties wearing a plaid shirt and a hard hat stood by the visitor parking slot. He held a second hard hat in his hand.

I parked.

He walked to the passenger side, tapped on the glass, a cheerful smile on his face.

I rolled down the window.

"Chester Lewis." He stuck his hand inside. "Plant manager here at McCarty Creek."

"Hi. How are you doing?" I shook. "Special Agent Jon Cantrell."

Chester didn't say anything else. He glanced back toward the admin building a couple of times.

"Let's go inside where it's cool and talk," I said.

He turned his full attention my way. "Inside?"

I nodded.

He looked back toward the building again.

"You rather talk somewhere else?" I asked.

He opened the passenger door, hopped inside the SUV. "Let's take a spin, Special Agent Cantrell. I'll give you a tour."

"Call me Jon." I put the transmission into reverse, turned around.

"How about we check out the boiler?" He pointed toward the tower. "That sounds like a good plan, doesn't it?"

I drove the way I'd just come. A few seconds later, we left the admin area and were back on what constituted the main road of the facility.

"Maybe I could give you a little lesson on power plants." He fastened his seat belt.

"I need to ask you some questions first."

"There's this talk I give to schoolkids," he said. "It's very informative."

"How come you wanted to get away from the admin building?" I asked.

No answer.

"It's a beautiful day," he said. "Great to be outside."

I didn't argue even though the temperature gauge on the Suburban read ninety-six degrees.

"Park over there." He directed me through the gate leading to the tower, to a spot between two tanks at the base of the structure.

I did as instructed, and we both exited the SUV. I put on the hard hat he gave me and followed him to a superstructure built as an outside layer on top of the boiler.

Right by the boiler, the air was hot and humid, much warmer than ninety-six degrees. Heat radiated from the massive structure, and a whooshing sound made conversation difficult. What looked like dirty talcum powder coated all the surfaces.

A freight elevator was attached to the outside of the superstructure.

Chester pushed the Up button, and the doors slid open. We stepped into a square room with plywood walls and a faded sign that read SAFETY FIRST. The temperature was hotter still, like the inside of an oven. He punched the button for the top, and a few very long and very hot seconds later, the doors opened, exposing a metal catwalk at the crown of the boiler structure.

We exited the elevator, and he directed me to a spot that was farthest from the boiler, an observation perch offering a view of the entire facility.

Up this high, there was a breeze blowing, and the ambient temperature felt like the North Pole compared with the enclosed sweatbox of the elevator.

"Great view from up here," he said. "Don't you think?"

I didn't say anything, just stared at him.

He pointed to the east. "That's the Crockett National Forest over there."

A blanket of green as far as the eye could see, the texture appearing as smooth as velvet from this distance. In the other directions, the green was marred by gray strips of highways and brown patches of buildings.

I decided to take a stab in the dark. I said, "Somebody leaning on you, Chester?"

No answer.

"Maybe telling you not to talk to the five-oh?" I asked.

A gust of warm air ruffled his short-sleeve dress shirt.

"The wife," he said. "She's in a bad way."

I didn't say anything.

"Ovarian cancer. The prognosis, well, it's not looking real good." He turned away, pressed both hands on the railing and stared out over the lake.

"Sorry to hear," I said. "That's a tough road."

We were both silent for a moment.

"You know how we make electricity here?" he asked.

I shook my head.

"Steam," he said. "The inside of the boiler—it's a bunch of steel tubes about as big around as my thumb. Maybe one inch total on the outside by a hundred feet."

I looked back at the structure behind us. The exterior was aluminum paneling crisscrossed with various wires and conduit.

"The tubes, they're welded together to form a forty-foot square, which makes up the inside of the boiler, and are then filled with water," he said. "At the bottom, we shoot coal dust into a flame. That boils the water, which makes steam that shoots out the top."

He pointed to a two-foot pipe wrapped in insulation. The pipe emerged from over our heads. It cut across the catwalk and then traveled down.

"Sounds like everything's under extremely high pressure." I tracked the steam outlet to a large structure that looked like a rocket lying on its side.

The structure was orange. On the top in large letters was the word Westinghouse.

"That's the turbine," Chester said. "That's what the steam turns to make the electricity."

Beyond the turbine lay a series of high-voltage wires feeding into metal buildings, similar to what Whitney had pointed out at the switching station.

"Steam by definition is under a lot of pressure," he said. "By the way."

"I wasn't talking about the steam, Chester."

"Oh."

"Those are transformers, aren't they?" I pointed to the metal buildings.

He nodded but didn't speak.

"The attack, Chester. Tell me what happened."

He looked off into the distance for a long moment, thoughts clearly churning in his mind.

"I'm not supposed to talk about that," he said.

"According to whom?"

He pursed his lips and stared at the canopy of trees.

A few moments passed. Then he said, "Somebody shot one of the main transformers."

I surveyed the area, an easy task given our height.

The tower and the turbine/transformer area were in the middle of a large open space, thousands of yards from the plant's perimeter and any possible sniper location.

"Do you know who?" I asked.

He shook his head.

The closest structures or likely hidings spots were the administration building, which was located in a slight depression, and a lake house on a hill about a hundred yards past the admin building.

"What's that place?" I pointed to the house.

Chester didn't respond.

"Is that where the shot came from?"

He nodded, a slight look of displeasure on his face.

"Is that part of the plant property?"

He pushed himself off the railing and patted his hands, and a small cloud of dust drifted off into the air. I wondered what was in the dust, what kind of pollutants were produced by burning coal.

"I don't want to lose my insurance, Jon. Not with my wife the way she is."

"I hate to be a hard-ass, but I'm a federal agent and you kinda have to talk to me."

He nodded but didn't speak.

"I represent the government of the United States, Chester. If anybody threatens you for talking to me, there's a world of hurt I can bring their way."

He took several deep breaths and said, "They told me it was a redneck who shot out the transformer. Told me not to worry about it."

The same story that Whitney Holbrook was peddling about Black Valley.

"Who told you that?"

No answer.

"Was it Price Anderson?"

His shoulders tensed for just a moment, and I knew the answer was yes.

"Tell me about the lake house."

"Back in the fifties," he said. "The man who started the company used it as a vacation spot. Great fishing right by the hot-water outflow."

The home was brick, overlooking the lake and a small dock. At the back there appeared to be a patio area with a barrel smoker and a couple of picnic benches. It was a pleasant setting.

"Nobody comes out there much anymore," Chester said. "Management uses it every now and then—fishing, I guess."

"Is there a record of who comes and goes?"

"There's separate access. From a different road. Requires a code."

"So someone could get in there without you knowing it?"

He didn't reply. After a moment, he nodded.

"Someone who had the right code, one they got from management?"

He started whistling softly, what sounded like the theme from *The Flintstones*.

We were silent for a moment. Chester said, "You want to see the rest of the plant?"

I shook my head. "No. I want to see the lake house."

- CHAPTER TWENTY-EIGHT -

Sarah composes an e-mail to her daughter with her phone, even though by the time Dylan is old enough to understand the message, e-mails will probably be as relevant as cassette players.

Dylan is in surgery, and Sarah wants to explain why things are the way they are, to help the child understand the reasons her mother can't always be there.

Also, Sarah wants to express her feelings in a healthy way, like that therapist in high school talked about after the incident with the baseball bat and the cheerleader who was putting the moves on Sarah's boyfriend.

Right now, everything is jumbled up inside Sarah's brain, and maybe by putting it down in writing the confusion will be lessened.

Maybe.

She takes a long swig of her Bloody Mary and begins:

Dearest precious Dylan:
You have no idea how hard it is for me to see you lying in a hospital bed like that.

If I could take the pain away from you I would. I wonder if your broken leg is somehow a punishment for what I've done or actions that other members of our family have committed. Whatever the case, you must understand that you are not to blame. You are pure & I hope you always will be.

You don't know yet about our family, about what we came from. There are dark things in our blood. I don't know how else to say it. Every family has their secrets, but ours seems to have been burdened more than most.

You asked if you would see Papa in heaven if you died, which amazes me, since he passed away five years before you were even born. I must have talked a lot of about him for you to want to see him that bad.

He was quite a man, your great-grandfather. He grew up in the Depression, which you'll learn about in school. Times were hard then & people had to do whatever they could to make a living. His own mother & father, my great-grandparents, died when he was just a boy. He lived on the streets of Texarkana for much of his child-hood, a period of time he never liked to talk about, so I can only imagine the hardship and suffering he endured.

But out of hardship comes strength, says the Bible (or maybe Shakespeare???), & he learned to survive & to make something of himself. He worked hard every day of his life & made a lot of money, providing a good life for his family. (When you're older, you'll hear people say Papa's fortune was built on blood money, because of the way he started out. I suppose that's true. A lot of the blood was his own, though.)

Sarah pauses for another sip of her drink. She's sitting by the beer taps in the bar across from the hospital, the place where Elias started the fight with the man in the Jiffy Lube shirt the night before.

Fortunately, it's just before lunchtime, so a different bartender is working and very few people are here.

A shaft of light cuts through the gloom as the door opens and a man enters. He's in his early thirties, but the years have been hard, as evidenced by the puffy face and dark circles under his eyes, both clearly visible even in the dim lighting. Lots of late nights and bad decisions have gone into that face.

Sarah watches the man survey the room, deciding where to sit.

He's wearing a pair of khakis and a golf shirt with a corporate logo on the breast. Despite the fact that no one else is at the bar, he slides onto the stool next to hers.

Sarah knows his type. He's a salesman, no doubt, fast-talking and insincere. An expense-account Romeo.

She's pretty sure she slept with someone who worked for the same company, a man she'd picked up at a hotel bar in Tulsa. He'd been wearing a similar shirt.

The guy next to her has on too much cologne, as well as a tacky gold bracelet on his right wrist, opposite a knockoff Rolex.

Sarah ignores him, trying to focus on her e-mail. In the back of her mind, she wonders if she gives off some weird pheromone that attracts a certain type of person—traveling salesmen and functional drunks, losers and dim-witted fuckwads—men who shroud themselves in body spray and bad double entendres.

She orders another Blood Mary, returns to the e-mail.

Papa was a violent man, & I'm afraid I've inherited that tendency from him. Sometimes violence is . . . I'm not sure how to put this . . . like a glass of milk when you have an upset stomach—soothing.

The salesman next to her orders a Dos Equis with extra limes. He speaks a little louder than necessary, glancing at Sarah as he talks to the bartender, trying to get her attention.

Sarah returns her concentration to the e-mail:

You will not read this until you are older and your leg is all healed. When that happens, maybe you and I will leave Dallas for a new life. Maybe we'll go to New York or Europe. Wonderful things await both of us, if only we can break free from this godforsaken place. This I promise you, Dylan. I will not allow our family's past to be inflicted on your future.

The salesman squeezes a lime wedge into his beer bottle. Some of the juice sprays Sarah's arm.

"Sorry about that." He hands her a cocktail napkin. "What are you working on so hard?"

A wave of pressure builds at the base of Sarah's neck, climbing its way up into her skull until her temples feel like they might explode.

She puts the phone down and wipes her arm, pointedly not responding to his question.

"So," the salesman says, "you come here often?"

Sarah can't tell if he's trying to be funny or not. Probably not.

Usually she can keep under control the self-loathing that comes from sleeping around. Unless the clichés start to pile up. For some reason, those make it all seem so tawdry and senseless. The salesman leers at her, fiddling with his gold bracelet.

Sarah's heart rate slows. She's in the zone, the sense of control making everything rosy. She's got a lot on her mind at the moment—an injured child, a dead cop in a motel room in Waco, a maybe-dead lesbian serial killer named Cleo—so the last thing she needs to be doing is making fuck-fuck eyes with some fruity-smelling loser. But what's a pussycat to do when the mouse wanders over and starts swinging its little paws at you?

"Boy, it's hot in here." She unfastens the top button of her blouse. "How about you buy me a drink, stud?"

The salesman's eyes open wide for an instant like he's just realized he's got a winning poker hand. He signals the bartender. "Another beer for me and whatever the lady is having."

Lay-dee. What an ass-munch. Sarah imagines she can actually hear the man's erection growing underneath his no-iron khakis.

The drinks arrive. Sarah wonders where the nearest hotel is.

"You work around here?" The salesman drains half his beer in one swallow.

"I don't work." Sarah runs her tongue around the rim of the glass. "I prefer to play."

The salesman's eyes go wide again and stay that way.

"What's the fragrance you're wearing?" she says. "Eau-de-fuck-me?"

He blinks several times but doesn't speak.

C'mon, Sarah thinks. *Am I gonna have to book the room myself and drag you to the bed?*

The thought makes her tired.

The salesman takes another pull of beer, regains a modicum of his game. "Well, aren't you a spicy enchilada?"

"You want to get out of here?" she says. "Find someplace a little more private?"

"Maybe we could finish our drinks first and, you know, talk a little."

The wind disappears from Sarah's sails.

"Oh, that's sweet." Her voice is tight and angry. "Like we're on a date. Two normal people who aren't in a bar in the middle of the day looking to hook up with whoever's got a pulse."

Silence.

Sarah takes a swig of her Bloody Mary. The throbbing in her skull is keeping time with the flicker of the TV over the bar. She should go back across the street and see her daughter. Not stay in this damn shithole, writing e-mails that will never be sent.

"Hell, lady." The salesman shakes his head. "How come you're so mean?"

Sarah drains the glass. "I'm not a lady."

The salesman doesn't say anything. Sarah feels her face get hot with anger and alcohol.

"I was just making conversation," the man says.

"You were trying to fuck me." Sarah's voice is matter-of-fact.

The salesman doesn't speak. He looks at her strangely.

"It's okay." Sarah touches his arm. "I was trying to fuck you, too."

The salesman shifts his weight, leaning away from her slightly.

"This guy tried to fuck me yesterday," Sarah says. "I had to shoot him."

The salesman's face turns white.

"You ever shot anybody?" she asks.

The salesman begins to shake.

"Don't worry." Sarah notices his distress. "I'm not gonna shoot you. I didn't bring my gun."

The man pushes away his unfinished beer. He throws a twenty on the bar, slides off the stool, and hoofs it to the exit.

Sarah watches him go. What the fuck? It wasn't like she actually pulled a gun on the guy. She returns to her e-mail, anger and frustration swirling around in her stomach along with all the booze.

The bartender scoops up the money and the beer bottle. He says, "Everything okay?"

Sarah nods, orders another Bloody Mary, wonders if the bartender knows where she might score some coke. A little pick-me-up would be good about now.

Her thumbs hover over the letters, but nothing happens. The words have disappeared from inside her, replaced by a dark emptiness.

She closes the e-mail and logs on to the website where she arranges meetings with her horndogs, the one where she met RockyRoad35. One of the features of the site is a notification system that tells you when someone else has been viewing your profile.

Sarah's profile has been viewed eleven times this morning alone, all by the same person.

RockyRoad35. A dead man.

- CHAPTER TWENTY-NINE -

Chester gave me a tour of the lake house, a three-bedroom home built sometime in the 1950s.

The walls inside were wood-paneled, floors covered in brown shag carpeting. The furniture was old and dusty. The air smelled like mothballs and fried onions.

There was nothing in the closets or any of the drawers except hangers and roach droppings. The kitchen cabinets contained a handful of glasses and plates that looked like they were from the set of *Leave It to Beaver*.

We wandered out to the back patio, which offered an elevated view of the boiler area, maybe four hundred yards away.

Not a slam-dunk shot like at the Black Valley substation. But not difficult either. Certainly doable.

"How many other Sudamento plants have lake houses?" I asked.

Chester shrugged. "I don't really know. Maybe three or four. The plant managers, we don't ever use them."

"Who does use them? People from the home office?"

"I guess. Doesn't seem like anybody is out there very much."

"Your security people," I said. "Do they regularly check on this place?"

Black Valley's cooling lake had a lakefront house, too, much smaller than this one, more of a shack. But the attack hadn't technically occurred on the plant premises. Maybe whoever was responsible had scoped out the plant from the lake house and then decided to strike the substation from the ridge behind Thompson's farm. An unoccupied home on or near the premises would make a great staging area for an attack.

"They're supposed to," he said. "But you know how that goes."

"What did the police say?" I asked.

"Police?" Chester cocked his head. "Here in McCarty?"

"So who investigated?"

"Sudamento sent some people from the home office."

"Price Anderson?"

"He was one of them, yes."

"And what did the Sudamento people say?"

Chester stared at the tower looming over the horizon and belching steam into a cloudless sky.

"Something about a rifle range being nearby. They said the bullet probably came from there." He paused. "We were only offline for a couple of hours."

"So nobody official came out here at all, did they? No police or federal investigators?"

He shook his head. "And there's no rifle ranges anywhere close."

I stared at the boiler.

"Mr. Anderson. He told me that his people would take care of everything," Chester said. "He told me that since the damage wasn't too bad, we shouldn't call the police."

I nodded but didn't reply.

"He said he'd already talked to the federal authorities about the situation. Said that if we get the police involved, then the newspapers might find out and that would hurt Sudamento's stock price."

I gave him my best blank stare.

"We didn't realize there'd been an attack at first," he said. "The heat readings on one of the units spiked, so I shut down the boiler and called the home office, like we're trained to."

I didn't say anything.

"I followed the proper procedures." He crossed his arms.

"How much Sudamento stock do you own, Chester?"

Overhead a pair of mallards glided toward the lake, wings cupped.

"Not much," he said. "Just our entire retirement account."

The retirement account for Chester and his cancer-stricken wife.

I walked around the patio, examining different angles and possible shooting positions. On the other side of the house was a gravel parking area that led to a dirt road.

I walked back to where Chester stood by the barbecue grill.

He pointed to the boiler. "Three transformers at the base. You see them?"

I peered into the distance. From four hundred yards away, the complex was an impenetrable mass of tubes, scaffolding, tanks, and wires. After a moment, I recognized the metal structures he'd pointed out from atop the boiler. Each was about the size of a large van.

"The shooter hit the heat sink on the one closest to us," he said. "One shot only."

"And that made the whole plant shut down?"

He nodded. "The juice had nowhere to go."

I stared at the three transformers. The shot would have been relatively easy. The gunman probably used the barbecue as a rest, sat in one of the patio chairs. Whitney was right; the attack was a dry run, a probe. Taking one plant offline wouldn't hurt the grid that much. They wanted to see what would happen if you shot a transformer.

"Fortunately, we had another unit on-site," Chester said. "They cost about three hundred thousand dollars each."

"How long would it have taken to get one here if you hadn't had a backup?" I looked at my watch. It was coming up on noon. I needed to go see the old drunk from the VFW hall.

Chester shook his head. "I don't know."

"Take a guess."

"Six months maybe." He shrugged. "They come on a boat from China."

- CHAPTER THIRTY -

The sunlight hits Sarah's eyes as she leaves the bar.

It's the noon hour.

She squints and puts on a pair of Dior sunglasses, not the cheap ones she uses when she meets a horndog.

Her head buzzes from the Bloody Marys, eyes half blind from the light.

She staggers into the parking lot, holding her cell phone.

Someone is accessing RockyRoad's account.

The voice of her grandfather rings in her skull: *They're looking for you, girlie.*

The phone feels hot against her palm, like all of the sun's energy is being directed into that tiny chunk of plastic.

You really think you could kill a lawman and get away with it?

"Shut. Up." Sarah squeezes her temples with one hand.

Even I never shot a damn cop. In Texas, at least. The old man cackles. *Louisiana, now that was a different story.*

"Please, just be quiet." Sarah wanders across the parking lot to the sidewalk by the street.

The bar is behind her, the hospital across Gaston Avenue. Traffic whizzes by.

A homeless guy with a grocery cart stares at her. He pushes the cart into the gutter to avoid an encounter.

How's your letter to Dylan coming?

Sarah sinks to her knees, the dirty concrete pressing against the artfully faded material of her True Religion jeans.

You're telling her all about me, aren't you? About her great-grandpappy?

"What do you want?" Tears stream down Sarah's face.

I want to keep you out of prison. What the hell do you think I want? One grandkid going to the joint is enough, dontcha think?

She stares at the screen. Her profile page is being accessed again, this time by someone called "Admin."

"The phone." Sarah jumps up, frantic. "They can track me through the phone."

"You okay, lady?" The homeless guy is still staring at her. He's a few feet away, a concerned expression on his face underneath all the grime.

She realizes how she looks. She's wearing a white silk blouse, $300 jeans, and Jimmy Choo pumps. An Hermès purse that costs as much as a used car hangs over one shoulder.

And she's crying in front of a bar so sleazy even the cockroaches are on parole.

"I'm fine, thank you. Everything's okay." She sniffles, backs away from the homeless guy.

A store that loans money on car titles is on one side of the bar. A taco stand is on the other. Between the taco stand and the bar is a strip of asphalt leading to an alley.

Sarah dashes away from the street, toward the anonymity of the alley.

The area behind the bar is shaded with trees and smells like old garbage, rancid grease, and human feces. It's full of overflowing Dumpsters, split trash sacks, and eight zillion crushed beer cans.

But no people. And she's not visible from the street.

Sarah heads to the nearest Dumpster. She smashes the cell phone against the corner of the trash receptacle.

Nothing happens. The screen doesn't break. The website is still visible.

She drops the phone on the pavement. Stamps it with her foot.

The device remains in one piece, screen still illuminated. The thin pumps she's wearing pack very little punch.

A wave of panic swells in her throat.

How fucking hard can it be to trash one fucking phone?

A pile of debris lies across the alley. Cast-off building material. Lengths of two-by-fours, pieces of broken plywood, a half-dozen bricks.

She strides across the alley, grabs a chunk of brick, returns to where she left the phone. She kneels, slams the brick into the middle of the screen, and is rewarded with a crunching sound as glass cracks and electronic parts scatter.

Relieved, she tosses the brick.

From the side of the alley closest to the street comes the sound of feet shuffling and metal rattling, somebody pushing a grocery cart.

Sarah looks up.

The homeless guy is back. And he's brought a friend, another street person. The second guy is wearing a dirty Dallas Mavericks sweatshirt with the sleeves torn off. He's got a shaved head and one eye the color of milk.

The first one, the person Sarah saw on the street a few minutes before, has matted dreadlocks. He's shirtless, wearing only a tattered navy blazer and dirty jeans.

Dreadlocks says, "You sure you're okay, lady?"

Sarah doesn't reply.

His buddy, the one with the milky eye, says, "How come you're smashing your phone?"

Before Sarah can say anything, Dreadlocks flanks out, moving away from his friend to the other side of the alley. His position blocks Sarah from running away.

"You got any money?" Milky Eye says. "We need to get a ride to the VA."

Silence. Sarah swivels her head, looking at each man in turn.

"My meds ran out," Dreadlocks says. "I don't feel so good when I don't take my pills."

"Leave me alone, please." Sarah lets her voice sound weak and timid.

"What's wrong?" Milky Eye cocks his head. "You got a thing against veterans?"

"How about I give you twenty bucks?" Sarah says. "Each."

"Your purse," Dreadlocks says. "How about you give us that?"

Sarah doesn't react. She evaluates her options. Adrenaline burns off some of the alcohol in her system, and she feels a calmness wash over her.

"Maybe you could show us your tits, too?" Milky Eye rubs his crotch.

Sarah touches the Spyderco knife in her waistband, the lockback with a three-inch serrated blade that she used yesterday to free the naked girl from the serial killer's van.

When she'd been twelve years old, her grandfather had told her to never leave home without a weapon of some sort. As an example, he'd shown her the Python he always carried under his denim work jacket.

At fifteen, her grandfather had hired an ex–Green Beret to teach Sarah how to take care of herself on the streets. At seventeen, she'd been in a beer joint in Texarkana when a man had tried to rape her. She'd used a pool cue and what the Green Beret had taught her and broken the man's pelvis and both of his arms.

"Twenty bucks each." Sarah slides the knife from her waistband. "That's what I'm offering. Take it or leave it."

"What's that?" Dreadlocks points to the Spyderco.

"It's a knife." Sarah flicks open the blade. "I don't want to hurt you, but I will."

"Shit." Milky Eye laughs. "Look at this bitch, thinking she's tough."

Sarah's still kneeling by the remains of the phone. The brick lies about a foot away.

"We're gonna have a good time with Miss Richie Rich." Dreadlocks moves toward her. "Wonder if she's ever pulled the train before."

The Green Beret used to talk about the heightened sensitivity you'd feel if you knew that trouble was coming.

Sarah can hear their ragged breathing, smell their unwashed bodies. She sees the individual specks of dirt on their faces.

Without warning, she rolls to the right, away from Dreadlocks, and scoops up the brick with her free hand. She stands.

Milky Eye is about eight feet away. He's moving slowly toward her, arms out.

She throws the brick at his face, not putting a lot of power into the toss. It's more about accuracy, and her aim is true.

One corner of the brick hits the man in his good eye.

He falls to the ground, screaming like somebody punched him in the balls.

Dreadlocks's mouth hangs open.

Sarah rushes him, the knife held in her right hand, blade down.

Dreadlocks raises his left arm to block her attack, his right reared back to strike.

Sarah knocks the left arm away with her left hand and punches toward the man's neck with her right, slashing his throat with the blade.

Dreadlocks's eyes go wide. He stares at the blood gushing from just below his chin.

Sarah stands a few feet away, catching her breath.

After a long moment, Dreadlocks stops looking at the blood arcing from his throat. He turns to Sarah. He reaches for her. Then, he falls to the ground, dead.

Milky Eye is still screaming like a girl.

Sarah runs to where he lies.

His hands are pressed to his damaged eye, throat exposed.

She stares at the man, the enormity of what has occurred in the last few seconds dawning on her. Her life is a wreck, and deep in her heart she understands she is the only one to blame.

In the distance, a siren sounds. Either an ambulance on its way to the emergency room or the police about to apprehend her.

The injured man at her feet screams louder.

"Fuck this," Sarah says. She slices through the cartilage and other tissue that forms Milky Eye's windpipe.

The screaming stops. Blood jets and then pools on the ground.

Good girl. The voice of her grandfather.

- CHAPTER THIRTY-ONE -

In the parking lot of the McCarty Creek Generating Facility, I sent Whitney Holbrook a text requesting a list of Sudamento plants that had lake houses as part of the grounds. I asked if it was possible to mark those that had separate access.

Every power plant had to have a body of water to act as a cooling agent. How many of those bodies of water had lake houses and how many of those houses had separate access was anybody's guess.

The more I thought about it, the more the presence of a lake house seemed like a factor worth investigating. Like a fever indicated a cold was coming on, I had a hunch that a lake house might be a sign that a plant was prone to attack. A comfortable shelter that was rarely checked, near the target, a place for the attackers to hide while fine-tuning the assault.

Whitney didn't respond.

I drummed my fingers on the steering wheel.

The old drunk from the VFW hall—the man who might or might not have witnessed my deputy's killer steal a car—lived in Italy, Texas. The town, located forty or so miles north of Waco, had about as much in common with the country in Europe as did an Olive Garden. But it was only about ninety minutes away if I used the lights and siren.

The next closest Sudamento power plant was an hour south, the opposite direction. The list Whitney had given me indicated that the facility had a smaller generator, only three hundred megawatts compared to Black Valley with fourteen hundred. Hardly worth visiting, in my opinion, especially since I didn't know if it had a lake house, the presence of which was as close to a theory as I had at the moment.

Thirty seconds passed. No response from Whitney.

I dropped my phone on the console, activated the red and blue lights in the grille of the Suburban, and headed to Italy.

Seventy-five minutes later, I stopped at a Quickee Mart just outside the town limits and bought a burrito, which I ate while filling the SUV with gas. When the tank was full, I drove to the address Whitney had given me.

The guy from the VFW hall lived in a double-wide trailer a couple blocks from the high school. His name was Delbert G. Littlejohn. DOB June 12, 1946. According to the local appraisal district, the owner of the trailer was Susan Marie Littlejohn, a daughter I guessed, since she was born in 1969.

The Littlejohn domicile appeared well tended. The lawn was mowed, the beds full of flowers. A late-model Kia was parked in the driveway, behind an elderly Ford pickup with two bumper stickers—Made in the USA and Vietnam Veteran.

I parked across the street in front of a vacant lot overgrown with weeds.

It was a little after noon, and the temperature gauge read ninety-nine degrees. I fastened the Peterson County sheriff's badge to my belt, got out, and walked across the road.

On the porch, hand reaching out to knock, I heard raised voices from inside, a man and a woman shouting.

I knocked anyway.

Footsteps.

The door opened, and a woman in her midforties appeared. She wore blue medical scrubs and had shoulder-length hair dyed the color of wheat.

I introduced myself. "Is Delbert Littlejohn at home?"

She swore under her breath and turned to the interior of the trailer, yelling, "Are you happy now? The damn police are here."

Unintelligible shouts in return.

The woman turned back to me. "What's he done now?"

"Nothing. But I need to talk to him. May I come in?"

She sighed wearily and opened the door.

The interior of the home was tidy, the air smelling of pine disinfectant and bacon. Gray sculpted carpet that was freshly vacuumed, wood-paneled walls adorned with framed prints of mountain scenes. A leather sectional sofa in front of a flat-screen TV.

"I got a shift at the dialysis center in Waxahachie," the woman said. "Starts in thirty minutes. I can't stay."

Waxahachie was a town on the interstate about twenty-five minutes away.

In the doorway on the other side of the room stood an old man in a bathrobe. He looked like death was knocking on his door, but he was too tired to answer. His face was blotchy where it wasn't pale, his hair greasy. A swollen gut, broomstick legs.

"Don't be conned into getting him something to drink." The woman picked up her purse from the dining room table.

"Is he all right to be by himself?" I said.

"Hell no." She walked to the door. "But we're not exactly full up with options."

"Is there anything I can—"

The door slammed shut. The old man and I looked at each other.

"What do you want?" he said.

"Yesterday at the VFW hall. You saw a car get stolen."

"You got any beer?"

"No."

"Then I don't know what you're talking about."

Silence.

Delbert Littlejohn shuffled into the kitchen area. He turned on the tap at the sink, filled a glass, and sucked it down in one long gulp.

"You had anything to eat today?" I asked.

He shook his head. "There's a bar in town that makes a good burger. How about you give me a ride? She hid the keys to my truck again."

"That's not gonna happen."

"Then you can leave." He drank another full glass of water.

"I can't do that, Mr. Littlejohn."

He wobbled over to the couch and sat down.

"Based on my observations," I said, "you appear to be a danger to yourself."

He looked up, his eyes forming slits.

"I'll have to take you to the hospital for a seventy-two-hour psych hold."

"You son of a bitch." His face turned red. "Who the hell do you think you are?"

I smiled. "I'm the guy who's gonna throw your ass into an alcohol-free environment for the next three days."

He swore again and then turned on the TV with a remote. A daytime talk show appeared on the screen.

I walked over to the sofa. Pulled the remote from his hand. Turned off the TV.

"They'll give you an IV full of vitamins and minerals," I said. "It makes the detox a lot easier."

A few moments passed.

"What do you want to know?" He slumped his shoulders, defeated.

"Everything you can remember about the woman who took the car."

A long pause.

"I was pretty drunk," he said.

"Yeah. I gathered that."

"Charlie, he never loans his car out. She tried to tell me she was borrowing it."

"What did she look like?"

"White girl. She was pretty."

"How about her age? How tall was she?"

He licked his lips and frowned, clearly trying to dredge up the memories. "Maybe, uh, twenty. Average height."

The woman I'd talked to for a few seconds behind the motel was in her thirties at least. I wondered if this had been a wasted trip. Thousands of cars got stolen every day in Texas, more than a few of them by women, some of whom no doubt wore ball caps.

"It was hard to tell what she looked like on account of she was wearing these big sunglasses and a hat."

"What kind of hat?" I asked.

He rubbed his chin but didn't answer.

"A Stetson? Or a sombrero?"

"A ball cap." Delbert looked proud of himself. "A Washington Redskins ball cap."

I tried not to look disappointed. It wasn't the same person. Pretty hard to misidentify something like that. The Cowboys' colors were blue and silver, Washington's red and gold.

"She was good-looking. Did I tell you that?"

I nodded. Glanced toward the door, thought about the long drive back to the office.

Delbert said, "And I bet she had a body underneath that rain jacket."

I turned away from the door. "What rain jacket?"

"She wore this ugly raincoat kinda thing."

"Like something you might buy at a dollar store?" I asked.

"Yeah. Exactly."

"And a Washington Redskins ball cap?"

"I remember the cap clearly." He nodded. "Thanksgiving, 1974. Drew Pearson caught a fifty-yard pass with thirty seconds to go. Cowboys beat the Skins, twenty-four to twenty-three."

I didn't say anything.

"Never forget that day," Delbert said. "Me and my little girl Susan. Her mama had just died." He paused. "That's how I remember the woman who stole Charlie's car was wearing a Cowboys ball cap."

I stared at his eyes. "I thought you said it was a Washington Redskins cap?"

"Did I?" He looked confused.

"Yeah."

He shook his head, the expression on his weathered face that of a lost little boy.

"So what kind of cap do you think it was?" I kept my voice soft. "Think real carefully."

"I . . . I don't know." Tears welled in his eyes.

"What else can you tell me about the woman? Anything at all."

He shook his head and started to weep for reasons I couldn't begin to fathom. Alcoholic mood swings, low blood sugar, a lifetime of bad choices?

I went into the kitchen, opened the refrigerator, and found a box of leftover pizza that didn't look very old. Pepperoni and sausage. I brought the box to the living area and set it down in front of Delbert. He jerked open the lid and devoured what was there like he'd just been released from the gulag.

When he was finished he closed the box and said, "It was definitely a Cowboys cap."

I nodded. "Anything else you remember?"

He stared off into space. "She wasn't a Monte Carlo kind of girl."

"What do you mean?"

"Not sure why, but I didn't get the impression she was boosting the car for the money."

A set of disjointed images flickered through my head. The woman in the ball cap and shapeless coat. A narrow hallway in a motel on the interstate. The Buick LaCrosse, an inexpensive automobile.

After a moment, I realized the woman I had seen didn't belong in that hallway or driving that car. She gave off a different vibe. Like she was used to better things.

"Did she seem like a rich girl?" I asked. "You know, playacting at being something else."

"Yeah." He nodded. "That's a good way to put it, now that you mention it."

We were both silent for a few moments.

I stood up to leave. "You gonna be all right if I go?"

He didn't reply, brow furrowed.

I headed to the door.

"One more thing," he said. "It was really strange."

"What?"

"Seemed like she was talking to somebody who wasn't there." He shook his head. "Sounded like it was her . . . grandfather?"

- CHAPTER THIRTY-TWO -

Sarah wipes the Spyderco on Milky Eye's shirt and tosses the knife into the Dumpster.

Then she plunges down the alley, heading away from the bodies of the two homeless men, trying to escape from all that she is and all that she will become.

She has no phone or weapon. She's dressed like she's going to the yacht club. Her only child is undergoing surgery at this very moment.

At the end of the alley, she stops. She's sweating, breath coming in heaves.

Across the street is a decrepit strip mall housing a tattoo shop, a store that sells electronic cigarettes, and a medical supply company.

She has to get out of sight.

The two bodies will be found, sooner rather than later. Even though the victims were homeless, not usually a high priority for the authorities, there were two of them, both with their throats cut in broad daylight.

The police will have to investigate. Soon the alley will be full of ambulances and homicide detectives. The trail she's left is too big, too many markers pointing back to her.

She waits until her breathing slows, then walks into the tattoo shop.

A woman in her twenties is behind the counter. The woman is wearing a tank top to better accentuate the ink covering her arms, a green-and-red floral pattern that gives the feeling of an album cover from the 1960s—peace and love and patchouli.

Sarah and the woman are the only people in the store. The walls are covered with silk screens showing various tattoo designs.

"Can I help you?" The woman lights some incense.

"I need to borrow a phone, if I could."

The woman stares at Sarah, taking in her white blouse covered in alley grime and sweat.

"I'm happy to pay you." Sarah reaches into her purse, pulls out a twenty.

"Are you okay?" A concerned look on the woman's face.

"I had a flat tire," Sarah says. "I tried to change it myself."

The woman doesn't speak.

"Of course I left my cell on the charger at home." Sarah rolls her eyes. "I'm always doing that."

"Here." The woman slides a landline across the top of the counter. "You don't need to pay me."

"Thank you." Sarah dials Elias's number.

She could call the person she reached out to last night, or Walden, but with two dead bodies behind her, there's a limit to how involved she wants a non-family-member to be.

After a long time, Elias answers the phone with a wary hello.

"It's your sister," Sarah says. "I have a flat tire. I need you to pick me up."

Silence.

The woman behind the counter busies herself rearranging a cup of pens, obviously not wanting to eavesdrop but just as obviously not going to the other side of the room.

"I'm busy," Elias says. "Call one of your boyfriends."

"I was going to call Roger," Sarah says. "But I figured I'd try you first."

Heavy breathing from the other end. Roger is Elias's probation officer.

"You're a piece of work, sis." His voice sounds tinny. "Where are you?"

Sarah reads him the address off one of the business cards by the incense.

"Ten minutes." Elias hangs up.

Sarah slides the phone back across the counter. "He's on his way. Thank you."

"Would you like to sit down while you wait?" the woman asks. "Maybe have some tea?"

On the wall by the cash register is a silk screen with a pattern that looks vaguely familiar. An ornate rose over two interlocking circles with crosses protruding from the bottom, nearly identical to the tattoo on Cleo's neck.

"That one." Sarah points to the screen. "What does it mean?"

"The power of hope and love," the woman says. "The crosses at the bottom, it's a lesbian thing."

"Hope and love." Sarah nods. "Yes, I can see that."

The flower bursts with color, petals seeming to reach out, yearning to touch the viewer, offering guidance and safe passage.

For some reason the springtime image makes her think of fall mornings at the house in Bowie County, frost on the grass, the smell of breakfast cooking. A time of peace. She's a little girl. She doesn't yet understand the emotional trauma adults are capable of inflicting on one another. Or on a child.

The woman, a confused expression on her face, stares at Sarah.

Hope and love, Sarah thinks. These are the important things in life. Hope, love, and family.

With a start, she realizes she won't be able to see Dylan when her daughter comes back from surgery. She has to change clothes, get cleaned up from the mess she made in the alley.

"Are you sure you're okay?" the woman asks.

A lump of emotion wells in Sarah's throat. She needs to get a lawyer. Or leave Dallas for good.

If the police do their job, Sarah might not ever see Dylan again.

In her head, the voice of her grandfather. *Get out of the damn tattoo parlor!*

Sarah looks around the store like she's seeing it for the first time.

"Who are you talking to?" the woman says.

"What?"

"Just now. You were mumbling something about Dylan."

Sarah's skin gets cold. In the far corner of the store she sees a tiny TV camera.

The woman squints at Sarah's waist. "Is that blood on your shirt?"

Sarah looks down. Several red droplets stain the white material just above her hip. Two homeless men, throats cut, blood gushing. How could she have avoided being tainted by what she's done?

"It wasn't my fault." Sarah doesn't know if she's thinking those words or saying them.

"Maybe I should call an ambulance." The woman picks up the phone.

Sarah's grandfather: *GET OUT OF THERE!*

The woman dials.

Sarah presses down on the receiver's cradle. "No, that's okay. I'll wait on the street."

The woman doesn't speak. Her eyes are wide, taking in every detail, no doubt.

"Thanks for your help." Sarah smiles and leaves the store.

Outside, the sky is cloudless, a merciless sun beating down on the cracked sidewalk. An ambulance, siren blaring, rushes by, headed toward the emergency room.

Sarah tries to get her head right, project an image of confidence. She imagines herself shopping in an expensive part of town, strolling with friends, not a care in the world. With that in mind, she walks to the corner and waits.

Three minutes later, right as the first police car turns down the alley, Elias stops and Sarah gets into his pickup.

Elias is not alone, and Sarah realizes that once again she has made the wrong choice.

- CHAPTER THIRTY-THREE -

I arrived at the Black Valley Generating Station midafternoon. Figured that would be where the action was, so to speak, and I was right.

Vehicles and people swarmed across the entire site.

A news van from Waco was parked on the side of the road just outside the main entrance. A woman with puffy blond hair stood with the smokestacks in the background, holding a microphone and looking into a camera operated by a bearded guy wearing khaki shorts.

I pulled up to the gate, and an armed man wearing a blue T-shirt marked FEDERAL AGENT on the back waved me through.

Inside the perimeter were dozens of Sudamento repair trucks and almost that many black Suburbans, the latter sprouting antennas like weeds.

As I drove toward the main office, my phone dinged with a text message.

I slowed, picked up the cell.

A blocked number. The message: *Eliz is fine.*

Breath caught in my throat. Piper was telling me about our daughter, Elizabeth.

There was no place to park in the lot by the administration building, so I stopped on the side of the road behind another black Suburban.

I typed a reply: *Where are you?*

No answer.

I typed some more. *Please come home.*

Nothing. A helicopter flew overhead. Vehicles rattled down the gravel road.

I waited a moment longer and sent one last text. *Tell E. her daddy loves her.*

An enormous sense of loss settled on my shoulders. An empty spot inside me, like something had been cut away from deep within.

As much as possible, I tried not to think about the situation. I didn't dwell on Piper's foibles, the idiosyncrasies that made her who she was. Made her the woman I loved at one time.

You get involved with somebody like that—caring and beguiling and volatile all in the same breath—you have to understand that everything can change with a shift in the winds.

My cell dinged again, a short reply. *OK.*

I let my breath out. Didn't realize I'd been holding it. I swallowed the emotions in my throat and exited the SUV.

The administrative office was not very grand as headquarters go, maybe a little larger than an insurance office in a midsized city.

In addition to the Sudamento trucks and black Suburbans, there was a late-model Range Rover parked near the front.

Inside, chaos reigned. Federal agents and Sudamento employees hustled from office to office, talking on cell phones and walkie-talkies. Administrative assistants scurried about, carrying files and clipboards. The air was cool but smelled of sweat and coffee.

In the middle of the building was a large conference room dominated by a table with seating for thirty. Every chair was taken, and people stood with their backs to the walls, looking toward the front of the room.

At the head of the table stood a man in his forties who was using a laser pointer to indicate various items on a large monitor. The image displayed was a satellite view of the area around the plant, including the substation that had been attacked, maybe two or three square miles total.

The man wielding the pointer wore an expensive-looking suit with no tie and looked like the kind of guy who would drive a Range Rover, upper management.

Whitney Holbrook stood against the back wall.

I eased into an empty spot beside her while the man with the pointer droned on about market share, kilowatt-hours, and Sudamento's fiduciary responsibility to its shareholders.

The people in the room were an even mix, about half feds and the remainder Sudamento employees. All of them were paying close attention to what the man was saying.

Whitney looked at me, a quizzical expression on her face. She whispered, "What's wrong?"

I didn't reply. The cell was still in my hand, and I realized I couldn't stop glancing at the screen.

Gently, Whitney pulled it from my grasp. She looked at the text messages. "This is about your daughter?"

I nodded.

"Let's get out of here." She put a hand on my arm, directed me to the hallway.

Outside, the atmosphere was less tense, not quite as crowded.

An agent walked by. Whitney waved him over and said, "Is that hacker from Homeland still around?"

The agent nodded.

She handed the man my phone. "The last text message. I need the number and location of the sender." She looked at me. "You okay with that?"

After a moment, I nodded. There was nothing on my phone that I wouldn't mind others seeing. If a device was connected to a cell tower or Wi-Fi, it was pretty much a given that someone had access to the contents.

Whitney spoke to the agent. "Last time I checked, Hacker Boy was playing video games and eating microwave pizza. See if you can impress upon him the need to make this a priority."

The agent nodded. He took the phone and strode down the hall to an exit door.

"Speaking of text messages," I said, "you never answered mine."

Whitney pulled a phone from her pocket. She stared at the screen but didn't speak.

"Price didn't tell you about the attack at McCarty Creek, did he?"

"We didn't find out until later." She shook her head. "Service wasn't interrupted because of that incident."

"He should have told you, though," I said. "Seeing as how that's your job, keeping the grid intact."

"There's lots of things that Price should have done."

I didn't know if she meant personally or professionally.

"What's he hiding?" I asked.

"I don't know."

"You're a federal agent, Whitney. You're supposed to be in the knowing business."

"It's not that easy," she said. "You of all people should understand that."

A Sudamento employee walked by, jabbering into a walkie-talkie.

"It's the golden rule," she said. "The corporation with the most gold makes the rules."

"Why would Sudamento not want to find out who's attacking their plants?"

"How long were you in the conference room just now?" she said. "Thirty seconds?"

I shrugged.

"And how many times did the guy in the fancy suit mention stock prices?"

I didn't reply. Three or four at least.

"The market's extremely volatile right now, especially the energy sector. Any big downswings in value aren't good for the economy."

"What's that mean, you don't get to do your job?"

"It means my job is complicated."

A burst of noise from the far end of the hallway as the exit door opened and Price Anderson stepped inside. Standing beside him was the ex–Special Forces guy from the other day. Both were dressed like private military contractors in Baghdad, circa 2006. Khakis, blue button-down shirts, heavy boots, flak jackets. They each carried M-4 rifles.

I looked at Whitney. "What's going on?"

"The part that makes everything more complicated," she said.

"What do you mean?"

"The head guy is here," she said. "Sudamento's CEO."

- CHAPTER THIRTY-FOUR -

Sarah slams shut the passenger door of Elias's pickup as the second squad car turns into the alley.

They are on the corner by the tattoo parlor, down the street from the hospital where her daughter is recovering from a broken leg.

"What's with the five-oh?" Elias says. "Have you been a bad girl?"

A pair of dead hobos in the alley. "Bad girl" is an understatement.

Sarah ignores the questions and stares at the figure in the middle of the bench seat, who's huddled up against her brother.

A black man in his early twenties. He is thin, a wisp of a human being, delicate features. He's wearing a pair of chinos and a collarless white shirt. The shirt is really a tunic, reaching to the man's thighs, and resembles what you might see someone in Pakistan wearing. As if to emphasize the Middle Eastern effect, the man is also wearing a Muslim skullcap of the same color.

Despite his clothes, Sarah senses he is not from the Middle East or of the Muslim faith.

"Who is this, Elias?" Her tone is wary.

"Alfie." The man holds out a hand, palm down. "Charmed, I'm sure."

His voice is as slight as his body. Feminine. Breathless.

"No-no-no." Elias shakes his head. "Your name is not Alfie anymore. It's Amin."

"Sorry." Alfie/Amin giggles, still holding his hand out. "It's a pleasure to meet you."

Elias pulls away from the curb. He turns onto Gaston Avenue. Their path will take them past the hospital and the bar.

Sarah doesn't shake hands. She leans forward, stares at her brother. "What the hell is going on? You win this guy at the state fair or something?"

Amin extends his middle finger. "Well aren't you just being a hateful little bitch."

The stress of the past two days explodes in Sarah's head, a starburst of yellow and black that makes her vision cloudy and her ears ring.

She grabs the man's hand and twists, rolling the thumb outward. "Shut up, *Amin*, or I'll punch you in the throat."

The man in the skullcap screams. After a few seconds, Sarah lets go, but he continues his high-pitched bellowing, cradling his hand like it had been stuck in hot oil.

Elias jerks the wheel of the pickup and squeals to a stop in the parking lot of the bar.

He looks at the diminutive man and says, "If you don't quit screaming, I'll get your parole violated so fast the Aryan Brotherhood will be trading your ass for a six-pack of banana pudding by dinner."

Alfie lowers his caterwauling to a whimper.

Sarah can see red and blue lights flashing behind the bar. "Keep driving. This is a bad place to stop."

Elias stares at the lights. "What'd you do?"

"You think I'm going to talk about anything in front of your little pal?"

"It's cool." Elias pulls away from the bar. "Alfie won't be talking to anybody."

The expression on her brother's face makes Sarah's stomach queasy. Alfie doesn't seem to notice.

Everyone is silent for a moment. Then:

"I want some ice cream," Alfie says. His tone in petulant, an angry child.

Sarah realizes the younger man is not quite right in the head.

"That's a great idea." Elias speeds down the street. "Let's find you a snack."

Alfie looks at Sarah. "You almost broke my hand."

A moment passes.

"Don't talk to me, Alfie." Sarah watches the city peel by. "It's better for everybody that way."

Elias attracts strays like a watermelon does flies on a hot summer day.

Needy, insecure people with the word "victim" written on their foreheads. This one is no different from the ten who came before him.

A couple of turns later, Elias pulls into a Braum's ice-cream store and parks. He hops out, hands Alfie a ten-dollar bill. "Get anything you want."

"Even a swirl?"

Elias nods. Alfie squeals with glee and scampers out of the pickup, skipping across the parking lot.

Elias slides back behind the steering wheel.

"Alfie's not long for this world, is he?" Sarah says.

"Are any of us?"

"You know what I mean."

"He's serving a larger purpose," Elias says. "Let's leave it at that."

"He's just a child."

"He drove over his mother with a riding lawn mower when he was sixteen," Elias says. "She was getting ready to send him back to one of those camps where they pray away the gay."

Sarah doesn't reply.

"When the praying didn't work, they used electroshock therapy."

The people in Elias's world all have horrible backstories. *Mommie Dearest* parents, abusive authority figures, and an endless string of improbably bad life choices. Why should Alfie be any different?

"I took Alfie under my wing the first night he was inside," Elias says. "They woulda split him in two before he'd been there a full day."

"You want a medal for being the humanitarian of the year?"

"How long do you think you'd last inside?"

Sarah doesn't answer. She'd rather die than go to prison. Fortunately, her brushes with the law have always been smoothed over with either money or her grandfather's influence.

Neither speaks for a few moments. They watch Alfie through the plate-glass windows of the store.

"You have to admit, he's kinda cute," Elias says. "You know how I am about brown sugar."

Sarah shakes her head, shifts in her seat.

Inside the store, Alfie accepts a large ice-cream cone with one hand. With his other, he scratches his crotch. Sarah looks away. She stares out the back window, happening to glance into the bed of the pickup. There, she sees a half-dozen or so fifty-pound bags of fertilizer.

"Wonder whatever happened to Odell?" Elias cut his eyes toward his sister, an eyebrow arched.

Odell was a few months older than Sarah, half black and half Mexican. He lived in a tar-paper shack behind a juke joint near the Red River. He was a sweet boy, tall, arms and legs ropy with muscles.

Sarah and Odell got to be friends when she and her grandfather would visit the juke joint. One time, they kissed. By Sarah's next visit, Odell was gone, never to be seen again in Bowie County. Sarah hopes he is still alive, but she has her doubts.

Elias chuckles softly to himself, obviously realizing he's scored a hit on his sister.

A flash of rage engulfs Sarah. She clenches her fists, wishing she had a knife at that moment.

On the floor of the pickup, her heel hits something hard hidden underneath an old blanket. She reaches down and removes the cover.

Their grandfather's old thirty-thirty and one of his submachine guns. The stock of the thirty-thirty is battered, bluing worn from the barrel. Underneath the two weapons is a plastic sack from RadioShack, full of items.

"Why do you have all that fertilizer in the back?" she asks. "And Papa's guns?"

Elias doesn't reply.

"Do you want to go back to prison?"

No answer.

"Or is this just some elaborate ruse to cause me more pain?"

"Everything's always about you, isn't it?" he says. "You're the star of your own movie. Center stage, twenty-four/seven. My little sister."

A moment passes. A weight presses down on Sarah's shoulders. The lies, the hurt she's caused. The face of the man in the locked car that summer day so long ago.

Elias says, "You never told me where his Python is."

Sarah doesn't respond.

"The guns were his trophies. You realize that, don't you?"

"I don't want to hear your bullshit."

"Now they're mine."

Sarah shakes her head, not wanting to listen but not getting out of the pickup either.

"He was a good man." Sarah crosses her arms. "I don't want to listen to you talk bad about him."

Elias laughs. "You really buy into all that chamber-of-commerce crap?"

"He provided for us," Sarah says. "We don't want for anything because of him."

The smile slides from Elias's face, his mood shifting like a leaf in a storm.

"We are rich because of him." Sarah wipes a tear from her eye.

Elias's nostrils flare with each breath, a sign he is angry. Talking about their grandfather usually brought that emotion to the surface. Elias's narcissism is so severe he cannot abide when another person refuses to see the world through his particular filter.

Alfie/Amin emerges from the store, an enormous cone of ice cream in one hand.

Sarah pinches the bridge of her nose. "Back where you picked me up. There are two dead guys in the alley."

Silence.

Elias says, "Witnesses?"

Sarah shakes her head.

"What about the place you called me from?"

"The tattoo parlor." Sarah remembers the TV camera, the observant woman behind the counter. "That could be a problem."

Alfie saunters toward the truck, licking the cone like he doesn't have a care in the world.

"What's gonna happen to him?" Sarah says.

"You really want to know?"

She doesn't respond.

"You should lawyer up on the front side," Elias says. "Don't wait until the last minute like before."

"I hate talking to lawyers." She sighs. "It's like I've done something wrong."

"Suit yourself."

Alfie stops for a bite of his ice cream. He takes an extra-aggressive lick on his cone, and the scoops of ice cream fall, hitting the pavement with a splat.

"What an idiot." Elias shakes his head.

Alfie starts to cry.

- CHAPTER THIRTY-FIVE -

The administration building. Black Valley Generating Station.

I watched Price Anderson and his associate, the ex–Special Forces operative, flank out like they were Secret Service agents. Their eyes scanned the people in the hallway, hands on their weapons.

Whitney and I were outside the conference room about thirty feet away.

The agents and Sudamento employees around us stopped what they were doing and turned their attention toward the door leading to the outside.

Behind Price came a man in his forties.

He was small, maybe five-six or seven, a wiry hundred forty pounds. He was clad in a pair of faded Wrangler jeans and a short-sleeve plaid shirt that looked like it came from the close-out section of Target.

The Sudamento people in the hallway stopped talking.

The new arrival was wearing a hard hat and heavy work boots. He took off his hat and tucked it under his arm.

His eyes swept the hallway before settling on Whitney Holbrook standing next to me.

He strode toward us, and the people in the hallway moved out of his way, staring after him like he was a celebrity. Price Anderson and his sidekick trailed after him, guns at the ready.

"Agent Holbrook." He held out his hand. "Nice to see you again."

His voice was newscaster smooth. Low and controlled, brimming with energy.

Whitney shook his hand and then introduced us. "This is Jon Cantrell, the sheriff of Peterson County."

"Eric Faulkner." The man in the plaid shirt shook my hand. "Nice to meet you."

He looked me in the eyes as our hands grasped. His gaze never wavered, holding mine for a couple of seconds longer than was necessary or polite.

"Sheriff Cantrell and I were just discussing the earlier attack," Whitney said.

"Earlier attack?" Eric Faulkner asked.

"McCarty Creek," I said.

In the background, I could see Price Anderson's eyes narrow. Eric Faulkner didn't reply.

"What happened yesterday," Whitney said. "There seems to be some similarities between the two."

Faulkner stared at her for a long moment. Then he turned his head slightly and snapped his fingers. "Price."

"Yes, sir." Price Anderson jumped forward, the barrel of his M-4 dragging along the drywall.

"McCarty Creek," Faulkner said. "What's the status?"

"Looks like an accident," Price said. "A fluke."

"Explain." Faulkner fixed an unwavering gaze on his underling.

"There's a shooting range nearby," Price said. "Our ballistics investigation indicates the bullet that damaged the transformer came from there."

High-powered rifle rounds could do strange things, ricocheting off a sliver of rock and traveling miles in the opposite direction. But Chester, the manager of McCarty Creek, had told me there was no rifle range in the vicinity. He'd been certain the shot came from the vacation home that was part of the facility.

I said, "What about the lake house on the proper—"

"The MO's completely different." Price cut me off. "There was no disruption of the telco lines at McCarty Creek."

"And you're sure about the rifle range?" Faulkner said. "We know for a hundred percent the bullet came from there? That the range was even open at the time the incident occurred?"

Price hesitated for an instant, then nodded.

"Double-check." Eric Faulkner pointed to the door.

"Now?" Price said. "That's two hours away."

No one spoke. Eric gave his underling the laser stare again.

"I could send some people," Whitney said.

"Nonsense." Eric Faulkner shook his head. "My chief of security has assured both of us that the McCarty Creek incident is—oh, what shall we call it—an anomaly. He should verify his claim."

Price Anderson's lips were pressed together into a thin line. His fingers flexed, nostrils flaring with each breath.

A long moment passed.

Price took several deep breaths. "Sir, with the threats and all, I think it would be better if I stayed on-site with you."

"I'll be fine." Eric Faulkner looked at me and then at Whitney Holbrook. "I'm surrounded by law-enforcement officers."

"As you wish, sir." Price Anderson stared at me for a few moments and then left.

After he was gone, I said, "Threats?"

Faulkner shrugged. "Sudamento has a market cap in excess of the GNP of half the countries in Africa. Threats go with the territory."

The manager for Black Valley appeared from the conference room. He looked at his watch and then at Eric Faulkner.

"I need to address the troops." Faulkner started toward the conference room.

"We're going to want to talk to you some more," I said. "Sooner, rather than later."

He stopped and looked at me like I was an animal in a zoo—a curiosity, Jo-Jo the Talking Bear, or a chimpanzee who smokes cigarettes.

I'd seen the look before on the faces of men destined for an eight-by-ten cell on death row. People who spend their entire lives without ever grasping the basic human concept of empathy.

- CHAPTER THIRTY-SIX -

Sarah sits at the desk, cell phone in hand.

The surface is scarred and stained.

Each blemish dredges up a separate memory. A pen jabbed in anger, a spilled cup of coffee, initials chiseled into the wood with the knife her grandfather had given her. Mundane little slices of life.

On the far wall is a faded poster of Bon Jovi, circa his big-hair era, the late 1980s. The poster hangs over a Sony Trinitron TV that probably weighs three hundred pounds.

Sarah's high school years.

Her mother is dead. Her father is in LA, following a path to enlightenment that included transcendental meditation, organic cocaine, and a dancer named Troy from Madonna's 1990 Blond Ambition tour.

Sarah and her brother had been left in the care of their grandfather at the farm in Bowie County, attending the local high school. Outsiders, once again, in their preppy Dallas clothes, at odds with the locals whose idea of high living was dipping snuff, dual-axle pickups, and Saturday nights at the Whataburger.

The desk sits in front of a bay window in her old room. The window overlooks a circular driveway and the long gravel road leading to the highway.

The front yard is filled with magnolias and crepe myrtles, while live oaks grow along the gravel road.

A helicopter sits on a concrete landing pad in the field to one side of the gravel road. The chopper is part of her husband's fleet. Sarah uses the craft from time to time to make the trek to the farm.

Nothing has changed since her last visit six months before.

Even though no one lives there, people still come and clean the house, mow the lawn, tend the pool. The money comes from one of Elias's trust funds. Why he cares so much, Sarah can't imagine.

Her brother and her grandfather never got along. The old man saw too much of his own son in Elias. The substance abuse and the narcissism, an inability to focus on a single task. His same-sex attraction, an abhorrent condition to people of her grandfather's generation.

Sarah misses the old man. His absence is like a physical ache. He would know what to do in her current circumstances.

She glances again at today's edition of the *Dallas Morning News*, the article about Cleo Fain, the serial killer found on the side of the road with a dead girl in her van.

Cleo had been attacked by persons unknown, suffering a severe concussion. But she is alive, recovering in a Dallas hospital. Cleo, the dyke who changed the tire on the stolen Monte Carlo, knows what Sarah looks like. Everything is a link back to the dead deputy in that motel room.

Sarah pushes the worry from her mind. She opens the e-mail program on her phone, begins another message to her daughter.

Dear Dylan:

I am so sorry I couldn't be there when you got out of surgery. The doctors told me that everything went well & you were very brave. Fortunately, Rosa is there to take care of you & make sure you have everything you need.

I was not at the hospital because I had to take care of some family issues with your uncle Elias. When you are older, you will understand how the problems of others often intrude on your own life.

Your uncle & I used to get into trouble when we were children, & I suppose not too much has changed. I wish you could have known him before he went away, back when he still had a glimmer of kindness in him.

When your leg is healed, I am going to take you to our place in Bowie County, your great-grandfather's home. I think you might like it here. There are horses to ride & fields to play in. And a river full of fish!

The farm is where I met your father, nearly fifteen years ago. He was a young businessman at the time, just starting out. In some ways not unlike your great-grandfather, in other ways completely different.

He came to see Papa, looking for money. People often did that, Papa being a shrewd investor with a good eye for business deals & such. You see, that's how Daddy got his start in business, how we got the big house on Strait Lane—the money from Papa made all that possible.

Sarah puts the phone down.

In the part of the yard cupped by the circular drive is a sitting area—several lawn chairs and a picnic table.

It was there that she'd seen for the first time the man who would become her husband. She'd been sitting at this very desk.

He'd been wearing a suit—his only one, she later found out—and leaning close to the old man, making his pitch.

A handsome man, even from a distance. Sarah could sense something different about him, a fire deep inside, a desire to succeed. Perhaps the biggest indicator of his future success was the fact that he had actually been able to get a meeting with her grandfather, then in his eighties and frail, his body wearing out while his mind remained sharp.

Then Elias had arrived, barreling down the gravel road in that stupid Lexus convertible he loved so.

The memory of her brother's anger washes over her like a tsunami.

He'd been furious at their grandfather for the meeting, furious that the old man was considering investing with the young firebrand who would become Sarah's husband. Elias had ideas, too—business opportunities that required start-up capital. The trust funds generated a nice monthly income but couldn't be broken, the massive sums unable to be accessed.

But Papa wouldn't invest with his own grandson, and Elias had chosen a different path, a road that eventually led to a manslaughter charge and five years in prison.

Sarah stands and goes to the bed, where the gun is.

She'd reluctantly given the Python to Elias when he dropped her off at the house earlier that day. He felt attached to the weapon as much as she did, one of Papa's "special toys," as the old man used to say. She'd thought about stalling, telling him she couldn't find the gun, but that would only cause more trouble. Once Elias had gotten something in his mind, he didn't give up.

In its place, she'd found a Ruger .38 Special in the back of the old man's gun closet.

Sarah needs a gun, so she's going to take the Ruger with her. She loaded the weapon with the same type of ammunition as she'd used in the Python, target rounds. Low recoil. Deadly, but easy to control.

She looks around her childhood room once more.

How did her life go so wrong?

- CHAPTER THIRTY-SEVEN -

Black Valley Generating Station. In the conference room of the administration offices, Eric Faulkner received a standing ovation when he walked in. He appeared to bask in the adoration, beaming and waving to the people around the expansive table. Elvis was in the building.

Whitney Holbrook and I took up position in the rear, our backs to the wall, and watched the show.

There were maybe sixty people squeezed into the room.

Faulkner started by addressing the terrorism rumors.

Next to me, Whitney tensed.

Faulkner told the crowd that a man who appeared to be a Chinese national had been captured at the scene.

Whitney let out a long breath.

Faulkner continued: The man had a Koran in his possession but had died before he could be interrogated. Preliminary tests indicated he had gunshot residue on his fingers, meaning he was one of the shooters.

Whitney shook her head, breathing shallowly. She was clearly angry, and it was easy to understand why.

The fact that a suspect had been captured was a secret, not to mention the person's supposed nationality. The information was available only on a need-to-know basis and then only to law enforcement. Faulkner had just given out a significant slice of intel to a bunch of civilians.

Whitney looked at me. "How did that happen? I didn't even know about the gunshot residue yet."

"He probably talked to a senator," I said. "And the senator rattled some chains at Homeland. That's how leaks like this usually happen."

Whitney swore. Not loud but not soft either.

Several nearby Sudamento employees looked at us, disapproving expressions on their faces.

"What the hell is he doing?" she whispered.

"I dunno." I shook my head. "Maybe he's trying to shore up the stock price somehow."

"I don't care." Whitney's voice was low and angry. "He's fucking up the investigation."

"From his perspective, it's not about the investigation," I said. "It's about the money."

Faulkner continued his speech, asking everyone to keep working hard. He thanked them for their help getting the plant back up and running, as well as assisting in the investigation. He employed a curious mix of analogies—sports metaphors, religious exhortations, comparing Sudamento to a family.

Near the end of his remarks, he spoke directly to the agents present. His choice of words made himself and the company the center of the universe—"thank you for helping with our investigation"—as if the officers present were there at his request.

Either he was trying to assert control over the situation, not an unlikely scenario, or he was just an egotistical prick. Also a distinct possibility given the level of his achievements.

He concluded his remarks by telling everyone that a dozen RVs and tour buses were being brought in for rest breaks, as was barbecue for dinner.

The crowd cheered.

Whitney left the room, a grimace on her face.

I watched Faulkner shake hands and slap backs for a few minutes and then departed, finding Whitney outside. She was standing beneath the overhang by the back door.

"That didn't take long." She held up her phone so the screen was visible.

A news aggregator site. The headline read, BREAKING: CHINESE TERRORISTS SOUGHT IN TEXAS POWER OUTAGE.

It was late afternoon, and the air felt like syrup. Thunderclouds gathered in the distance, purple and angry.

I said, "It was bound to get out in the next day or two anyway."

"You don't know that for sure."

I shrugged. She was right. The feds could keep a secret for a long time if they wanted to.

"Now we're going to have to deal with the media." She swore again.

I decided to change the subject. "What's the chatter been like?"

"Chatter" was an all-encompassing term for enemy communications. The level and intensity of chatter was often more indicative of what was coming than the content of the messages. Immediately before September 11, 2001, there had been a huge increase in cell traffic between various jihadist groups. Now entire departments at the CIA and the NSA did nothing but study chatter.

"That's the weird part," she said. "Nothing unusual."

"So it's the lone-wolf scenario."

She nodded.

"And whoever it is, they only attack Sudamento properties."

After a moment, she nodded again.

"And I'm betting the attackers have a thing for properties with lake houses attached." I briefly explained my hunch. I ended by telling her that it appeared the only people who ever used the recreational facilities were part of the management team.

"Interesting theory." She stared into the distance. "That makes sense. Hide in plain sight, wait for the right moment."

I didn't mention how the attacks could be an inside job, especially since there didn't appear to be any signs of a break-in at the lake house. Sometimes it's better to let people arrive at a conclusion on their own timing.

The side door of a large van in the parking lot opened, and an obese young man in sweatpants emerged. He squinted like he hadn't seen the sunshine in weeks and then waddled toward us.

"You should investigate the company," I said. "And the CEO, Faulkner. Just to be safe."

"What am I looking for?"

"If we knew that, then you wouldn't have to investigate."

The obese man got closer.

"What about you?" she said. "What are you going to do?"

"I talked to the manager earlier," I said. "Other than a couple of plants in far West Texas, there's only one other Sudamento facility that has a lake house."

"Where?"

"San Saba. There's also a pretty big substation adjacent to the property, a nice target. I'll head there tomorrow. Right now, I'm going back to the office to check on the murder investigation."

The obese young man stopped in front of us. He was sweating profusely, breathing heavily. He pulled my cell phone from his pocket and handed it to Whitney.

"You're the one who wanted the trace, right?"

Whitney took the phone. "What did you find?"

"The texts came from a burner using an anonymous redirect service."

Whitney handed me the cell.

"Whoever sent the messages knew their stuff," he said. "They set up a reroute in a different part of the same network."

"What does that mean?" I asked.

"It means I don't know who sent the messages or where they were when they pushed Send." He wiped sweat from his upper lip. "Specifically."

"How about generally?" I said.

"Somewhere near Austin," he said. "That's the best I can do."

That meant Piper was close by, as was our daughter. She wasn't on the other side of the globe, as I would have suspected.

"Does that help?" the man said.

"I have no idea." I stuck the phone in my pocket and headed toward my SUV.

- CHAPTER THIRTY-EIGHT -

The Ruger feels different in Sarah's hand.

The grip is slimmer than the Python's, the barrel only two inches long. The weapon fits perfectly behind her hip, though, pressed between her flesh and the waistband of her jeans, covered by the black T-shirt she's wearing.

Sarah has a moment of coherence and realizes she is going to kill her one true soul mate. This thought fills her with sadness and an extraordinary emotion she didn't know she possessed. Regret.

She remembers the last time they were together.

The curve of his back, the sinews in his arm. The sweat on his brow and the smell of his aftershave. The way he pressed her arms against the headboard as he thrust into her. His nightmares as he slept pressed against her, the cries in his sleep, the shivering.

He is missing the same pieces as she, jagged little holes in his soul. Both of them long for a stylized idea of what life should be like, an image from a magazine, a happy family, smiling over the holiday turkey. A concept that doesn't exist anywhere except in the mind of some booze-addled advertising executive.

But the man has failed to do as she asked, and the anger that coils deep within her will cause her to lash out.

The Ruger will fire of its own accord, and she will be alone again.

As always.

A glimmer of happiness, destroyed by her own hand—her life a bad TV drama where the plotline never changes.

She is in a high-rise apartment in downtown Dallas, the floor-to-ceiling windows offering a stunning view of the city.

The apartment is one that she keeps under a different name. It is a place to be alone, away from the prying eyes of her nanny and the incessant whining of her daughter.

The décor is stark. Stainless steel and pale marble. Low-slung black leather sofas. White walls. Everything sterile. Serene.

Sarah is in the living room by the fireplace, reading an article on her tablet computer about the murder of two homeless men in an alley near Baptist Memorial Hospital.

One of the victims had been a veteran of the Iraq War, a Purple Heart winner ravaged by alcohol and drug abuse related to his time in combat.

The murders are drawing more attention than would be typical for a pair of hobos, Dallas's do-gooder mayor making the treatment of the underclass a priority of his administration.

She switches to another page and reads again the story of Cleo Fain, the serial killer found with a concussion on the side of the highway.

Cleo is expected to make a full recovery and stand trial for the murder of several young women.

How long, Sarah wonders, before Cleo tries to make a deal, offering up the details of her chance encounter with a woman who meets the description of the suspect in the killing of a law officer outside of Waco?

Sarah's phone chimes, a text message from the man who has failed her. He is on his way to the apartment.

She swallows her anger. She flips to another website, reads a rehash of the deputy's murder, tries to find hidden meaning between the lines.

Had they identified the woman in the Dallas Cowboys cap? Are the police congregating outside her house on Strait Lane at this very moment, looking to question her?

Her vision blurs. Fear and anger make the words on the screen watery.

The front door opens. A man's footsteps on the marble.

Sarah doesn't look up. She continues to scroll through websites. "Did you find him?"

"Him" would be her brother, Elias.

The man says, "I know it's hard for a rich girl like you to understand, but some of us have real jobs to do."

"I gave you the license plate and the make of his vehicle," she says. "How much easier could I make it?"

She'd asked the man to perform a simple task.

Locate Elias.

Stop him from shooting up power plants, his disjointed plan to wreak havoc as payback for a lifetime of wrongs. She doesn't mention that she had been in Elias's company after calling the man standing in her living room. Mentioning that would entail talking about the two dead bums, and Sarah figures that's a topic that she should avoid at all costs.

"It's a big state, Sarah. And your brother's pretty good at covering his tracks."

"You're worthless." Sarah sighs. "If it wasn't for your dick, there'd be a bounty on your head."

"You've had plenty of opportunities to stop him." A long pause. "But you never do."

The man can almost read her mind. He's always had that knack. Sarah doesn't reply. On the inside, she seethes.

"They're calling what he's done a terrorist act," the man says. "That changes things."

Sarah flexes her fingers, letting the anger wash over her.

"He has detailed maps of the grid," the man says. "He knows where the choke points are."

Sarah rubs her eyes.

"The next choke point," the man says. "The closest one to Dallas. That's the key. That's where he'll be."

Sarah knows she could have stopped Elias yesterday or the night before that. But that would require crossing her brother, something that she's never been able to do. Therefore, the need for someone like the man standing before her.

"San Saba," the man says. "I'll stop him there."

Sarah puts her tablet computer down, flexes her fingers.

"You look like you're about to try and rip somebody's eyes out," he says. "I hope, for your sake, they're not mine."

Everything is out of control. Cleo Fain. The dead deputy. Dylan's injury. And she hasn't tried to line up a meeting with a horndog in days. Of course she's angry.

"You want a drink?" the man asks.

Sarah pulls the Ruger from her waistband.

The man laughs.

"I should shoot you," Sarah says.

"That's your answer to everything, isn't it?" he says. "Guns or fucking."

She aims the Ruger at his face.

"Why do you care so much what happens to Sudamento anyway?" the man asks. "You like a good train wreck. This is shaping up to be a big one."

Sarah tightens her finger on the trigger. The metal presses against her flesh; the hammer creaks back.

The sense of control is delicious, savory. A life hangs in the balance. You do not fuck with SarahSmiles.

The man's eyes narrow, his only reaction. He says, "You can't control everything, Sarah. Sometimes, you've just gotta let go."

Her arm shakes.

The man walks across the room, takes the weapon from her hand, puts it next to her tablet computer on the coffee table.

"I'll take care of it," he says. "I promise."

"You'll stop him?" Sarah feels the tears well in her eyes.

The man nods. "I'll be the hero for once."

"Oh, Price." She stands, slides into his arms. "Thank you."

The head of security for Sudamento kisses her tenderly. He strokes her face. "Let's go to the bedroom."

Sarah kisses him back, mashing their lips together, grinding her pelvis against his. The anger is just a prelude to the sex. He knows her so well.

Price Anderson grabs her hand, pulls her toward the back of the apartment.

- CHAPTER THIRTY-NINE -

I returned to my office at the county courthouse, having had my fill of talk about the integrity of the grid, blown transformers, and the need to keep Sudamento stock prices high so the terrorists don't win.

Whitney Holbrook stayed behind to continue riding herd on the investigation and to coordinate the various federal agencies that were descending upon Central Texas like David Koresh and the Branch Davidians had risen from the ashes.

A stack of paperwork rested on my desk, reports to sign, interdepartmental memos, messages from the HR department. I took care of everything in short order and then went to my deputy's office.

The room looked like it had that morning except for one item that was missing, the desktop computer.

A receipt and an accompanying memo were taped to the door.

The machine had been taken to the Department of Public Safety IT lab in Austin. The techs there would try to find out the identity of SarahSmiles, or at the very least pinpoint the location from where she'd accessed that site.

I returned to my office, plopped in the chair, and looked at my cell phone, at the text message from earlier: *Eliz is fine.*

I stared at those eleven characters until my eyes became blurry.

After a period of time—I'm not sure how long—an e-mail dinged, a message from the Texas Rangers.

The ballistics report had come in.

Since an officer had been killed, they'd rushed the testing. The weapon used had been a Colt Python .357 Magnum. The fatal bullet had been a low-powered .38 Special, what's known as a semi-wadcutter. A target round.

Based on the lead content and design of the projectile, the lab had determined the bullet was old, manufactured around a quarter century ago by the Remington Company.

These facts were interesting but not very revealing as to any potential suspects.

The next part of the message was, however.

The lab had run the bullet striations, each as unique as a fingerprint, through a national database and learned that the same weapon had been used in an unsolved murder in 1991.

That crime had occurred in Bowie County in the far northeast section of Texas. The victim, a black male aged forty-three, had owned a bar and was believed to be involved in gambling and prostitution.

The last section of the message was even more intriguing.

The bullet used in the 1991 murder was a Remington semi-wadcutter.

I leaned back in the desk chair and tried to imagine a scenario where the same gun and the same ammunition could be involved in two different murders twenty-four years apart.

Was there a serial killer out there, one who'd been able to remain undetected for all this time?

The MOs indicated not. The victim in 1991 had been shot three times, once in each kneecap followed by a final round in the head, right between the eyes. My deputy had been killed during an altercation of some sort, a single bullet to the chest.

The e-mail from the Texas Rangers ended by saying they would pursue the lead in Bowie County, but their resources were stretched at the moment because of the purported terrorist attack on the power grid.

I forwarded the e-mail to several law-enforcement friends, old-timers who'd been around during the early 1990s, asking if they knew anything about the murder in Bowie County. A long shot, but it made me feel like I was doing something.

Footsteps sounded outside my office.

I looked up.

Jerry stood in the doorway. He looked ten years younger. A smile creased his face as he bounced on his toes.

"Did you hear, Jon?"

I arched an eyebrow.

"We got a grant, a big one." His eyes glowed. "Uncle Sam has come to town and hit us with the money stick."

"That's swell, Jerry."

"We can get rid of that bad sewer line here at the courthouse." He sat down in the chair in front of my desk. "And rebuild those Section Eight apartments that burned."

We were silent for a moment, Jerry staring off into the distance, a rapturous look on his face.

I said, "Have you and the other commissioners fixed Kelsey's benefits?"

"Huh?" He came back to earth.

"What we talked about." I stood, ready to depart. "She needs the money."

A confused look on his face. Then: "I meant to ask you. How's the investigation going?"

Jerry had evidently forgotten that the grant money was a trade for my being on leave.

"We're making progress," I said. "I bet we have an arrest in a few days."

"That's great, Jon. I always had faith in you."

"The grant money," I said. "Has the cash come through yet?"

He didn't reply. The answer was obvious. Nothing involving the government happened fast.

"You be sure to take care of Kelsey." I stood and walked to the exit. At the door, I flipped off the lights and left Jerry sitting in the dark.

•   •   •

I picked up a burrito from the taqueria on the far side of the town square and then went home.

It was early evening, the heat of the day still thick despite the thunderclouds building. A breeze rustled the leaves on the sycamore tree in my front yard, blowing dirt and lawn clippings from the place next door.

Everything on the block appeared normal. My neighbors' vehicles were where they should be. The old Chevy Impala across the street. The pickups on either side of me. The Toyota and the Honda down the block.

In front of the house on the far corner was an old Jeep Cherokee I'd never seen before. But the couple who lived there had a lot of family in the area, so there were always a lot of different vehicles coming and going.

I got out of the Suburban and went inside. Once across the threshold, I dropped the burrito sack and pulled my Glock.

Someone had been there.

The place felt different, disturbed somehow.

A chair in the dining room had been moved slightly. A stack of magazines on the coffee table had been knocked askew.

I stood perfectly still.

No sounds whatsoever except for the hum of the AC and the slight rattle from the refrigerator's compressor.

Clearing a house by yourself is no easy task. But we were short-staffed because of the deputy's murder and the power outage, so I didn't call for backup. Also, there was a certain amount of pride involved.

Instead I went from room to room and closet to closet, gun held high against my chest and muzzle out, my free hand opening doors, moving curtains.

Everything was as it should be until I got to the back bedroom, what would have been the nursery. The room was empty except for a baby bed, a changing table, and a handful of toys.

In the middle of the changing table sat a stack of photographs, eight-by-tens printed on copier paper.

They were all pictures of my daughter, Elizabeth.

Cooing for the camera. Nestled against a stuffed animal. Sitting on a couch. She was smiling in all.

Breath caught in my throat. My heart ached.

Piper had been here. She'd moved the magazines and the chair, just enough to let me know. She was trying to tell me our daughter was okay.

I dropped the photos and ran outside.

The Jeep at the end of the block was gone.

- CHAPTER FORTY -

In the interest of discretion, I figured perhaps my next course of action would be best discussed in person.

At 9:00 P.M. I pulled into the parking lot of the Shangri-La Inn, a sixty-year-old motel where the FERC agents investigating the power outage were staying.

I counted twelve black Suburbans in the lot, the government SUVs easily outnumbering the other vehicles, a motley assortment of pickups and old American sedans.

The Shangri-La was the kind of place a murder victim in an episode of *Perry Mason* might have been found. Peeling cinder block, flickering neon, wheezing AC units mounted in the windows of each room.

I parked, got out of my borrowed Suburban, and strode to the room Whitney had finally managed to check in to, a ground-floor unit near the office.

She opened after the first knock, hand behind her back. She was dressed like a cat burglar—black jeans, a matching long-sleeve T-shirt, dark sneakers.

"Getting ready to do a little B and E?" I asked.

"What do you want, Cantrell? I didn't figure you for the booty-call type."

"Is that a gun behind your back?"

She hesitated and then nodded, letting her arm fall to her side, a pistol in hand.

"This isn't exactly the Ritz," she said. "I'm pretty sure the guy upstairs just OD'd on meth."

In a room nearby, a TV set came on, the volume all the way up.

Whitney said, "You were getting ready to tell me why you dropped in."

"I hate to ask, but I need a favor."

"Again?" She sounded put out. "What happened to the self-reliant Texan?"

"Do you want to do your own off-the-books digging?" I asked. "Or keep me on the payroll?"

She stuck the gun in her waistband. "Your wish is my command, Sheriff Cantrell. Tell me what you need."

I relayed the message from the Texas Rangers about the murder in Bowie County and how it might be connected to the death of my deputy. Asked her to reach out to the FBI for any information on the 1991 incident.

The case had an organized-crime feel, which meant there might be a file somewhere with a suspect list. Or an agent nearing retirement who might remember something.

She grabbed her phone and tapped out some notes as I talked. When I was finished she said, "The SAC in Shreveport owes me. If there's anything to know about that murder, he'll have it."

"SAC" stood for "special agent in charge," the head of an FBI field office.

"Thanks," I said.

"What else?" she asked. "You look like you're sitting on something."

I didn't say anything.

"Don't be coy," she said. "It's not your style."

"Somebody broke into my house." I explained about the pictures and the Jeep Cherokee.

"Your ex, right?"

I nodded.

"Did you get a plate?"

I shook my head. "It was red, a late-1990s model. Two door."

"You didn't call the state police, did you?"

"No."

I knew I didn't have to explain to her why. It doesn't exactly help the sheriff's street cred to have his ex portrayed as a stalker.

"I'll see what I can do." She typed an e-mail, pressed Send. "Now I have a question for you. Have you heard from Price?"

I shook my head.

"He's gone AWOL; nobody knows where he is." She picked up a crowbar from the dresser. "You want to help me break into his room?"

• • •

In the end, I persuaded Whitney not to use the crowbar.

They weren't real big on warrants and probable cause at the Shangri-La, so I flashed my sheriff's badge to the clerk and got the key.

Price Anderson's room was empty. No clothes or personal items. An unmade bed underneath a framed print of a longhorn steer in a field of bluebonnets. The air smelled faintly of pine disinfectant and unwashed sheets.

"When was the last time you saw him?" I asked.

"This afternoon. When his boss sent him to McCarty Creek."

"You've called, right?"

"Of course. Multiple times. Each call goes straight to voice mail."

"What do his people at Sudamento say?"

"They're in the dark, too. He was supposed to be in on several teleconferences, but he no-showed."

"You think he's been in an accident or something?"

"Maybe. But his room is prepaid for a week." Whitney looked around the empty unit. "Why would he pack up?"

I grabbed the wastebasket from underneath the desk, dumped its contents on the bed.

The trash was minimal. Several beer cans. A used-up tube of toothpaste and a half-dozen empty vitamin packs, the kind that you bought at a health-food store and that promised increased energy and sexual drive.

And three items that looked like credit cards, except each was missing a rectangle out of the middle, the empty space only a few millimeters in each direction, smaller than a postage stamp.

Whitney said, "Shit."

The three items were SIM card carriers. The term "SIM" was an acronym that stood for "subscriber identification module."

If you changed the SIM card in your phone, you changed the number. And your identity.

"Price is dirty," I said.

"We don't know that for sure." Whitney shook her head.

"Let's just call him unclean then."

Whitney sat on the chair by the desk, her shoulders drooping.

"Call McCarty Creek right now. See if he ever got there. In the morning, send a team to retrace his route. Maybe he had car trouble or something."

She nodded, a glum look on her face.

"Then you and I will head to San Saba like we planned."

No response.

"It'll be all right," I said. "There's probably a logical answer for the SIM cards and the fact that we can't reach him."

"It won't matter," she said. "He looks bent, and I was sleeping with him."

I didn't know what to say, so I kept my mouth shut.

She took a deep breath and smiled, the expression on her face obviously forced. "Breakfast in the morning?" She stood. "Before we make the drive?"

"Sure." I nodded warily.

"Pick me up at seven. Don't be late." She left the room.

- CHAPTER FORTY-ONE -

The diner on the outskirts of town was full of customers at twenty past seven in the morning when Eric Faulkner, the CEO of Sudamento, walked in with his bodyguard trailing behind him.

Faulkner wore a denim work shirt and faded jeans, while his security guy had on a dark suit. The juxtaposition of the two made them appear to be working from completely different playbooks, not an uncommon occurrence for Faulkner, if I had to guess.

All the seats were taken, even at the counter.

Whitney and I were in a booth at the back, eating breakfast. Bacon and eggs, biscuits with sausage gravy, coffee.

Faulkner surveyed the room and then strode toward us. His bodyguard stayed by the front door.

He stopped at our table and gave us each the laser stare. He settled his gaze on Whitney and said, "What's the status of the investigation?"

"Good morning." I pointed to the insulated carafe by my plate. "You want some coffee?"

He cocked his head and looked at me, a puzzled expression on his face.

"You're the sheriff, right?"

How quickly they forget. I wore civilian clothes, the badge out of sight on my belt.

"Yeah, that's me. Sheriff Jon Cantrell."

"The investigation is ongoing," Whitney said. "We have several avenues to pursue."

"What exactly does that mean?" he asked.

"It means we have some leads," she said. "But we don't know who's responsible for the attacks yet."

Faulkner's skin was pale and drawn, and the dark circles under his eyes were especially harsh in the fluorescent lighting of the diner.

"Price Anderson," I said. "What did he find out at McCarty Creek?"

The waitress came over before he could answer. "You want something to eat?"

"A glass of milk and two slices of dry toast," he said.

The meal of a cancer patient or someone under a lot of stress.

He slid in next to Whitney, uninvited.

I said, "Please, join us."

"Price never checked in from McCarty Creek." Faulkner spoke with a lowered voice. "His phone's off, too."

Whitney and I looked at each other.

"When's the last time you talked to him?" Whitney asked.

Faulkner didn't reply. He drummed his fingers on the tabletop, taking shallow breaths.

"You okay?" I said. "You're not looking so good."

The waitress brought a plate of toast and a glass of milk.

"What?" Eric Faulkner looked around like he'd just woken up from a nap.

Whitney said, "How much sleep did you get last night?"

Faulkner drank half the milk, rubbed his eyes. "Do you believe in karma? Either of you?"

I shrugged. The CEO of a Fortune 500 company did not strike me as the type of person to ponder the metaphysical side of existence.

"I've got an earnings call in a couple of hours." He took a bite of toast. "They're gonna want my head."

"The attack wasn't your fault," Whitney said.

"It's all about perspective." He slapped the table. "Actions that appear innocent to one person take on a different meaning when you're looking at them from across the room."

Silence.

"Sudamento has a market cap of seventeen billion," he said. "Do either of you understand the way the piranhas on Wall Street work?"

"Have you broken any laws?" Whitney asked. "Is there any reason for someone to want to hurt your company specifically?"

"The Chinese man who died," he said. "Is that one of your *avenues*?"

Neither Whitney nor I responded.

"They can't throw me out of my own company if it's terrorism," he said. "The CEO of American Airlines didn't lose his job after 9/11, did he?"

The waitress brought a fresh carafe of coffee.

"Who has access to the lake house at McCarty Creek?" I said.

"How the hell would I know?" His voice was shrill. People at nearby tables glanced our way.

"Well, it is your company," I said.

"I've got bigger things on my mind." He pointed his index finger at me. "Our stock has gone down twenty-three percent in the last week alone."

The waitress came back over, asked if there would be anything else. I shook my head, and she left a check.

"The vultures are already circling." He rubbed his eyes. "Another attack would kill us."

"Has Price Anderson ever disappeared before?" I asked.

Faulkner shook his head again.

No one spoke for a few seconds.

"Can you think of any reason Price would want to hurt Sudamento?" I asked.

Whitney gave me a deadpan stare.

"He's worked for me for five years now, ever since he came back from Iraq." Faulkner rubbed his chin. "He's a good employee. Loyal, honest. I'd trust him with my life."

The bodyguard walked to our table, a cell phone in hand. He leaned down, whispered into his boss's ear.

Faulkner looked at Whitney. "I have to go. One of our biggest investors wants to talk before the earnings call."

He left.

"Bastard." Whitney pointed to the check. "He didn't even pay his share of the tab."

- CHAPTER FORTY-TWO -

Sarah wakes at dawn in the master bedroom of her high-rise apartment. Before she gets out of bed, she turns on the tablet computer and searches for any fresh stories about the murdered deputy, the serial killer Cleo Fain, or the two dead hobos.

Nothing new has appeared overnight.

She slides from underneath the covers, pads to the window, and opens the curtains.

The apartment is on the northern edge of the central business district, and her bedroom looks to the south. The center of Dallas is a forest of glass and concrete, a pleasing shade of yellow in the early-morning light.

A sense of calm settles over Sarah. Everything is under control. She's going to skate through this crisis.

Price will stop Elias.

The deputy's murder investigation will stall. Progress already appears to have slowed. She covered her tracks well, so the odds of anyone putting her together with the dead man in the motel room are getting slimmer every day. Except for the good-looking sheriff in the parking lot, no one who counts saw her.

And as for Cleo Fain, well, who's going to believe a serial killer anyway?

Sarah calls the nanny and checks on Dylan. Her daughter is still asleep but doing well after the surgery. Rosa doesn't even ask when Sarah will be visiting today, a minor victory.

Next, Sarah puts on workout clothes—a pair of yoga pants, sports bra, Nike trainers—and takes the elevator to the gym on the third floor. There, she runs on the treadmill while watching the morning news shows on the tiny TV monitor mounted over the control panel.

The exercise soothes her. The higher her heart rate, the more peaceful she feels.

After forty-five minutes, she returns to her apartment on the thirtieth floor. Sweaty but content, she pads toward her unit, key in hand.

The door to each dwelling is recessed from the hallway, small alcoves that give the illusion of privacy and make the building seem less like a hotel.

Sarah is about ten feet from her unit when from across the hall a woman steps out of the shadows, fumbling with a cell phone.

She is Latino, in her midforties. Stout, almost six feet tall.

"Hello." Sarah smiles politely.

The woman is wearing a pair of Wrangler jeans and a starched khaki shirt. On the breast pocket of the shirt is a gold badge, five stars inside a circle.

"Hi, how are you doing?" The woman moves into the middle of the hall.

Sarah approaches her door, keeping an eye on the interloper.

The woman is wearing a tooled leather belt with a matching holster on her right hip. The holster contains a stainless-steel semiautomatic pistol with mother-of-pearl grips.

"Is that your apartment?" The woman puts her cell phone away.

Sarah doesn't reply. Her skin grows cold.

"My name is Sergeant Moreno. I'm a Texas Ranger."

Sarah forces another smile.

"I'm looking for Debbie Wilson," the Ranger says.

This is the name Sarah used to rent the apartment. Her college roommate, freshman year, who died in a car wreck right after graduation.

"Are you Debbie?" Ranger Moreno asks.

Sarah shakes her head.

"Who are you then?" The woman's tone is amicable despite the intrusive nature of the question.

"I'm, uh, a friend of hers."

"What's your name . . . friend?"

"S-Sarah."

Moreno points to the door of the apartment. "Is Debbie at home, Sarah?"

Sarah doesn't reply. The sense of control has blown away like a tornado just hit town. Why is this Texas Ranger here, asking about the name she used to lease the apartment?

"Somebody who called herself Debbie Wilson bought a Buick LaCrosse last week," Ranger Moreno says. "The address she used was this apartment."

Sarah can actually feel the blood rush from her face. She imagines how white her skin must look. The LaCrosse was the car the sheriff had seen her get into at the motel. She'd left the vehicle at the abandoned Whataburger next door to where she'd boosted the old Monte Carlo.

She'd planned to report the LaCrosse stolen but had forgotten. Too many distractions.

"Debbie's not here right now." Sarah's voice sounds small, hoarse.

"When will she be back?" Ranger Moreno moves closer.

"I'm not sure." Sarah steps toward the door. "She didn't say."

"You live here with Debbie, huh? You two are roommates?"

Sarah slides her key into the dead bolt. Her hand shakes. "Uh, no. I'm just visiting."

"From where, Sarah?" Moreno leans against the side of the alcove, watching Sarah fumble with the lock. "Where's home for you?"

The door opens.

"I'm sorry you missed Debbie." Sarah steps inside, turns to face the Texas Ranger. "I'll tell her you stopped by."

Moreno glides across the floor to the entryway, her feet on the threshold. "May I come in, Sarah? I need to ask you some more questions."

"I have an appointment in just a little while. I need to get ready."

"This won't take long."

"Sorry, I have to go." Sarah starts to shut the door.

Moreno sticks her hand out, stops the door from closing. "What's your last name, Sarah?"

Sarah doesn't reply. She tries to shut the door again, but the Ranger's push is too strong.

"I need your full name for my report," Moreno says.

"Anderson. Sarah Anderson."

She's imagined something like this happening many times, scenarios where she has to outwit the police. In her fantasies, she always has a ready answer for any question because she is SarahSmiles.

The reality is so different. The fear has lowered her IQ, made everything fuzzy, hard to process. Price's surname is the first thing that pops into her mind.

"Thanks." Moreno smiles. "One more question."

Sarah realizes her mistake—what she used as her first name, part of the profile ID for the website where she met the deputy. Her stomach ties itself in knots.

"You okay?" Moreno asks. "You're looking a little queasy all of a sudden."

"Low blood sugar," Sarah says. "Shoulda had something to eat before I worked out."

The Ranger stares at her for a moment and then says, "Do you by any chance own a Colt Python?"

- CHAPTER FORTY-THREE -

From the passenger seat of Whitney Holbrook's Suburban, I watched the countryside blow by.

San Saba was 120 miles west, on the northern plateaus of the Texas Hill Country.

The terrain was mostly flat, with the occasional rocky out-cropping. Sun-browned grass covered the pastures, dotted with post oaks and stunted groves of cedar elms. Several low mesas shimmered in the distance, wavy from the heat.

As soon as we left the diner, Whitney Holbrook had turned on the red and blue flashers in the grille of the SUV. She kept the speedometer pegged at a hundred, even on the narrow two-lane highways, and we hit the San Saba town limits eighty minutes after watching Eric Faulkner leave the diner.

The Suburban's GPS routed us down Main Street past the town square.

The central business district was full of old stone buildings, some occupied by lawyers' offices and antique shops, others vacant.

The Sudamento plant was on the west side of the county, about three miles past the town. According to the grid map, a substation was located about a half mile beyond the plant. Six different generating facilities fed their electricity into that substation, nearly 7,200 megawatts, or enough juice for 3.6 million homes.

The entrance to the facility lay at the end of a gravel road. The earth on either side of the road had been carved into shallow canyons thousands of yards long, the result of the strip-mining operation that provided coal for the boilers.

The gate was open, but Whitney stopped at the guardhouse anyway, a one-room wooden structure with large windows on all four sides.

No one appeared to be in the guardhouse.

She tapped the horn.

No response.

She glanced at me, a worried expression on her face.

"Wait here." I opened the door, got out.

The air was hot and still. In the distance, a buzzard glided over a pasture.

I walked around the front of the Suburban.

The entrance to the guardhouse was ajar, cold air spilling out.

I pulled my Glock from its holster, eased toward the opening, stepped inside.

The smell hit me first, then the noise.

A whiff of copper followed by the buzz of flies.

Two bodies lay on the floor, shoved under the front counter to keep them as out of sight as possible.

They were wearing Sudamento security uniforms. Each had massive trauma to the chest area, such as might be caused by a large-caliber rifle.

I scanned the rest of the shack. Yanked open the bathroom door, saw it was empty.

When I turned around, Whitney was standing in the doorway, gun in hand.

"Call it in," I said.

She didn't move, just stared at the bodies.

"*Go.*" I pointed to the Suburban.

In the distance, a *whoomph* sound.

We both craned our necks, looking in every direction for the source of the noise.

A few seconds later, the lights in the guardhouse flickered and then went out.

"Shit." Whitney dashed to the Suburban.

I followed her, jumped into the passenger side, fastened my seat belt.

The map we'd looked at the day before showed the lake house on the far western edge of the site, about halfway between the boilers and the substation.

Whitney grabbed her phone, called what sounded like one of her colleagues, asking for an airlift of agents to the San Saba plant.

I dialed 911. A sleepy-sounding woman answered.

I told her my name, identified myself as a federal agent, and said there was an attack underway at the power plant outside of town. I told her to contact the sheriff ASAP and implement whatever protocols they had in place for a terrorist event.

Another explosion sounded. This one was softer, farther away.

Before the 911 operator could answer, the line went dead.

Whitney and I looked at each other. She said, "Did your phone just die?"

"They blew the communication lines," I said. "Just like McCarty Creek."

In the distance, the exhaust towers of the plant continued to bellow steam, everything appearing to be normal.

I pointed to the west. "The lake house is that way. Take the road to the boilers and then turn right."

"We should wait for backup."

"There's no backup coming, Whitney, not for a long time anyway."

Her face was pale, teeth chattering. "W-w-what should we do? I-I've never worked without b-backup before."

"We're gonna find the bad guys," I said. "That's our job."

A jolt of adrenaline ran through my system. You didn't get many chances like this, the opportunity to investigate a crime scene as it unfolded. She took several deep breaths.

"We'll back each other up." I spoke in a soothing tone. "It'll be fine. I've been in this situation before."

She nodded. Put the SUV into drive.

The color was starting to return to her face.

"You should know I've never shot my gun anywhere but the range." She stepped on the accelerator. The SUV headed toward the heart of the plant.

"Keep your finger off the trigger," I said. "Until you're ready to fi—"

We were about five hundred yards away when the boilers exploded, all twelve stories.

A supernova of light filled the sky, followed by what sounded like the inside of a sonic boom.

- CHAPTER FORTY-FOUR -

Dust swirled. My ears rang.

I blinked, regained my vision.

Clouds of black smoke in the distance.

From high above us, the heavens opened up and the debris from the towers rained down. An onslaught of metal and pipes and wires, thumping the ground, pinging the metal of our SUV.

I looked to either side.

The Suburban had run off the road. We were in a shallow ditch a few dozen yards past the guardhouse.

Next to me, Whitney was slumped over the steering wheel, not moving. She hadn't been wearing her seat belt.

"Whitney?"

No answer.

I grabbed her shoulder, eased her back. She had a nasty bruise on her forehead but was breathing, her airway unobstructed.

I placed a finger on her neck, felt the pulse. It was strong and rapid.

"W-what happened?" Her voice was hoarse.

"There was an explosion," I said. "You remember where we are?"

It was even money as to whether she had a concussion or not.

Either way, no ambulance would be on its way for a long time. There were no hospitals in San Saba, and we were too far away from population centers for any type of rapid response.

"The power plant." She opened her eyes. "It's gone."

"Let's switch places," I said. "I'll drive."

She touched her head and nodded. As gently as possible, I pulled her into my lap. Then I slid over to her spot behind the wheel.

Once she was in the passenger seat, she opened the console and pulled out a large device that looked like a cellular phone from the 1980s.

"S-satellite phone." She dialed a number. "I have to c-call this in."

She had enough manual dexterity to dial—a good sign—but her speech slurred.

I engaged the four-wheel drive and jammed on the gas.

All four tires spun. Dirt spewed everywhere.

After a couple of seconds, we shot out of the ditch and headed across open ground, moving at a right angle to where the towers used to be.

The terrain was flat but bumpy, covered in low brush that scraped the sides of the Suburban as we went.

Whitney told whoever was on the other end of the sat phone what had happened. She managed to rattle off a bunch of code words and acronyms, government-speak for a terrorist attack, all hands on deck. Her voice was strong, but she sounded tipsy.

She glanced at me, phone still against her ear. "Where are we going?"

In the distance, the power plant lake shimmered like a sea of diamonds.

"The blast scene," Whitney said, looking behind us. "We need to see about survivors."

I kept driving.

"Please, Jon." She touched my arm. "We have to help with the wounded."

"There aren't going to be any survivors from a blast like that." I maneuvered around a stock tank. "Anybody who's still alive needs to be found first, which means bulldozers and search dogs."

She didn't say anything. Just stared at me with wide eyes, like she was trying to process the words.

"Then they'll need to be transported to the nearest trauma center, which is, oh, maybe two hundred miles away."

She looked at the phone.

"We're going to the lake house," I said.

She stared at me blankly. One eyelid drooped.

"They're still here, Whitney."

"How do you know?" she said.

"Because people who do things like this usually stick around to watch."

She didn't reply. Instead she put the phone on the floor and buckled her seat belt.

I pressed down on the accelerator. The Suburban bumped and jumped across the uneven ground. I drove through a stand of mesquite trees, and about ninety seconds later, the SUV burst through a barbwire fence at the rear of the lake house.

The home was low and squat, like someone had mashed a two-story house into a single floor. Beige brick siding, a large back patio next to the attached garage.

Whitney gasped.

Parked in the driveway by the garage: a gray Chevy pickup. The same type of vehicle the farmer by Black Valley had mentioned seeing.

I stopped by an old live oak about fifty yards from the house. Whitney grabbed her pistol.

"No." I shook my head. "You stay here."

"I can handle myself."

"You've got a concussion." I opened my door. "Your attic's a little dusty. Call the cavalry on the sat phone. Tell them we've spotted the suspect's vehicle."

She looked at the gun in her hand. Her mouth was open.

I pulled the weapon from her fingers, put it on the dash. "Then lie down and be still."

She touched the bruise on her forehead, which had grown into a nice-sized goose egg.

I got out. Jogged to the rear of the Suburban.

There, I found a locker with four MP-5 submachine guns and a couple dozen clips full of ammunition. Hanging from a rod across the rear were eight or ten pieces of clothing. Half were bulletproof vests, the rest blue Windbreakers marked FEDERAL AGENT on the back.

I found a vest and a Windbreaker in my size and put both on, ignoring the heat. Then I loaded one of the subguns with a thirty-round magazine and stuck a spare clip in my back pocket.

Whitney appeared next to me, wobbly.

I put a hand on her elbow, led her back to the passenger side, got her seated.

"Stay here," I said. "Wait for the troops."

She stared at me, a blank expression on her face.

"Please." I touched her hand. "This is where you'll be safe."

She nodded once, and I jogged toward the lake house as the remains of the power plant burned behind me.

- CHAPTER FORTY-FIVE -

Sarah parks her Mercedes in the handicap space in front of a restaurant in Preston Center, one of the city's swankier North Dallas neighborhoods.

It's a little before noon, and there are a lot of empty spaces, but Sarah's give-a-shit meter is broken, so she picks the closest spot.

Malcolm's is a white-tablecloth kind of place named after the owner, a Louisiana expat who died the year before when the gas tank of his Escalade "malfunctioned" and exploded.

A black awning covers the front door of the restaurant, sheltering the red carpet that leads to the curb. A jewelry store and a plastic surgeon's office are on either side.

Several hours before, Sarah had told the Texas Ranger that she doesn't own any guns and finally managed to shut the door of the apartment. She'd showered and then picked out her clothes with care, a black linen sundress and a strand of pearls her husband gave her for their fifth anniversary. Her Hermès purse, the Ruger stuffed inside, is on her shoulder. On her other shoulder is a small duffel bag made from vinyl, the kind you might take to the gym.

Two types of people frequent Malcolm's. Men in the real estate business, Rolex-wearing deal junkies. And gamblers. Sarah has an appointment with one of the latter, an attorney named Stodghill.

The inside of the restaurant is decorated with oil paintings of nude women reclining on chaise lounges and English gentlemen on horseback hunting foxes.

This early, only about half the tables are occupied. Ninety percent of the patrons are males, a hundred percent of whom are drinking.

Sarah approaches the hostess station, where the maître d' is standing.

"I need to go to the back room," Sarah says.

The maître d' makes a big show of consulting his reservations book.

"You know who I am," Sarah says. "Quit acting like you don't."

The man snaps his finger, and a waiter in a tuxedo instantly appears. The waiter escorts Sarah to a heavy wooden door on the other side of the dining room.

The waiter opens the door with a flourish, and Sarah steps into a separate room that doesn't resemble a white-tablecloth restaurant so much as it does a sports bar.

Ten flat-screen TVs on the far wall, each tuned to a different sporting event. Tables are all arranged so that the seats face the televisions. There's a bar on one wall with a bartender and two heavyset guys in tracksuits scribbling notes on clipboards, talking on cell phones. The tracksuit guys aren't taking drink orders; they're handling bets.

All the tables are empty except for the one in the middle, the best spot in the house.

Two people are sitting there. Stodghill, a man in his forties wearing a starched white button-down shirt, pressed Levi jeans, and black lizard-skin boots. Next to him is a girl in her early twenties dressed like a stripper—skintight red minidress and matching platform shoes.

Stodghill is eating raw oysters and drinking beer, watching a soccer game.

Sarah sits down uninvited on the right side of the attorney. The girl is on his left.

Stodghill looks over at the new arrival, one eyebrow raised.

Sarah is no stranger to lawyers. She's dealt with dozens of them, the big firms in the skyscrapers downtown, people in $5,000 suits who handle her trust funds.

Those people all play by the rules, which is not something she needs at the moment.

Stodghill is a defense attorney who maintained a small office between a dry cleaner and a discount cigarette store. His last big case ended with his client, a crooked city councilman, going free after a mistrial. One of the jurors, an elderly Baptist deacon with no criminal record, was discovered to have ten pounds of marijuana in the trunk of his Toyota Camry.

"I thought we'd be meeting alone," Sarah says.

"This is Darcie," Stodghill says. "She's my fiancée."

Sarah leans across the table. "Hey, Darcie. You've got blow on your face."

The girl, who up close appears to be in her late teens, has some white powder on her nostrils and upper lip. She instantly covers her nose with one hand.

Stodghill shakes his head.

"Where'd you two meet?" Sarah says. "A hooker rodeo?"

Stodghill speaks to the girl. "Go clean yourself up."

Darcie gets to her feet and wobbles on her platform shoes toward the restrooms.

"Is she even old enough to drive?" Sarah asks.

"Her Oklahoma ID says she's eighteen." Stodghill drains his beer. "You want to keep busting my ass about my private life, or tell me why you had to see me so fast?"

Sarah puts the duffel bag on the table. "There's three hundred thousand in there. Half of it is to pay for my fee. The rest is a retainer for a new client you're about to start representing."

Stodghill stares at the bag for a moment before he places it under his seat.

"Dallas is getting a little hot for me." Sarah stares at the wall of TVs, trying to figure out where to begin.

"How hot are we talking about? You about to be arrested?"

Sarah shrugs. "I don't know. Maybe."

Stodghill signals the waiter. He orders a pot of coffee. When the waiter leaves, he says, "Start at the beginning."

- CHAPTER FORTY-SIX -

I could smell the destroyed power plant, a heavy mixture of burnt creosote and fried insulation.

A couple thousand yards to the east, a huge cloud of black smoke wafted upward, the remains of the boilers. To the west, maybe three hundred yards away, was the substation. Smoke trickled from several of the transformers closest to the lake house.

The terrorists had blown up the plant, another Sudamento property, and then disabled the substation—a two-pronged attack.

A bomb for the plant, shoot out the transformers at the substation.

The people responsible were getting bolder, certainly more dangerous. No telling how many had died in the explosion—five or ten at least.

I approached the rear of the lake house, threading my way through a small patch of brush.

The patio appeared empty.

I ran crouched over to the driveway. Stopped, took cover at the rear of the gray pickup.

In the bed of the truck were several empty fertilizer bags. In the right combination, fertilizer plus diesel fuel would yield an Oklahoma City–style bomb, one certainly big enough to take down a couple of boilers. The vehicle itself was unoccupied.

At the rear of the house was a sliding glass door that was open about two feet. Vertical blinds blocked the gap.

I moved as quickly and as quietly as possible across the patio. At the open door, I led with the muzzle of the subgun, pressing through the blinds.

The interior of the house was dark. No electricity.

I stepped inside and pressed my back against the wall by the door, letting my eyesight adjust to the gloom. Underneath the bulletproof vest and Windbreaker, sweat dripped down my torso.

I was in the back half of the structure, a large area that served as a combination kitchen and family room. Immediately in front of me were two couches and several easy chairs, all covered with sheets. To the right was an open area full of kitchen appliances from the 1960s.

The air smelled like mildew and stale sweat. The house was completely silent.

A hallway led toward the front, the direction of the lake.

I eased that way.

The hall ended in another living area. The far wall was glass, dirty and smudged, offering a clouded view of a large wooden deck built out over the shoreline of the lake. Beyond the deck the water shimmered.

The living room was empty. The deck was not.

Price Anderson sat in a chair by the railing. He was bound and gagged, facing the wrecked power plant, as if someone had wanted him to watch the destruction.

At the corner of the deck, farthest from the remains of the plant, were two people.

One was on his or her knees, facing the house, head bobbing back and forth over the crotch of a second person. The second individual had his back to me. His pants undone, hands holding the first person's head.

On a glass-topped table by the two people were several items. A lever-action rifle and a submachine gun, an old MAC-10. And an electronic device that looked like what you'd use to fly a radio-controlled airplane. Or remotely set off one or more bombs.

There was an open sliding door in the middle of the glass wall.

I stepped onto the deck, keeping my subgun pointed toward the two people getting their freak on in the great outdoors. They were oblivious to my presence.

Price had been roughed up. Clothing torn, one eye swollen, a cheek bruised. He saw me but didn't move or make a sound.

I aimed at the pair on the other side of the deck, shouted, "FREEZE! POLICE!"

The person on his knees was a man.

He squealed and jumped back, wiped his mouth. He was dark-skinned, in his twenties, wearing a white tunic and skullcap. Small, about as threatening as wet paint. He looked like an extra hired to play a terrorist on some cable TV show, a non-speaking role.

His partner, however, was a different story.

He was tall and lanky and mad as a tiger getting a bath. He yanked his zipper up and turned to face me.

Cops see crazy all the time, the base level for about half the people on the streets. Crazy usually equaled dangerous, and this guy was Olympic-level looney.

His eyes glowed with anger, rattling in their sockets. His breathing was rapid and shallow. Crude prison tattoos adorned his forearms.

"You couldn't wait until I was finished?" He didn't appear concerned that a weapon was pointed his way.

He was a me-me-me guy, which wasn't all that surprising. There was usually a lot of narcissism in prison, in addition to the crazy.

"Hands on top of your head." I brought the MP-5 to my shoulder. "Both of you."

"Do you know who I am?" Crazy Man said.

Another question, this one the hallmark of the sociopath. *I am so important. You must know me. You must bow to my wishes.*

I said, "You're the guy I'm getting ready to shoot if you don't do what I tell you."

He laughed.

The small man in the skullcap pointed at me and said, "Allah is great."

Under the circumstances, the words would have been menacing, except for his lisp and Texas accent.

"Shut the hell up, Alfie." Crazy Man shot a murderous look at his friend.

"Step away from the table," I said. "Both of you."

Neither person moved.

Crazy Man pointed toward the smoldering ruins of the plant. "Do you know how easy that was?"

Behind me, Price grunted.

"They don't even guard it properly," Crazy Man said. "It's like they *wanted* me to blow it up."

I took a step closer.

Two suspects who refused my commands. As soon as I tried to restrain one, the other would attack.

"You fuck with me, this is what happens." Crazy Man's face was flushed, fingers clenched. "It should have been mine. All mine."

I had no idea what he was talking about.

The table with the guns was maybe a foot away from his hand.

Price grunted again, louder.

I took another step closer, the subgun still pressed against my shoulder.

Crazy Man laughed. "You think you're gonna take me in?"

He was closest to the guns, so I decided to shoot him first. I aimed at the middle of his chest, tightened my finger on the trigger.

Footsteps from behind me in the house, splitting my attention.

I looked away for a nanosecond as Whitney Holbrook appeared in the doorway, a subgun pressed to her shoulder. She screamed, "DON'T MOVE!"

Everything started to happen in slow motion.

I returned my attention to the two suspects.

The little guy in the skullcap had a revolver in his hand, a weapon that seemed to have appeared out of thin air.

Crazy Man grabbed for the MAC-10 on the table.

I brought the muzzle of my gun back to Crazy Man. Took up the rest of the slack in the trigger.

The guy in the skullcap fired, and what felt like a brick slammed into my stomach.

There was no sound associated with any of this. The only thing I could hear came from behind me, Price Anderson grunting frantically through his gag.

I staggered backward as spits of flame erupted between Whitney Holbrook and Crazy Man, both firing their subguns at each other.

Finally, after what seemed like hours, I managed to squeeze the trigger of my MP-5, firing a short burst toward the little man in the skullcap, not my original target.

Black holes blossomed in the man's tunic as he yanked the trigger again, and another bullet slammed into my chest.

I staggered away from the house, hit the deck railing.

My chest felt like an elephant had been tap-dancing on my torso.

I fell to the wooden surface, landing on my side, facing the house and the chair where Price Anderson was tied. I was beneath the last rung of the railing, my back on the edge of the deck, the water about thirty feet below me.

Price cranked his head my way, eyes pleading.

I didn't understand why. I wanted to ask, but my lungs weren't working.

He looked down.

My eyes followed his, and I saw what was underneath his chair.

Two sticks of dynamite and an electronic device of some sort.

I reached an arm toward him, which was enough to upset my balance on the edge of the deck.

The fall to the water seemed to take an eternity.

I thought about my daughter and Piper. I wondered who the man with the crazy eyes was.

The water felt warm. I didn't try to fight it when my head went under the surface.

From a long way off came the sound of an explosion.

Then everything went black.

- CHAPTER FORTY-SEVEN -

On the largest of the TV screens, Sarah watches smoke billow toward the sky, black and oily.

She's in the back room of Malcolm's, sitting at the table with her attorney, Stodghill, and his fiancée, the woman dressed like a stripper.

About half the TVs are tuned to news channels, all of which are covering the explosion on the outskirts of San Saba. One of the network affiliates out of Waco has a chopper circling the blast area, and this is the feed most of the channels are running.

The bartender is staring at the TV. The bookies have quit talking on their cell phones, stopped scribbling notes, engrossed in the footage of destruction.

Before the news of the explosion interrupted everything, Sarah had told Stodghill her story—an abbreviated, sanitized version, because even a lawyer who advertises on a billboard across from the county jail has some ethics.

She explained that she might be a suspect in the killing of a deputy in a motel in Central Texas, as well as in the murders of two homeless people near downtown Dallas.

Stodghill took notes on a cocktail napkin, asking the occasional question, particularly about witnesses and physical evidence.

Sarah didn't say anything about the gun she used or the throwaway phones. The phones had been smashed with a hammer and tossed into Turtle Creek, a few miles south of their current location. The Python, her grandfather's weapon, Elias took.

She also told him about the only potential witness, the only reliable one anyway—the sheriff she encountered leaving the motel. Stodghill asked if she knew the officer's name. She told him: Jonathan Cantrell. Stodghill put his pen down and stared at the tabletop, his brow knitted in thought. Before he could respond, the news about the attack on the power plant had appeared on one of the TVs, and everything changed.

Now they've switched from coffee back to beer.

Sarah and Stodghill watch the screen while Darcie taps on her cell and smacks her gum, seemingly oblivious to what's happening.

"Damn terrorists." Stodghill drains his glass.

Sarah tries to muster some feeling about the destruction of the power plant, a slice of concern or empathy for those affected. She gets nothing.

She does, however, feel a wellspring of anger building, wrath at what her brother has done and what her lover, Price, has failed to stop.

After a while all she feels is dirty, as tainted as the black smoke wafting heavenward.

The camera on the news copter shifts to a one-story house on the shore of the lake by the power plant. The home has a large wooden deck jutting out over the water. In the middle of the deck is a ragged hole like a huge fist had been punched through the wood.

In the driveway sits a pickup that looks like the one used by Elias and Alfie.

The realization hits Sarah like a turning page. Without being told, she knows her brother is dead.

An emptiness that is more than words can describe invades her mind, growing larger and larger.

Behind the pickup are several squad cars, vehicles that appear to belong to the local sheriff or police department. Behind the squad cars are two ambulances.

On the bottom of the screen, a ticker runs the latest updates.

Two Suspects in San Saba Terrorist Attack Confirmed Dead. Two Law-Enforcement Officers Wounded. Third Body Unidentified.

Stodghill holds up the empty beer pitcher, catches the bartender's eye.

Sarah says, "Darcie, why don't you go powder your nose again."

The young woman sighs loudly. "Are you like the boss of me or what?"

Stodghill points to the restrooms. "Go."

The woman pouts but does as requested, sashaying across the room.

Stodghill says, "I assume what's coming next is attorney-client privilege."

"I need to ask you a question," Sarah says. "A hypothetical."

The lawyer nods.

"What if the gun used to shoot the deputy at that motel is found in possession of the people who blew up that power plant?"

He doesn't reply. Instead he stares off in the distance, stroking his chin.

Sarah says, "That would get me off the hook, wouldn't it?"

- CHAPTER FORTY-EIGHT -

The smell of rubbing alcohol. An intercom blared in the distance.

The bed was warm, the covers snug.

I didn't want to be awake. I wanted to continue the dreamless sleep, adrift in the vast nothingness.

Then I heard the gurgle of an infant—a happy sound—and a soft shush from a familiar voice.

I opened my eyes.

Piper Westlake was sitting by the window, bouncing a baby on her lap.

Elizabeth, our daughter.

I blinked, tried to focus. My head hurt.

They both looked healthy.

Piper had cut her hair, short and spiky. She'd dyed it, too—brunet, no longer blond. She wore a pair of faded jeans, pointy-toed cowboy boots, and a Butthole Surfers concert T-shirt. She'd always been tall and lean, but she looked even more so now. Her arms were sinewy, her skin tan.

Elizabeth was wearing a peach-colored romper and tiny Chuck Taylor tennis shoes. Her arms were plump with baby fat.

"You're alive," Piper said.

I coughed, tried to clear my throat. "I hope so." My voice was croaky.

"You gave us quite a scare."

"How long have I been here?" I looked around. Saw a hospital room that looked vaguely familiar.

"Almost two days now. You nearly drowned."

I sat up. My head spun. A bandage encircled my left bicep.

"You've got a concussion, a bullet graze to the arm, and some bruised ribs."

"Are we in Waco?" I glanced around the room again.

Piper nodded. Elizabeth stuck her foot in her mouth.

"How's the kiddo?" I asked.

"She's good." Piper's voice was flat.

"How are you?"

"Sleep deprived. But other than that okay." She paused. "You shouldn't try to talk too much. Lie back down and take it easy."

We were both silent for a moment as our daughter chewed on her shoe.

I said, "Can you see a Bed Bath and Beyond from the window?"

Piper craned her neck, looked outside. She nodded.

This was Kelsey's room, the widow of my murdered deputy.

Karma had come full circle. Or something. I eased down, closed my eyes. When I opened them again, it was dusk outside and another woman was sitting where Piper had been.

She was dressed like a law-enforcement officer—a khaki shirt with a badge on the breast, a Colt semiautomatic pistol on her hip.

I blinked to bring her into focus. When I could see better, it was dark outside, and she was gone.

The door to the room opened and a nurse entered, carrying a tray of food. A doctor followed. The nurse took my vitals while the doc told me I was lucky to be alive. I picked at the meal, eating only about half. I drank several glasses of water.

Bits and pieces came back to me. The man with the dark hair and the crazy eyes. His companion, a small guy, dressed like an Islamabad street vendor.

The doctor told me I would make a full recovery but that I would need to rest for the next few days to allow my brain to heal.

I remembered the explosion at the power plant. Whitney arriving—

"What about the agent who was with me?" I asked the nurse. "Whitney Holbrook?"

"You need to rest," the nurse said.

"Is she okay?"

The nurse and the doctor looked at each other. The doctor said, "She survived the attack. But she's suffered a much worse concussion than you did."

"How much worse?"

The doc sat on the foot of my bed. "Look, Agent Cantrell. I wish I could tell you more, but we're pretty strict about the HIPAA laws around here."

A wave of pain in my skull made my vision blurry.

They prepared to leave.

"Would you send Piper back in then?" I said. "She was just here."

"Who?" the nurse asked.

"Piper Westlake."

Blank stares from both of them.

"Midthirties, about five-eight. Wearing jeans and a, um—a concert T-shirt." I paused. "She had a baby with her."

The doc made a note on my chart. "No one's been in your room, Agent Cantrell. The police have a guard outside your door."

"There're federal agents all over the hospital, too," the nurse said. "Half the state's on lockdown because of the terrorist attack."

My head felt like someone was trying to dig their way out from behind my temple. I rubbed my forehead, willing away the throbbing.

The doctor peered at my face. "Let's give you a little something for the pain."

"I'm okay."

The nurse had already injected a substance into my IV.

A moment later, everything became hazy and pleasant, a golden sheen on the surface of life.

"We're going to wake you up in a few hours," she said. "Make sure your head's doing okay."

I nodded and smiled. She was so nice. Painkillers were so awesome. The doctor was nice, too. He was nice and awesome.

They left. A moment later, the door opened, and the woman with the badge entered.

She stood by the bed. "How are you feeling?"

"Awesome," I said. "And sleepy. Who are you?"

"I'm a Texas Ranger," she said. "My name is Moreno. You and me, we need to talk."

- CHAPTER FORTY-NINE -

I woke at seven the next morning to sunlight streaming into the hospital room.

My body had turned a corner. The ache in my head was nearly gone. The bruised ribs were only a minor throb, and the flesh wound in my bicep itched now instead of hurting.

I felt the need to be moving, to check on Whitney Holbrook and get the details on the attack at San Saba. But even more than that, I was eager to leave the hospital. I wanted to find Piper. Continue the investigation into who killed my deputy.

My clothes were in the closet, stiff and smelling of mold from being in the lake.

I was wondering how to quickly and easily get a new set when a nurse entered the room and corralled me back in bed. Once there, she checked my heart and blood pressure and administered several tests to determine how the recovery from my concussion was progressing.

I did everything to her satisfaction, so I asked her when I could check out. She told me the doctor would be along shortly.

She left, and an orderly brought in a breakfast tray. I devoured the meal almost before he left the room. As I drank the last of the surprisingly good coffee, the door opened yet again and the Texas Ranger from the night before, Moreno, entered.

"How are you feeling?" she asked.

"Like I'm ready to get out of here."

"The feds want to debrief you about the attack." She moved to the window. "I thought I'd slide in before your dance card got full."

"You're part of the team investigating the murder of my deputy, aren't you?"

She nodded.

"What do you have for me?" I pushed the tray away.

"A math problem," she said. "Certain things aren't adding up right."

I got out of bed, walked to the window. Bed Bath & Beyond wasn't open yet.

"The two rounds that hit your bulletproof vest," she said. "They were fired by the same gun that killed your deputy."

My head got dizzy. I shuffled back to the bed, sat down.

"The guy that shot you," she said. "He was a three-time loser from Tyler, currently on parole."

I rubbed my forehead, the headache returning all of a sudden.

"Alfie Washington, that was his name," she said. "You ever run across him before?"

"No."

"Alfie killed his mother when he was sixteen. He was about as Muslim as Jerry Falwell."

"Where the hell did he get the gun?" I said.

"Doesn't matter." Moreno turned away from the window. "Nobody's going to spend much time figuring that out."

I looked at her but didn't speak. Too much was going on in my head to form a coherent sentence.

"They've closed the books on your deputy's murder," she said. "Alfie Washington's gonna go down as the shooter."

"That's ridiculous."

"I agree, but it's a nice, neat package that everybody can get their head around." She sighed. "The story is, he was meeting people online and hooked up with your deputy, who didn't realize Alfie was a dude."

"The guy that shot me was not SarahSmiles." Even as I spoke the words I wondered if Alfie and SarahSmiles could somehow be tied together.

Nothing about that made sense, however.

Sarah was a loner. And where was Alfie when Cleo Fain was attacked on the side of the road?

"The day your deputy was killed, Alfie Washington's cell phone pinged a couple of towers near the murder scene."

"I saw someone leaving the hotel. *She* was not a black man."

"Oh yes." Moreno smiled. "The woman with the Dallas Cowboys hat who may or may not have been using SarahSmiles as an alias to meet men."

"There has to be a record of her IP addresses when she logged on to the site," I said. "Do they match Alfie's phone?"

A few moments passed before Moreno shook her head.

"So who is SarahSmiles?" I asked.

"Nobody knows." She paused. "And the Texas Rangers have stopped trying to figure that out."

I swore.

"Alfie Washington represents a twofer," she said. "He killed your deputy and was part of one of the most audacious terrorist attacks since 9/11."

Noise from the hallway. Feet shuffling, voices talking.

Moreno strode to the door. She opened it a notch and said to the people outside, "Agent Cantrell is feeling a little dizzy. Let's give him another few minutes, okay?"

I heard grumbling, but no one came in.

Moreno shut the door. "I'm not done with you yet."

"I need you to get me some clean clothes. Mine were ruined in the lake."

She ignored my request. "Tell me everything you remember about the woman you saw leaving the motel."

"What's it matter? The Rangers have stopped looking."

"Officially, yeah." She smiled. "Some of us don't like to give up, though."

The expression on her face was friendly but determined. Despite her age—midforties—she was an old-school cop. A dog with a bone. Not going to let go until they pried it from her jaws.

I told her everything, starting with the text at the diner telling me where my deputy's pickup had been spotted.

At the rear entrance of the motel, a woman in a shapeless blue raincoat and oversized sunglasses and a Dallas Cowboys ball cap. Attractive, somewhere in her thirties. Maybe five foot six or seven.

Her weight was hard to determine because of the jacket, but I had the impression of someone who was fit, weight proportionate to her height. Her legs appeared toned underneath the jeans she'd been wearing. No eye color because of the glasses. Her hair was brown or black, again hard to tell because it had been wet. She'd gotten into a Buick LaCrosse with dealer tags.

Moreno stopped me at that point. "Do you know anybody named Debbie Wilson?" She rattled off an address in downtown Dallas, an expensive high-rise apartment.

I thought for a moment and then shook my head.

"A person with that particular name and address purchased that Buick LaCrosse the week before."

"What about the Monte Carlo?"

Moreno didn't say anything, a puzzled expression on her face.

I told her about the tip from the feds, the drunk who'd gotten his Chevrolet stolen from a VFW hall on the interstate. I told her that I'd interviewed a very unreliable witness, an alcoholic in his seventies who'd seen a woman wearing a rain poncho and a Cowboys cap in the car. How he'd said the woman gave the impression of being rich.

"A rich girl, huh?" Moreno got a far-off look on her face.

"My takeaway, too," I said. "The way she carried herself, her tone of voice. The TravelTimes Inn wasn't her usual lodging choice. She was used to the finer things in life."

Moreno paced the room.

"I sent an e-mail about all this to my contact at the Texas Rangers."

"Typical." She shook her head. "That never made it to anybody in the field. Where was the VFW hall?"

I told her.

"That's next door to where we found the LaCrosse." She yanked her cell from her belt, tapped out a message.

The door opened, and a man in his fifties stepped into my room without knocking. He wore a dark suit and carried a briefcase in one hand, a cell pressed to his ear with the other. He nodded hello but continued his phone conversation.

"He's with Homeland Security." Moreno lowered her voice to a whisper and continued to fiddle with her cell. "We can talk later, but I've got one more question now."

The door opened again. No one came in, but I could hear voices in the hall. The feds weren't going to be stalled any longer.

Moreno held the phone for me to look at. "I managed to take a picture of Debbie Wilson's 'friend' who was staying at her apartment."

The image on the screen was that of a woman in her thirties walking down a hallway. She was attractive with shoulder-length hair the color of chestnuts. Her body was fit, evidenced by the tight workout clothes she was wearing.

Moreno said, "Is this the woman you saw leaving the motel?"

My vision tunneled and my throat got tight. If that wasn't the same person, it was her sister. The long, thin nose, the jutting jaw.

I nodded.

"You sure?"

"Sure enough. Who is she?"

"No idea. The apartment's been vacated."

"Agent Cantrell?" The man in the dark suit stood at the foot of the bed. "Are you ready to begin your debriefing?"

I didn't reply. Too much going on in my concussed skull to answer that question right then.

The man looked at Moreno. "We'll need the room cleared for the interview."

Moreno stared at him for a moment and then left.

- CHAPTER FIFTY -

Three people in my room, sitting in folding chairs at the foot of my bed.

The man in his fifties, Harris, an investigator with Homeland.

A much younger guy in an ill-fitting gray suit. Operating a video recorder mounted on a tripod, the lens aimed at me.

And a fortysomething woman dressed like Whitney Holbrook had been on the first day we'd met—dark skirt and matching jacket, white blouse, minimal makeup. She identified herself as an FBI agent, no name given. She was carrying a thick briefcase.

Harris asked how I was feeling and then the basics—name, address, job description, et cetera. When he finished with the preliminaries, I said, "Tell me about Whitney Holbrook. How is she?"

Harris and the FBI agent exchanged glances.

"Agent Holbrook was wearing a bulletproof vest but took four rounds to the chest," Harris said. "She fell off the deck when the guy in the chair exploded. Hit her noggin pretty hard."

The second blow to the head in only a few minutes.

"I want to see her."

"Maybe later. We've got a lot of ground to cover right now." He pulled a yellow pad from his briefcase. "Walk us through the day of the attack."

I told them everything that I remembered in as much detail as possible. Picking up Whitney at the motel. Going to breakfast at the diner. Eric Faulkner arriving.

At the mention of Faulkner's name, the FBI agent and Harris retreated to a corner of the room and had a whispered conversation. About a minute later, they returned and sat back down.

Harris said, "Mr. Faulkner's state of mind. Give me your impressions."

"He appeared agitated."

"Agitated how?"

"Agitated that someone had almost killed one of his geese that lays the golden eggs."

"You're referring to the attack on the Black Valley substation?" the FBI agent asked.

"Does he have any other geese?" I said.

They both stared at me, their expressions blank, uncomprehending.

"Yes," I said. "I was talking about the attack on Black Valley."

Harris scribbled some notes.

The FBI agent said, "Did Faulkner give any hints that he might know who was responsible?"

I pondered the question, remembering our conversation. After a moment, I said, "No. Not in the least."

Harris said, "Keep going. You finished breakfast and . . ."

I continued. Whitney driving to San Saba. The two dead guards. The explosion of the towers. Whitney running the

Suburban into the ditch, hitting her head. How I drove the rest of the way.

Harris said, "How did you know to go to the lake house?"

"A hunch."

No one spoke for a moment. Harris and the FBI agent glanced at each other. The guy running the video recorder fiddled with the settings.

"You feel like talking about what happened next?" Harris asked. "We can take a break if you want."

"Let's get it over with."

He nodded, and I told them about entering the house, seeing Price Anderson tied to a chair, encountering the two suspects—the small man in the skullcap and the guy with the crazy eyes. Whitney busting in right as my finger was tightening on the trigger.

"Do you know an individual named Elias King?" Harris asked.

I shook my head.

"How about a man named Frank King?"

"The guy from East Texas?" I asked. "The King of the Red River?"

"Yeah." Harris nodded. "That's the one."

Everybody knew who Frank King was, one of the richest men in the state when he died. He'd amassed a fortune in real estate, timber, banking, and oil. Supposedly, he'd gotten his start after World War II running cigarettes and moonshine back and forth across the Arkansas state line.

"I know who he was," I said. "Most people in Texas do. But I never had any dealings with the man."

The FBI agent pulled a manila folder from her briefcase. The folder was the size of the Houston phone book, if there still was such a thing.

"This is what the bureau has on Frank King," she said. "A summary, actually. The files themselves take up two cabinets."

"So he was dirty," I said.

"Filthy." She nodded. "A murderer and a thug. Whitewashed everything with money, became so-called legit when he strong-armed his way into controlling a bank."

"The revolver that Alfie Washington shot you with," Harris said. "It was used in several killings in northeast Texas in the 1970s and '80s."

I remembered the e-mail from the Texas Rangers several days before, the message about the unsolved murder from 1991. Bowie County. A man who owned a bar and was believed to be involved in gambling and prostitution.

The FBI agent continued. "Frank King was a suspect in all of them."

"No witnesses of course," Harris said. "Because even as an old man, he ran that part of the world with an iron fist."

"So how did that same gun end up killing my deputy?"

"Elias King was Frank's grandson," Harris said.

"I'm not following."

"Elias was the second terrorist in the attack on San Saba," Harris said. "The guy Whitney Holbrook shot on the deck of the lake house."

Crazy Eyes. With the thick black hair and the pointed nose. I could actually feel my jaw drop open.

"Elias King was a felon," he said. "Manslaughter. Killed a guy in a bar fight. Used a broken beer bottle on his throat."

"That makes no sense." I shook my head. "The grandson of a mobster goes terrorist? How . . . why?"

"Good question," Harris said. "We're still trying to connect the dots on that particular angle."

No one spoke for a few moments.

"All the money in the world, trust funds out the ass." The FBI agent looked out the window. "And he ends up a hood who likes to make shit go boom-boom."

"Maybe it's genetic," Harris said. "Who knows?"

More silence. Harris and the FBI agent flipped through their respective yellow pads.

"There's an outlier in the bell curve, though," I said.

They looked at me.

"So Frank King kills a bunch of people with that Python. Then his grandson inherits the weapon and gives it to Alfie Washington, who puts a couple rounds into my bulletproof vest."

Harris nodded.

"My deputy's killer had the same gun," I said. "And a woman using the alias Debbie Wilson and/or SarahSmiles left the scene, got into a Buick LaCrosse."

The FBI agent sighed loudly.

"I've been in law enforcement for almost twenty-five years," I said. "I know the difference between a white woman in her thirties and a black cross-dresser barely out of high school."

The FBI agent began to pack up her stuff.

"There was no woman, Cantrell." Harris shook his head. "That case is closed. You need to move on."

- CHAPTER FIFTY-ONE -

Sarah watches the man get out of bed.

He is in his twenties and naked. Fit as only someone that age can be. A flat belly, muscular arms ringed with tattoos that look like barbed wire, hair thick and brown.

"Damn, lady." He picks up his underwear from the floor. "You fuck like Jenna Jameson."

"You ever done it with a porn star?"

He shakes his head. "But I've seen her plenty on the Internet."

Sarah crooks her index finger at him. "Come back to bed."

"I got work to do." He steps into his boxer shorts.

"I'll give you the day off." She giggles. "Then I'll get you off."

The young man's name is Ronnie or Donny; she can't remember which. He's an assistant manager for the landscape company Sarah's husband has hired to redo one of the side yards.

It is midmorning and they are in the master suite of the house on Strait Lane.

Other than Walden, Sarah has never had an encounter at home before. But since the death of her brother and the closing of the investigation into the murder of the deputy—the man she knew briefly as RockyRoad35—she has loosened her rules.

She is SarahSmiles after all. She is invincible.

And more than a little tipsy, she realizes as she swings her legs out of the bed and picks up a hand mirror on the nightstand. A small mound of cocaine rests in the center of the mirror.

She holds out the drugs. "You want one for the road?"

The man stares at the coke, face indecisive. Finally he shakes his head.

"That's bad shit," he says. "A little goes a long way."

Sarah chops up a line with her American Express Black Card, just a short one. She snorts it with a cocktail straw. A moment later, everything hums pleasantly.

She puts the mirror down. Snakes one hand up the leg of Ronnie/Donny's underwear, cups his balls.

"You sure you don't want to come back to bed?" She pouts.

The man closes his eyes, sways a little.

Sarah can feel him grow erect again. She smiles.

After a moment, he pushes her hand away and steps back, reaching for his clothes on the sofa.

"I told you. I gotta get back to work."

The AC is turned down low, and there's a fire in the fireplace despite the temperature outside. The glow from the flames provides the only illumination in the room.

Sarah stands. She is naked. In the mirror across the room, she sees her body glistening in the dim light.

The yellowish-purple bruise on her arm from where the dyke hit her with the tire iron is nearly healed. She looks good and she knows it.

"Aw, c'mon, Donny." She steps toward him. "Just one more time. Then you can go back to work."

The man slips into his pants. "My name is Ronnie."

"Whatever." Sarah rubs her nose. "Just get back in bed."

Ronnie puts on his shirt. Grabs shoes and socks from the floor.

Sarah is incensed. The coke burns the back of her throat, and her stomach feels upset from the bottle of wine she's had this morning.

"If you don't get back in bed, Ronnie/Donny or whatever the fuck your name is, I'll have your ass fired so fast you'll end up in another time zone."

Ronnie backs away from her, shoes in hand.

Sarah is shaking. Anger clouds her vision. People don't tell her no. She is her grandfather's offspring; this lesson was learned at his knee.

She flings open the drawer of her nightstand, grabs the Ruger.

Ronnie says, "W-what the hell are you doing?"

Sarah aims the gun at his chest but doesn't answer. What is her plan? Is she going to rob him? Or just make him taste the fear?

The young man jerks open the bedroom door and dashes out on bare feet, his shirt half buttoned.

Sarah runs after him, naked, gun in hand.

He disappears around a corner. Footsteps echo through the cavernous living room.

Sarah stops. At the end of the hall, by the archway leading to the rest of the house, stand Rosa and Walden.

Rosa is carrying a stack of towels. Walden is empty-handed. They both stare at her, mouths agape.

Sarah lowers the Ruger. "What the hell are you two looking at?"

Her voice is ragged, hoarse.

Neither of her employees speaks.

Sarah realizes she is completely naked. Her body is coated in sweat. She tastes blood in the back of her throat.

She staggers back into the bedroom, slams the door and locks it.

There's more wine and more coke waiting for her, lots more.

Fuck Rosa and fuck Walden and fuck Ronnie/Donny. She doesn't need them or anybody. She is SarahSmiles. She sits on the bed and chops up another line, ignoring the tears streaming down her cheeks and the blood dripping from her nose.

- CHAPTER FIFTY-TWO -

Harris, his FBI colleague, and their video-camera operator left.

The doctor came in a few minutes later and said that if I promised to take it easy, he would release me. I promised and went to take a shower.

When I was finished, I put on a robe and exited the bathroom.

The first thing I saw was the Texas Ranger, Moreno, sitting on the foot of my bed and holding Elizabeth, my daughter.

"Crap," I said. "The hallucinations are back."

"What are you talking about?" Piper was on the far side of the room.

I blinked several times, swung my head back and forth between her and the child.

"Your wife and I met in the hallway," Moreno said.

"We're not married." Piper stared out the window.

Moreno patted my daughter's knee. "Cute little kid you've got here."

"Yes, she is." I took the child from Moreno's lap, held her close. A feeling of peace and well-being came over me. Elizabeth squirmed and tried to grab my nose.

"I got you some clothes." Piper turned around, held up a paper sack. "And a gun."

My duty weapon was with the crime-scene techs investigating the shooting at the lake house.

"You were here earlier," I said. "I thought that was a dream. How'd you get past the guards?"

"Really?" Piper rolled her eyes. "You'd ask me that?"

I didn't say anything. I should have known better.

Piper Westlake was the most self-sufficient person I had ever met. She'd knowingly walked into firefights that would have left a Navy SEAL running the other way. Getting into a guarded hospital room was nothing, a stretching exercise before a race.

She tossed the sack on the bed, and I handed her Elizabeth.

"Cleo Fain," Moreno said. "You know who that is?"

"The serial killer." I nodded.

"She liked sorority girls, if I remember right," Piper said. "There were a bunch of BOLOs out on her in the last year or so."

"You're a cop, too?" Moreno said.

"Dallas PD most recently." Piper paused. "It's complicated."

"What about Cleo Fain?" I said.

"She's in custody, a hospital in Dallas. Wants to make a deal in exchange for info on a woman who assaulted her on the side of the highway."

"Can't imagine she's in any position to be doing any horse trading," I said.

"The woman who attacked her was driving an old Monte Carlo," Moreno said. "Lime green."

I walked to the window, stared outside. The parking lot for Bed Bath & Beyond was about half full.

"I've got to be in Sweetwater in the morning." Moreno stood. "A triple homicide. Can't throw any more time at a closed case."

I turned around. "What hospital is she in?"

"Parkland. Up in Dallas. I e-mailed you the information." Moreno headed to the door. "Nice to meet you both."

She left.

Piper and I were alone with our child. We stared at each other for a few moments. I was filled with questions: Where Piper had been. The murder of my deputy. The fallout from the attack. I didn't know where to start.

So I said, "Why'd you cut your hair?"

She didn't answer.

"You planning to stick around?" I opened the sack.

She'd been raised an orphan, a succession of foster homes. She preferred to be off the grid and could disappear in the time it took for the dinner check to arrive, going completely underground, using false names and ID cards that would put a secret agent to shame.

"That Texas Ranger explained to me what's been going on," she said.

I got dressed. Piper knew my sizes and tastes. Wranglers and a white cotton button-down shirt. Low-heeled boots. A Glock .40 caliber, three full magazines, an inside-the-waistband holster.

"You're gonna go after this SarahSmiles person, aren't you?"

"Wouldn't you?" I jammed one of the mags into the Glock.

A member of my department had been murdered. No one was going to answer for that unless I pressed on.

She nodded.

"Why'd you come back?" I put on the boots. They fit perfectly.

"I heard you were injured."

"That almost sounds like you care whether I live or die."

"Don't make me out to be a coldhearted bitch, Jon. If I was going to be with anyone, it would be you. We've been over this before."

Elizabeth started to cry. Piper shushed her, stroked her head.

I headed to the door. I wanted to see the hallway, to be in motion. The room felt claustrophobic all of a sudden. Sitting in its narrow confines made me think about missed opportunities and roads not taken.

Piper said, "Wait."

I stopped, a hand on the knob.

"I'm moving to Mexico." Her voice was soft.

Breath caught in my throat.

"There's a company that needs a security chief for their CEO in Latin America."

I didn't reply.

"The CEO is a woman, a few years older than me. The money's good, and they'll provide child care and benefits out the ass."

"Where in Mexico?" My voice sounded hoarse.

Silence.

"Don't try to find me," Piper said. "It's better this way."

"Elizabeth is my child, too. I have a right to know."

"We leave in a week," she said. "I thought maybe you and I could spend some time together before we go."

A knock on the door.

I opened it.

Eric Faulkner stood in the hall. He wore what I assumed was his standard uniform, a plaid shirt and faded jeans. His face was gray and drawn like he hadn't slept in a while. He was alone.

"I wanted to come before now," he said. "Just to say thank you."

"I was just doing my job," I said.

He glanced over my shoulder. "I'm interrupting. Sorry."

No one spoke.

His arrival wasn't going to change anything. Piper and my daughter were leaving. I wanted to be with them while I could. But I also wanted to go to Dallas and interview Cleo Fain.

"Your family?" Faulkner nodded toward Piper and Elizabeth.

I hesitated for a moment before nodding back and introducing them.

"I'd like to invite you to my home," he said. "All of you. We're holding a small ceremony to honor Price Anderson."

Elizabeth gurgled and clapped her hands.

"Given everything that's happened," he said, "I realize that throwing what amounts to a party might seem a little callous."

"A man in your position," I said. "You have to keep up appearances." I hoped that didn't sound too sarcastic.

"Exactly. Glad you understand." He sighed heavily. "It's a horrible thing, what's happened. So many deaths. I think a little closure would be good for everybody."

The last thing I wanted to do was spend time with Eric Faulkner. I needed to go to Dallas, to see Cleo Fain.

Piper came up beside me, Elizabeth on her hip. Eric Faulkner cooed at the child.

"Tomorrow afternoon." He handed me a slip of paper. "Here's my address."

Faulkner lived in Dallas.

"We'll be there." I put the paper in my pocket. "Thanks."

"Sorry about your colleague," he said.

"What are you talking about?"

"Agent Holbrook."

I felt the blood drain from my face.

"You didn't know?"

"Know what?" My voice was raspy.

"She died an hour ago."

- CHAPTER FIFTY-THREE -

Parkland, the hospital where President Kennedy died, had moved.

The new facility, open only a few months, was across the street from the old one and resembled a huge gray set of Legos. Four or five blocky buildings attached to each other at right angles, forming an L shape around a massive parking garage.

I was in a waiting area on the fourth floor, in the wing used by the Dallas County jail.

Everything was white and bright—tile and plastic and metal—except for the chairs, which were upholstered in what appeared to be purple burlap.

Piper was next to me, bouncing Elizabeth on her lap.

Across from us sat a woman in her thirties who was missing several teeth and two fingers from her left hand. She smelled like an ashtray and looked like a stripper from Sturgis, wearing a sleeveless Harley T-shirt with no bra and leather chaps.

Piper said, "This is a great place to bring a child, Jon."

It was early afternoon, the day after I'd been released from the hospital in Waco. We were due at Eric Faulkner's home in a couple of hours.

"Maybe if we were a real couple," I said, "we could have lined up a babysitter."

"So this is my fault somehow?" Piper asked.

"I didn't say that."

"But you were thinking it."

Back together for less than twenty-four hours and we were already bickering. Why was it so hard to be together with the one that made you better than what you were alone?

Elizabeth began to cry. The Sturgis stripper moved to the other side of the room.

I opened the file in my lap and read the first few pages again.

That morning, Piper and I had contacted a number of people in our network of law-enforcement officers, courthouse rats, and private investigators, an unsavory group who'd given me several bits of information that might help in my upcoming interview.

On the far side of the waiting area were an elevator and a reception station for the jail's hospital, a glass enclosure with a uniformed officer sitting behind a computer monitor.

I closed the file and waited.

A few minutes later, the elevators opened and two people exited.

The first was a man with muttonchops, wearing a brown plaid sport coat and square-toed cowboy boots. He was a Dallas PD homicide investigator.

The second person wore jeans and a beige linen jacket. This was Cleo Fain's attorney, Stodghill, a lawyer perpetually on the edge of disbarment for a variety of ethical infractions.

I slid up behind them as they talked to the officer behind the bulletproof glass.

"Hello, Stodghill." I smiled. "I didn't realize you were taking court-appointed gigs these days."

We'd had dealings in the past, none of them pleasant.

He looked at me and muttered under his breath. Then he said, "My retainer's been paid—not that it's any of your business."

The homicide detective asked who I was. I flashed my FERC badge and said, "I'll be sitting in on your interview with Cleo Fain."

He protested, but there wasn't much he could do. A federal badge trumped the local PD. I had no idea if my credentials were still in force, since the person who'd hired me was dead, a fact that bothered me more than I wanted to admit. But at this point, I didn't really care if I was still a legitimate federal agent. As long as I had that badge, I intended to use it.

The detective and I handed over our pistols. A jailer opened a metal door and admitted the three of us into the secure area that smelled of rubbing alcohol and sweat. He led us to a room at the end of the hall where a woman with a bandage on her head was handcuffed to a bed.

We entered. Stodghill sat in a chair next to his client. The homicide detective and I stood at the foot of the bed. The detective pulled a set of pictures from his briefcase, grainy eight-by-tens of a woman in a store of some sort, maybe a tattoo parlor.

The woman bore a resemblance to the person I'd seen leaving the motel where my deputy had been murdered. My pulse ratcheted up a notch, but I didn't say anything.

The detective asked Cleo if she recognized the person.

Stodghill shook his head. "Don't answer that."

"I thought you and the DA had worked something out," the detective said.

"Our discussions with the district attorney's office are not germane to this meeting," Stodghill said. "My client will not be answering questions about that photo."

"W-what?" Cleo Fain spoke for the first time. "I thought—"

"Shh." Stodghill patted her hand. "Everything's under control."

I looked at the detective. "Give us a moment, will you?"

He shrugged and walked out.

When the door closed, I turned to Cleo Fain. "Did you recognize that woman?"

"Are you deaf, Cantrell?" Stodghill wagged his finger at me. "She's not saying a word about that photo."

Cleo looked at her attorney, a concerned expression on her face.

"Yes, she is," I said. "Trust me."

"This is a typical Jon Cantrell bluff." Stodghill patted his client's hand. "All hat, no cattle."

I said, "She's going to tell me everything she knows about that woman for three reasons."

Neither of them spoke.

"First, it doesn't sound like there's any deal in the works with the DA." I wondered but didn't ask who'd paid Stodghill's fee. Could it be so easy that he was connected somehow to SarahSmiles? Maybe, but it didn't matter. I'd have to tear his spleen out before he'd tell me.

The attorney crossed his arms, a cocky expression on his face.

"Second," I said, "everything we say will be off the record."

Stodghill snorted.

"And third, Ms. Fain is going to talk to me because her attorney is going to tell her to as he leaves this room."

"That's not gonna happen." Stodghill shook his head. "No way I'm leaving you alone with my client."

Cleo Fain spoke for the second time. "I d-do what my lawyer says. P-period."

Her voice was weak. Words stuttering.

"How's your head feeling?" I asked.

"F-fuck you, f-fed."

"I had a concussion a couple of days ago, too," I said. "Hurt like a mofo."

No one spoke. Stodghill's face was granite, obviously figuring that he'd won.

I opened the file I'd brought with me and removed a single piece of paper, a picture of a young woman with large brown eyes and a scowl on her face. Across the bottom of the page were the words WASHITA COUNTY JAIL.

I handed the picture to Stodghill. "You know who that is?"

He was silent for a moment. Then his face reddened. He tossed the paper at me.

"You son of a bitch. That's my fiancée, Darcie."

"Darcie Mullins?" I asked. "From Lawton, Oklahoma?"

He glared at me, nostrils flaring with each breath. After a moment, he nodded.

"You're wrong, counselor. That's not Darcie Mullins."

He frowned, a confused expression on his face.

"That's Darcie's kid sister, Laverne. She's been using her older sister's ID." I paused for dramatic effect. "Laverne is seventeen."

Stodghill's eyes grew wide, his skin pale.

"She's underage," I said. "And you've driven her across state lines."

Stodghill took several deep breaths, flexed his fingers.

"What's g-going on?" Cleo looked at her attorney.

"Give us the room, counselor." I pointed to the door.

The attorney stood, mouth hanging open. He recovered and said, "Five minutes."

"That'll work." I nodded.

"Wait." Cleo sat up in bed. "What's happening here?"

"Answer his questions." Stodghill marched to the exit. "I'm gonna get a cup of coffee."

The door shut behind him.

"It's just you and me, Cleo." I smiled.

"M-my attorney. Why isn't he in here?"

I shrugged.

"I have rights." She pointed a finger at me.

"Not today," I said. "Today you get to tell me everything you remember about the woman who hit you."

She looked at her wrist handcuffed to the bed. Then she began to talk.

- CHAPTER FIFTY-FOUR -

Eric Faulkner lived in the most exclusive section of North Dallas.

His home was the size of a palace, completely at odds with his workingman mode of dress.

The design was some sort of Spanish-Mediterranean-Vegas hybrid. Fountains and colored tile, oversized balconies, stucco archways. The grounds had been landscaped with palm trees, bougainvillea, and a lawn so lush the grass looked like an ad in a golf magazine.

There were eight or ten vehicles in the circular driveway.

I parked Piper's Jeep Cherokee behind a Mercedes. Piper was next to me, Elizabeth in the rear in a car seat.

"Look at that house, will ya?" Piper whistled softly. "It's bigger than the Vatican."

I didn't say anything. The people who moved about in this world were not my preferred social companions.

"What's the etiquette in a situation like this?" she asked. "Do we leave our guns in the car or what?"

I was wearing a pair of khakis and a blue button-down. It was hot out, so I hadn't brought a sport coat. The Glock Piper had brought me was on my hip in a clip-on holster, plainly visible.

Piper carried a smaller pistol in her back pocket, not as visible but still noticeable.

"We always carry our guns," I said. "Why is today different?"

"Because I don't want Elizabeth to think that's the way normal people operate."

A good point. I realized we both wanted our daughter to take a different path in life, one that wasn't filled with violence.

I was about to reply when a man approached the car. He was in his thirties and had the appearance of ex-military. I rolled down the window.

He stood by the driver's door and said, "You must be Agent Cantrell."

I nodded.

"I'm Walden, head of house security. Welcome to Mr. Faulkner's home."

"Hi." I introduced Piper, pointed to the back. "And this is our daughter, Elizabeth."

It felt good to say that, even if they were only going to be around for a few more days.

"Nice to meet you all," he said. "C'mon in. It's hot out here."

I hesitated, and he seemed to read my mind. "Keep your piece if you want."

I looked at the other cars, all expensive luxury automobiles.

"You're on safe ground, though," Walden said. "I've got two guards on duty."

Piper and I glanced at each other, unsure how to proceed. We were out of our element, mingling socially with a man who had enough money to afford a home like this and a security staff. A lifetime of never being a real part of anything left us both with a desire to fit in.

Plus, after what had happened at San Saba, I was tired of guns. So I pulled my holster off and put it in the console. Piper did the same with her weapon.

Together we got Elizabeth out of her car seat. Piper propped her on her hip. I carried the diaper bag.

We followed Walden toward the front door.

"Mr. Faulkner has a daughter, too," Walden said. "Dylan—she's four. Poor little thing broke her leg a couple of days ago."

Elizabeth burped at this nugget of information.

"There's a playroom upstairs," Walden said. "Lots of toys."

Elizabeth, who was just starting to understand her voice, said, "Ummmm . . . arrghh."

We all laughed and continued walking up the driveway.

"You can leave her up there if you want a break," Walden said. "The nanny's working today."

"That might be a good idea," Piper said. "Babies shouldn't be at funerals."

"It's not really a funeral. More of a wake." Walden opened the front door. "Welcome."

- CHAPTER FIFTY-FIVE -

Sarah wipes the blood from her upper lip and stares out the front window.

In the nether regions of her mind, she understands that cocaine can make you paranoid, especially if you haven't slept or eaten in a couple of days.

Intellectually, she grasps the concept, but what's happening in front of her eyes is reality, and the reality is Olympic-level crazy, *One Flew over the Cuckoo's Nest* wacko.

The sheriff who saw her at the motel, Jon Cantrell, just parked in her driveway.

He's talking to Walden. They're both looking at the house.

Sarah realizes what's going on.

They are coming to get her.

Despite the Python being discovered at the scene of the terrorist attack, despite the assurances from her attorney, she is about to be arrested.

She rubs her nose with one hand, grips the Ruger with the other. Her teeth chatter.

From the passenger side of his vehicle, a woman with short brown hair emerges. She is tall and thin and pretty. The woman removes a baby from the back of the SUV. The sheriff is under-cover, a clever ploy.

Sarah snorts another line and looks back outside.

Jon Cantrell, the woman and her child, and Walden are walking toward the house.

Toward her.

She grabs her cell and dials the attorney. The call goes straight to voice mail.

Her heart races. She slams the last few inches of wine in her glass and chops up another line of cocaine. She has to get her head straight, to think of a plan.

She's been in her bedroom suite for days now, ever since she saw Walden and Rosa staring at her. Her husband has been staying in a different part of the house. No one has bothered her. She's been alone. Just the coke and the wine and the memories of her childhood.

An image of her daughter flashes in her mind, the cast on her leg white against her peach-colored flesh. She's tried to be a good mother to the child, but she's failed, just like all the adults in her life did when she was the same age.

All but one. Her grandfather.

"Dylan, I love you so." She says the words out loud, the first time she's spoken in hours.

She wants desperately to leave the room and to run away. But she doesn't. Instead she tries her attorney again—no answer—and snorts another rail of coke.

- CHAPTER FIFTY-SIX -

The inside of Eric Faulkner's home was just as impressive as the outside.

A huge living area with fireplaces at either end dominated the first story. Marble floors, a vaulted ceiling, clusters of leather sofas artfully spaced throughout.

There were maybe twenty people in the room, scattered here and there. They were drinking and talking quietly. Servants in white jackets moved about, carrying trays filled with cocktail glasses and appetizers.

Eric Faulkner greeted us in the entryway. He wore jeans, a white dress shirt, and a slightly nicer pair of work boots than what he usually had on in the field.

"Nice to see you again, Agent Cantrell." He shook my hand. "You want a drink?"

"We're good," I said.

He smiled at Elizabeth, tickled her chin. "Walden told you about the playroom upstairs?"

Piper nodded.

"You want to check it out?" He looked at his security guy. "Hey, Walden. Take the kiddo upstairs."

Walden nodded. He gestured toward a sweeping staircase that looked like a set piece from *Gone with the Wind*.

Piper looked toward the second story and then at me. I shrugged and nodded.

"I'll be back." She headed toward the stairs, Walden walking beside her.

When they were gone, Faulkner said, "You sure you don't want a drink?"

"Okay. Maybe a beer."

Before the words had left my mouth, a man in a white coat appeared with a bottle of Heineken wrapped in a cocktail napkin. He also had a can of Diet Coke for my host.

Eric Faulkner stood next to me, surveying the room, sipping his soft drink.

"Half these people were friends of Price's." He paused. "The other half, well, they're here to watch me crash and burn."

"I'm not following."

"Sudamento's board of directors." He took a gulp of his drink. "They're gonna shit-can me next week."

"It was a terrorist attack. An act of God." I shook my head. "That wasn't your fault."

"You know who Elias King is?"

"The guy who masterminded the whole thing," I said. "A demolitions expert and an ex-con."

Faulkner chuckled and rubbed one eye. He looked ten years older than when I first met him only a few days before.

"We've managed to keep it out of the media for now, but Elias was my brother-in-law. My wife's only sibling."

There was a little tidbit that Harris the Homeland investigator hadn't let me in on.

I tried not to look surprised. That helped explain how the attackers knew which plants had lake houses and what transformers to take out. They had inside knowledge.

Faulkner was right; the board of Sudamento had to be planning to fire him.

"How's your wife taking all this?" I looked around the room for a woman who might be his spouse. No likely candidates presented themselves.

"She's in her room." He drained his Coke. "She's, uh, sick."

- CHAPTER FIFTY-SEVEN -

Sarah stands behind a pillar at the entry to the playroom, watching from afar as the tall, thin woman with the short hair talks to Rosa.

The infant is playing with some blocks on the floor.

Dylan is in her room with a babysitter, a part-time assistant for the overworked nanny, according to the various texts and e-mails Sarah has received from her staff. She hasn't seen her daughter in several days. Strangers in the same house. She wonders if Dylan has a remote chance of turning out normal, not fucked up like her mother and her now-dead uncle.

Sarah has gotten dressed—a pair of navy slacks and a rose-colored silk blouse—and combed her hair. In the mirror of her bathroom, she's noticed that she looks a little pale and her eyes are a tad red, but she is still attractive. She is SarahSmiles, able to seduce any man she wants to.

The Ruger is stuck in her waistband, covered by the blouse.

A new Spyderco lockback knife, the blade sharp enough to shave with, is in one of her rear pockets. The other contains a wad of cash and her passport. The beginning of a plan rumbles around in her brain.

She wants to hurt someone, hurt them badly. Another's pain validates her own, lessens it somehow.

Maybe kill the sheriff, then run away, the next flight to a country that doesn't extradite.

She remembers the feeling after the deputy died in that motel room, the one besides the sense of fear, an utter sense of control. She wants that feeling again. That would be a better high than the coke.

She touches the Ruger through the fabric of her blouse, the feel of the weapon almost arousing, pressed tight against her flesh.

The woman with the short hair kneels beside the infant, kisses her forehead, and then stands, heading toward the door and where Sarah is located. She is leaving the child in the care of Rosa.

The woman gets close.

"Hello." Sarah steps away from the pillar.

The woman stops. Her eyes go wide like she's surprised or something.

"My name is Sarah-Jane Faulkner." Sarah holds out her hand. "Welcome to my home."

"Hi. I'm Piper Westlake." The woman makes no move to shake hands. Instead she stares at Sarah's face.

A long silence ensues. Sarah tries to stop the tremor in her arms.

"You'll have to excuse my appearance." Sarah rubs her nose. "I'm recovering from a head cold."

The woman nods, her face blank.

"Have we met before?" Sarah asks. "You look familiar."

"I don't think so." Piper Westlake shakes her head. "I don't mean to get all up in your business, but do you need to lie down or anything?"

Sarah doesn't answer. In the background she can see Rosa staring at her, the infant playing at her feet.

"I'm fine."

Piper doesn't reply.

"Let's go downstairs, shall we?" Sarah points to the exit.

"Okay." Piper takes a look back at the infant and follows Sarah out.

"That your child?"

Piper nods.

"I have a daughter, too. She's a little older. That's a fun age, when they're not quite walking yet."

"Except for the dirty diapers," Piper says. "And not sleeping through the night."

They descend the staircase. Sarah uses the handrail.

At the bottom, Sarah sees that the party has moved to the far side of the room, to a sitting area overlooking the patio and the pool.

Two men stand in the space where the foyer turns into the living room.

Her husband. And the sheriff, Jon Cantrell.

Piper Westlake moves to Cantrell's side, linking her arm with his. They whisper with each other.

Are they talking about her? Are they getting ready to arrest her?

Sarah touches the Ruger underneath her blouse. She could shoot him right now, a single round to the back of the head. But would that really solve her problems? She wishes she'd done another line of coke. Her thinking isn't as clear as it should be.

Her heart is racing, however. Her vision is sharp, and she hears everything with an extra layer of clarity.

Her husband turns to greet her. Next to him, Cantrell shifts his feet, beginning to turn as well.

She touches the gun. When Cantrell sees her face, he will recognize her as the woman at the motel, and then she'll have to kill him.

She'll have no choice.

- CHAPTER FIFTY-EIGHT -

Footsteps behind me. One or more people descending the stairs.

I was visiting with our host. We were near the front door.

Piper walked up behind me and slid her arm around mine.

Faulkner turned and said hello to someone behind us.

I glanced at Piper. "Everything okay upstairs?"

"Yeah. Everything's, um, fine." She had a puzzled expression on her face, one that I couldn't decipher. "Upstairs anyway."

She turned and looked toward the staircase.

I followed her gaze and found myself staring into the face of a woman I'd never seen before, one who gave every indication she was about to die.

She appeared to be in her early forties but looked a decade or more older. She was gaunt, like a cancer patient who'd lost the will to eat. Her hair was greasy and lank, the color of burnt wood. Her face was pale and lined. Her eyes red-rimmed and sunken.

Eric Faulkner said, "Sheriff Cantrell. This is my wife, Sarah-Jane."

"Hello." She dropped her hands from her waist to her sides.

"Hi." I smiled. "Nice to meet you."

"Why don't you go back to your room, dear?" Faulkner said. "You look tired."

That was an understatement.

She looked like a cadaver and smelled like she hadn't bathed in a week. She wore a light-red silk blouse. The arms of the blouse reached her wrists but had slits on the outside, baring the length of her limbs. The exposed flesh was pale, except for where it was mottled with bruises, including a particularly deep one on the bicep of her right arm, a yellowish-brown discoloration.

"I want to enjoy the party," Sarah-Jane said, voice shrill. "Price was my friend, too."

An awkward silence descended on the husband and wife.

Piper glanced at me, one eyebrow raised.

"It's not a party," Eric Faulkner said. "It's a ceremony to honor his memory."

"His memory?" Sarah-Jane snorted. "What do you even know about Price Anderson?"

Piper and I eased away. For reasons we couldn't even begin to fathom, an argument was about to ensue.

Walden, the security man, stepped between the two.

"Let me help you back to your room, Mrs. Faulkner." He grasped her arm gently. "You should lie down and get some rest."

"You'd like that, wouldn't you, Walden? Me lying down." She wrenched free from his fingers and stared at me.

"Sarah-Jane, please." Her husband pointed to a hallway. "You're embarrassing yourself."

She continued to stare at me.

"You okay, Mrs. Faulkner?" I didn't know what else to say.

"You're a sheriff, huh?" She smiled. Her teeth were gray.

I nodded.

"See you later, *Sheriff*."

She turned and staggered down a hallway leading to a different wing of the house.

Walden followed a few feet behind her.

"I'm sorry about that," Faulkner said. "She's not been well."

"Yeah, I sensed that." Piper nodded. "Her unwellness."

I put my beer on a side table. Piper and Faulkner continued talking, but their voices were muted and their words didn't make sense all of a sudden—background chatter in my brain.

A river of disjointed information ran through my mind, snippets flowing in and out of my consciousness.

The old drunk had described the woman who'd stolen the Monte Carlo as a "rich girl," the same phrase Cleo Fain used about the person who attacked her, a woman who appeared to be in her thirties in a similar vehicle. The picture the Texas Ranger had shown me, a person in an expensive high-rise belonging to a woman named Debbie Wilson. The photos Piper and I had gotten from a contact at the Dallas Police Department, images of a suspect in the death of the two homeless men, a woman in her thirties, taken from a video system at a tattoo parlor.

My own memories of the person in the Dallas Cowboys cap and the raincoat.

Why did all these bits of data make me think of Eric Faulkner's wife, a woman who bore little resemblance to the relatively healthy person I'd seen?

Sarah-Jane Faulkner. SarahSmiles.

A coincidence, surely . . . except that my deputy had been killed with a gun that belonged to her grandfather.

Piper touched my arm, startling me.

"You okay?" she asked.

Faulkner was standing a few feet away, talking on his cell.

Cleo Fain's words rang in my head. *I hit her with the tire iron. Her right bicep. Had to leave a nasty bruise.*

I looked at Piper. "She had a bruise on her arm."

"What? Who did?"

"Sarah-Jane Faulkner. The wife."

"What are you talking about?"

"What if Eric Faulkner's wife is SarahSmiles?" I said. "The woman who killed my deputy."

Piper rolled her eyes. "Other than the fact that she looks like she has stage nineteen cancer and probably has a rock-solid alibi, you might be right."

I didn't say anything.

"Does the wife look anything like the woman you saw at the motel?"

"Not really," I said. "But I only saw her for a few seconds."

Piper looked down the hall where Sarah-Jane Faulkner had gone.

"The wife has a bruise on her arm," I said. "And it's in the same place that Cleo Fain said she hit the woman in the Monte Carlo."

Piper frowned, scratched her chin.

Eric Faulkner ended his call and approached us.

"This is a weird question," I said, "but do you know anybody named Debbie Wilson?"

"No." He shook his head. "I mean, not really. That was the name of my wife's college roommate. But she died a long time ago."

Piper's eyes grew wide.

A couple of people approached Eric. He stepped away from us and began talking to them.

"Where's Elizabeth?" I asked.

"Upstairs with the nanny. She's safe where she is for the moment. Let's check up on Mrs. Faulkner."

I headed down the hallway, Piper on my heels.

At the end of the corridor was a set of double doors, the entrance to the master bedroom. One of the doors was ajar.

I stepped inside.

The security man, Walden, lay on the floor by the fireplace.

His throat had been cut. Blood pooled around the top half of his body.

Piper swore softly. "We left the guns in the car."

We searched the suite anyway, moving quickly. We found a half-dozen empty wine bottles in the bathroom wastebasket and a hand mirror covered in white residue. But no Sarah-Jane Faulkner.

"Before we do anything else," Piper said, "we need to get Elizabeth."

From another part of the house, somewhere above us, came a scream.

- CHAPTER FIFTY-NINE -

Eric Faulkner met us at the foot of the stairs. Several guests milled about, craning their necks to see what was going on.

"Where's the rest of your security team?" I asked.

"Outside," he said. "What's happening? Where's Walden?"

I tossed the car keys to Piper. "Get the guns and find the other guards."

"Are you out of your mind?" She didn't move. "My baby's upstairs, Jon."

"She's my child, too." I shoved her toward the door, hoping she wouldn't see the fear that had to be in my eyes. "GO!"

Piper hesitated a moment, then dashed outside.

"Walden," Faulkner said. "Where is he?"

"He's dead."

"*What?*"

"Stay here." I took the stairs two at a time.

At the top was a large landing, hallways to the left and right. In the center, at the head of the stairs, was another set of double doors.

An enormous stuffed horse sat beside the doors, not far from the edge of the first step.

A playroom. That's what Walden had called it.

I flung open the doors and hopped inside, hugging the wall.

The room was huge, big enough to cover maybe a quarter of the downstairs area. Big enough that you'd have to shout to be heard on the other side.

Toys were everywhere, stacks and stacks, so many it was overpowering.

Pinball machines and pink wagons, stuffed animals and dollhouses, ginormous Lego sets, child-sized cars, scooters and bicycles, every form of Barbie ever invented.

A pathway threaded its way through the mounds of stuff, heading toward what appeared to be a balcony on the far side.

There was movement on the balcony. Too far away to tell what.

I headed that way.

About thirty feet down the path lay a life-sized doll, a woman in her fifties, splayed on her back. She was wearing a blue dress, the front of which was stained red from the knife sticking in her chest.

I knelt beside her, felt for a pulse.

She was alive but not for long. Her eyes flickered open and stared at me for an instant before they closed again.

"The infant. Where is she?" I spoke softly, tried to keep the panic from taking over.

She tried to speak, but nothing came out except a bloody bubble. Then she died.

A low whistle from the door.

I turned.

Piper stood there, two men behind her, the security guards. She cut her eyes from side to side, glancing at the men, a wary expression on her face.

Guard One said, "Sir. You need to come downstairs. We've called the police."

Without warning, Piper tossed my Glock toward me. Guard Two tried to stop her. Guard One aimed his gun at me.

The pistol landed on top of a stuffed bear a few feet away.

"Don't touch the weapon," Guard One said.

"I'm a federal agent." I picked up the gun. "You shoot me, you'll spend the rest of your life in prison."

He lowered the weapon slightly, indecision evident on his face.

"The police will be here soon," he said. "We need to wait."

From the balcony came the faint sound of a baby crying. Our baby. Elizabeth.

"That's my child," I said.

"We have procedures in place for an event like—"

Piper went full *krav maga* on Guard One, ripping the weapon from his grasp and throwing him to the floor. His shoulder popped from its socket.

More crying.

Guard Two reached for Piper's arm.

She punched his nose with the trigger guard of her pistol.

He fell to the floor, too.

I ran toward the balcony, Piper thumping behind me. Fear clutched at my chest, a terror unlike any I'd ever known. My child was in jeopardy.

The balcony was large, maybe thirty feet wide by twenty feet deep.

Sarah-Jane Faulkner stood with her back against the railing in the middle. She held Elizabeth in one arm, clutching the infant against her chest.

The other hand held a revolver, the muzzle of which was pressed against my baby's head.

A patio table and chairs stood between us.

Beside me, a sharp intake of air from Piper.

"Put the gun down," I said. "Nobody else needs to get hurt."

"You didn't even remember me," she said. "From the motel."

I didn't reply. Piper eased away from me, flanking out, trying to split the woman's attention, her gun raised.

"Nobody forgets SarahSmiles." Sarah-Jane Faulkner shook her head, obviously upset. "Except for you."

Elizabeth was crying, kicking her feet.

"Your deputy. He was a fucking animal. I did the world a favor."

"Put the baby down," I said, "and we can talk."

Sarah-Jane looked at Piper. "STOP MOVING!"

Piper was about five feet to my right. She froze.

"Whose child is this anyway?"

"Mine." I nodded toward Piper. "Ours, I mean."

"You brought your own baby along on an undercover operation?"

"What the hell are you talking about?" Piper said.

Elizabeth had quieted down a little, though tears were still dribbling down her face.

"You're here to arrest me," Sarah-Jane said. "You were plotting with Walden."

Drug-induced paranoia. She was a powder keg, and every puff of air was a shower of sparks. She would use the gun, either on us or the child. It was just a matter of when.

Sirens in the distance.

I brought the Glock up, closed my left eye. We were about fifteen feet away from each other.

"Did you meet my daughter?" Sarah-Jane asked, her voice choked with emotion.

The top of Elizabeth's head was level with Sarah-Jane Faulkner's throat. I could put one in Faulkner's temple and miss the child, an easy shot from this distance . . . if the targets were paper. I tried to figure out another play but drew a blank.

"My baby's father is dead," Sarah said. "And she'll never know."

I took up the slack in the trigger, an eighth of a millimeter play in the firing mechanism.

"My own brother," she said. "He killed the father of my only child."

"Price Anderson?" Piper asked.

Sarah-Jane Faulkner nodded.

"I'm glad we've got that settled," Piper said. "Now put my baby down, and I'll make it a clean kill. You won't feel anything."

Sarah-Jane Faulkner seemed to notice my Glock aiming at her.

"What the—*drop your fucking gun!*"

I increased the pressure on the trigger and said a quick prayer, promising God all my tomorrows if he would only make my aim true and save my baby today.

Sarah-Jane Faulkner cocked the hammer of her revolver.

BOOM.

A gun fired.

- CHAPTER SIXTY -

Two weeks later

Turns out I have a knack for tea parties.

Oh, the things we learn about ourselves as we grow older.

I was enjoying my second one of the day, sitting at a tiny table in Dylan Faulkner's playroom.

My companions—Winnie-the-Pooh, SpongeBob Square-Pants, and an elephant named Eloise—were not very good conversationalists. I chalked that up to the fact that they were stuffed toys, not that they had any inherent bias against middle-aged meat puppets like me.

Our hostess, Miss Dylan, sat at the head of the table, pouring tea. Her leg was still in a cast, jutting awkwardly out from her chair. A new nanny hovered in the background while a real estate agent took pictures in the hallway. The Faulkner family, what's left of them, was downsizing.

The tranquil image of a child's party was at odds with what I saw when I closed my eyes—two weeks before, the bullet from my gun impacting Sarah-Jane Faulkner's forehead just a few yards away on the balcony.

In my mind I could hear Sarah-Jane hitting the patio below as she tumbled from the second story. I could see Elizabeth falling from her grasp, dropping to the floor unharmed.

My aim had been true. My daughter was safe, and because of this I was unable to come up with words to express my gratitude to a God who up to that point in my life I wasn't sure I believed in.

Dylan asked me to pour for Eloise the Elephant, closest to my seat. I happily complied.

The parsing of Sarah-Jane Faulkner's life turned out to be a monumental undertaking, even with the muscle of the Department of Homeland Security behind the task.

Due to Sarah-Jane's connection to the targets of the attacks and the attacker, the feds were determined to find out everything they could about her. Even though every snippet of information indicated that Elias King had acted alone or with a single accomplice, the powers that be at Homeland Security wanted to make sure there was no organized terrorist threat.

Unfortunately for the investigation, Sarah-Jane had been very good about keeping her tracks hidden. She'd used burner phones, disposable e-mail addresses, and IP proxy services, changing everything on a regular basis like she'd been trained by al-Qaeda or Edward Snowden. All of those factors indicated a sophisticated operation.

On the other side of the equation were her criminal activities, armed robberies of a bunch of men looking to step out on their wives. Hardly the work of an ISIS sleeper agent or some neo-Nazi group pissed off about Ruby Ridge.

Eric Faulkner entered the playroom, a packing box under one arm. He smiled at us and waved. Dylan ignored him, continuing to fuss with the teapot and a plate of cookies. I'd managed to fill my own cup earlier, a generous slug of single-malt scotch from the bar downstairs.

Faulkner was no longer the CEO of Sudamento. He'd been forced out as he'd predicted, but according to the newspapers this had made him a wealthy man. Stock options had vested, severance bonuses triggered, golden parachutes puffed open.

Despite the loss of his job and the death of his wife at my hand, he appeared happier than when I'd first met him. The lines on his face had softened, and the color of his skin was healthier. He smiled more readily, like a great weight had been lifted from his shoulders, though there was a tinge of sadness in his eyes.

He put the box down and surveyed the room, now only about half full of toys. The expression on his face was that of a man wondering where to begin.

The investigation into Sarah-Jane Faulkner's actions was further muddied by the soap opera love triangle between Sarah-Jane, Price Anderson, and Price's employer, Eric Faulkner.

The affair had been on-again, off-again for years. The authorities had pieced together the course of their relationship through Price's phone records and travel logs. The investigators had even uncovered an appointment at an abortion clinic five years before, made in the name of Debbie Wilson, Sarah-Jane's deceased college roommate. Video footage from the clinic, archived by an overly obsessive security-minded facilities manager, showed Sarah-Jane arriving with Price and then hurriedly leaving a few moments later.

I drained my teacup and extricated myself from the tiny table.

Dylan said, "Where are you going, Jon?"

In the immediate aftermath of her mother's death, she'd been alone, lost in a swirl of first responders and hysterical colleagues of her father's. Piper and I had sat with her, with our daughter, Elizabeth, on Piper's lap, wrapped in her mother's protective embrace. Every few minutes, Dylan would reach out and hold my hand for a moment, as if to reassure herself that someone real was there, not just a fleeting image of an adult.

Dylan had seemed remarkably calm and accepting of the fact that neither her mother nor her nanny was around anymore.

Since then, I'd spent as much time as possible with her. I told myself that I was trying to help the Homeland Security investigators close out the investigation, and keeping the child occupied while they snooped around the house was beneficial to all parties involved. I also convinced myself that any use of my time that helped the child find a center for her young life was the least I could do, since I had been the instrument of her mother's death.

I didn't know if those reasons were accurate, however.

Maybe the truth was that subconsciously I was seeking a replacement for my own daughter.

"I'm going to talk to your dad," I said. "Be right back."

She watched me go, eyes unblinking. The thought of the road that lay ahead of her caused my heart to break just a little.

Eric Faulkner and I retreated to a corner of the room out of earshot.

"You're a very kind man," Faulkner said. "She really likes you."

A kind man. Except for that time I put a bullet into your wife's head.

I didn't reply, thinking of my own daughter, grateful she was alive.

"Price Anderson's family," he said. "They've gotten a court order for a DNA test."

I wished for another glass of tea.

"Apparently Price was convinced that Dylan was his child." Faulkner rubbed the bridge of his nose. "He told his brother that anyway, a couple of years ago."

With their son dead, the Anderson family no doubt wanted a piece of tangible evidence that he had existed. Or money. Too early to tell. Either way, I felt for Eric Faulkner. When it rains, it pours, as the old saying goes.

"What the hell is that going to prove?" Faulkner shook his head. "Dylan is mine. I don't care what any damn test says."

Two weeks before, as he came to the realization that his wife was really dead, the dominant feeling I got off him was relief mixed with concern for his daughter. Now he was about to find out the child he'd always thought of as his own was not.

"You're still her legal guardian," I said. "There's bound to be a way to stop a custody battle, especially considering . . . everything."

"So you believe it's true?" He looked at me.

I didn't say anything.

"I should have paid Elias to stay away from her," he said. "This is all his fault."

I couldn't even fathom how Elias King had been responsible for his sister's infidelity. On some level we all live in a special world filled with mirrors that flatter the image of how we'd like things to be. Why should Eric Faulkner be any different?

From what I had gleaned, Sarah-Jane and her brother were an eleven on a ten scale of damaged people. Both parents had been alcoholic, neglectful if not abusive. As a result, they'd been raised by their grandfather, an elderly thug with the moral code of Al Capone.

Faulkner shook his head. "You know that I told Elias about the lake houses, don't you? Gave him the access codes?"

I wasn't aware of that fact, but I had suspected it.

"He told me he wanted someplace to get away, to clear his head." Faulkner sighed. "Turns out he wanted to destroy me."

"Because his grandfather gave you money?"

Faulkner nodded. "He never got over that. He was blood; I wasn't."

Revenge. The oldest, most destructive motive of them all.

"Have you told all this to a lawyer?" I asked. "The feds may get it into their mind to come after you for aiding and abetting."

"I'm not stupid, Cantrell. Of course I've told my lawyer."

I didn't say anything.

"Sorry," he said. "I didn't mean to snap at you."

Dylan looked over at us. She smiled and waved. We waved back.

"I've made a deal to sell my Gulfstream," he said. "Won't close for a week."

Dylan poured another round of tea for her stuffed animals.

"The pilot needs to file a flight plan," he said. "Where should I tell him the destination is?"

There were some loose ends that required tidying up. Eric and I had talked about a particular situation that needed addressing. It was his idea to use the plane one last time for this matter.

"Logan International Airport. That's the first stop." I headed back to the party of stuffed animals.

• • •

Piper was gone again from my life, departing for Mexico a few days after the death of Sarah-Jane Faulkner. Elizabeth naturally went with her mother, leaving me alone.

I told Piper I would visit as soon as I could, and she didn't seem completely opposed to the idea. This I took as a positive sign.

I remained in Dallas, staying close to Dylan and Eric Faulkner.

For reasons only he could articulate, Eric looked upon me as his new BFF.

Maybe it was because his daughter had taken a shine to me. Or perhaps because he was secretly relieved that I had enabled him to be free of his cheating wife. It could have been because as a hard-charging type A businessman he'd never developed friendships with people outside the corporate jungle.

In any event, he and I had spent a lot of time together. He talked about the way things played out, trying to come to terms with the death and destruction caused by his brother-in-law. I listened a lot, played with his daughter, and thought about my own child.

So it seemed more or less natural that he would offer me use of the tools of a successful industrialist, specifically the private jet that was about to be sold.

This was how I came to be sitting on the front stoop of a house in South Boston.

The home was slender and tall, an oversized Cracker Jack box paneled in gray wood siding. It was located on a narrow street filled with similar structures, some freshly painted, most not. A flower box filled with dead flowers hung underneath the front window.

It was late in the afternoon, in the latter half of September, and the air had a chill to it.

A few houses down, a group of kids were kicking a soccer ball back and forth.

Next to me sat Connie Holbrook, Whitney's mother.

Connie was in her sixties with a red bulbous nose and cheeks that were spider-webbed with burst capillaries. She wore a Boston Bruins sweatshirt and Nike sneakers.

"You shure you don't want another beer?" She took a drink of her tallboy.

Her accent was thicker than her daughter's, reflecting a lifetime in this one particular neighborhood.

"I'm good, thanks."

She drank in silence for a few moments. Then she said, "What's the weather like in Texas now?"

"Still pretty hot."

Connie Holbrook nodded like this was important information. "Whitney, she didn't much like the cold."

I didn't say anything. We'd already spent half an hour inside, sitting by the bay window in the tiny living room and making small talk.

The living area was decorated with a cracked leather sofa and two recliners in front of a TV. On the opposite wall was a picture of the pope amid a cluster of family photos.

The largest photo was of a much younger Connie Holbrook and Whitney when she was about twelve, along with a boy maybe a year or so older. The snapshot had been taken at Disney World. The others showed the three at different ages and different places. Times Square, an empty beach, the Lincoln Memorial.

No father figure was present in any of the shots.

Back outside, I watched the kids chase the soccer ball past the stoop where we were sitting.

Several called out a greeting to Connie. She waved and told them to be careful for cars.

"Nice neighborhood," I said. "Whitney grew up here?"

"Yeah. This house." She patted the steps. "Couldn't get out of here fast enough, though."

The words had a hint of bitterness to them.

I let the silence drag on for a while. Then: "I got the sense that she liked to travel, to see new places."

Connie stared at the children, lost in thought.

I wondered again why I had come. The matter at hand could have been handled indirectly. I didn't really know Whitney Holbrook that well, but I'd felt the need to connect with who she was and where she'd come from. We all seek closure in different ways, I suppose.

She'd died alone in a hospital room, and the solitary nature of her passing made me sadder than her actual death for some reason.

"There's a man in Texas," I said. "His name is Eric Faulkner."

Connie looked at me. "The head of that company? Sudamento?"

"That's him. Anyway, he's going to send you some money in a few weeks."

"Why?"

"He feels responsible for what happened to your daughter."

"Is he?"

I didn't answer. After a moment, I said, "Maybe. I don't really know. Who's to say?"

"I don't want charity."

I shrugged. "Then you can send it back. Or donate it to the local food bank."

Connie Holbrook opened another tallboy. Held one up for me. I relented this time. We sat quietly for a while, drinking, staring at nothing.

"What happened to Whitney's father?" I asked.

"Birds of a feather, she and her old man." Connie shook her head. "Both of them wanderers."

I didn't say anything.

"He went to California to see his brother. Whitney, she was almost four." Connie took a long swig of beer. "Bastard never came back."

In the house across the street, a porch light winked on.

Connie stared down the block. "Whitney always wanted to get out of Boston. I never understood why."

Why do any of us want to leave home? To make our mark in the world? To see what we're made of? I kept these thoughts to myself. This woman had just lost her daughter. She was experiencing a pain unlike any other.

I wondered what Elizabeth was doing at this very moment.

"You and my girl," Connie said. "Were you two partners?"

"We worked together for a few days. The power plant thing in Texas."

Silence.

"Sudamento," she said. "The man who's sending me money for no reason."

I nodded. "That would be the power plant thing, yes."

"You the guy she was dating?"

I shook my head.

"She told me about her new boyfriend the last time we talked. Said he was a real nice fellow—a keeper, was how she put it—had a good job and everything."

Price Anderson. Quite possibly the only time he'd ever been described as "a keeper."

"The man she was talking about," I said. "He died in the attack as well."

"So, was he a good guy?"

I didn't answer.

"I'm guessing not, because Whitney had a bad picker." Connie drained her beer. "Kinda like her mother."

The light grew thin. Shadows lengthened on the street.

"They're gonna put a plaque up in Washington with her name on it," Connie said. "They want me to come to the ceremony in the spring."

"She was a good agent," I said. "They're doing the right thing by her."

"The right thing." Connie Holbrook snorted. "Except that she's still dead."

The children began to drift away, headed home for supper.

"Those pictures inside," I said. "Is that Whitney's brother?"

Connie nodded, eyes cloudy. We didn't speak for a while as darkness descended.

"Sean, my oldest, Whit's brother," Connie said. "He was on the United flight, the one that crashed in the field in Pennsylvania on September eleventh."

I didn't reply. There wasn't much I could say that would ease this woman's suffering.

"Where you going from here?" Connie asked.

"Mexico City," I said. "To see my daughter."

- ACKNOWLEDGMENTS -

Creating a novel is a collaborative affair. The raw material may have been mine, but the end result is a communal effort, thanks to a dedicated group of professionals who are as much responsible for what you hold in your hand as the author. To that end, I would like to thank the incredible team at Thomas & Mercer: Alison Dasho, Jacque Ben-Zekry, Gracie Doyle, Alan Turkus, Tiffany Pokorny, and Charlotte Herscher.

Several people who wish to remain anonymous provided insight into the operations of the typical power plant as well as the workings of the electrical grid, the high-voltage spiderweb that reaches to every corner of the nation. I would like to express my deep appreciation to each of you for your expert advice and time. Any mistakes are entirely my fault.

For their continued support of the Jon Cantrell Thrillers, I would like to thank Anne and Steve Stodghill—good friends, patrons of the arts, and aficionados of the printed word.

For their help with the manuscript, I would like to offer my gratitude to Jan Blankenship, Victoria Calder, Paul Coggins, Peggy Fleming, Suzanne Frank, Alison Hunsicker, Fanchon

Knott, Brooke Malouf, Clif Nixon, David Norman, Glenna Whitley, and Max Wright.

Special thanks to Richard Abate for helping me traverse the waters leading to this book's publication.

And finally, last but never least, thanks to my wife, Alison, for being there through it all.

- ABOUT THE AUTHOR -

Harry Hunsicker, a fourth-generation native of Dallas, Texas, is the former executive vice president of the Mystery Writers of America. His debut novel, *Still River*, was nominated for a Shamus Award by the Private Eye Writers of America, and his short story "Iced" was nominated for a Thriller Award by the International Thriller Writers. Hunsicker lives in Dallas, where he works as a commercial real estate appraiser and occasionally speaks on creative writing. *The Grid* is his sixth novel.